COZY CATS
CATS
COTTAGE plc

JOHN SCHROEDER

JOHN SCHROEDER – production genius and songwriter, the quiet man of British Pop Music, internationally acclaimed for his wide ranging success tells this endearing story that embraces the world of cats that have been a constant source of love and companionship throughout his personal life.

Schroeder was the producer and co-producer for no less than one hundred and seventy Artists throughout his career including such stars as Cliff Richard, The Shadows, Helen Shapiro and Status Quo. Virtually every field of popular music has been touched by his talents, from the orchestral jazz-based stylings of Sounds Orchestral through the pop-soul of Geno Washington to the exciting black rock of Cymande, an outfit that was the first British based black group to break the American R & B charts wide open. In addition to this he was also initially responsible for bringing the Tamla Motown label to the UK.

Roger St. Pierre

Cats have always been in and out of my life in one way or another providing love and support when it was most needed. At one time I found myself living with eleven of them! By chance I discovered the amazing therapeutic power of this animal when one of my mother's cats developed an unusual relationship with my father who was sadly both deaf and blind during the last five years of his life.

Music and cats seemed to be a winning combination as Andrew Lloyd Webber has so aptly proved.

The urge to write this story was like writing a song – totally irresistible, an exciting challenge and lots of fun. I can only hope that it will eventually enjoy as much success as some of the songs I have been lucky to have written during my career in music.

John Schroeder

BY THE SAME AUTHOR

Sex & Violins – My Affair with Life Love and Music

KIRAN AHMAD

It has been a real pleasure to work on this book, not only because I absolutely love cats and found the story both interesting and unique but also because John Schroeder is so passionate about his Cozy Cats Cottage world!

I actually studied Graphic Design at College but then thought it would be much more fun to illustrate so, after putting together my portfolio, I was fortunate enough to be taken on by The Maggie Mundy Illustration Agency which set me on the path to being a freelance illustrator. Over the years I have worked in children's books, packaging, card design, gift-wrap design and for various educational publishers.

I live in Kingston, Surrey, a really beautiful part of the UK, with my partner Laurence, and our daughter Eliza, 8, who is showing great talent and enthusiasm for painting and drawing. She was very impressed with the drawings, so it was nice to have an appreciative audience straight away!

I hope you enjoy this lovely book and that my drawings do the book justice.

Matador
5 Weir Road
Kibworth Beauchamp
Leicester LE8 0LQ, UK
Tel: (+44) 116 279 2299
Fax: (+44) 116 279 2277
Email: books@troubador.co.uk
Web: www.troubador.co.uk/matador

ISBN 978 1848767 225

British Library Cataloguing in Publication Data.
A catalogue record for this book is available from the British Library.

Printed and bound in the UK by TJ International, Padstow, Cornwall

Typeset in 11pt Aldine 401 BT Roman by Troubador Publishing Ltd, Leicester, UK

Matador is an imprint of Troubador Publishing Ltd

In memory of my dear wife Zoë who loved and adored cats and who passed away on Saturday May 21st 2011
May she rest in peace forever

With thanks and acknowledgement to Rirette Mudd for the amazing photograph of 'Pumpkin' who became the inspiration for the front cover of this book.

CONTENTS

PREFACE

The 'cock-a-doodle-doo' alarm clock thoughtlessly shattered the morning solitude.

It was 7.30 and the day she thought would never come was suddenly a reality. For the first time Angela Tillsworthy found herself consumed with a strange mixture of fear and excitement as it dawned on her that she and Buckingham were actually going to appear on national television and be seen by possibly thousands.

The brief was that they wanted to discuss and talk to her about her vision of the apparently underestimated therapeutic power of the cat, Cozy Cats Cottage plc and the The Tillsworthy Trust for the Prevention of Cruelty to Cats; the charity she had set up specifically for the prevention of cruelty to cats.

With slightly shaking hands Angela lovingly fed all six cats, but every one of them knew something unusual was going on. Six pairs of eyes inquisitively looked up at her as she consolingly picked up Buckingham and gently placed him in his cat box.

"Today, my gorgeous Bucks, you might well become a megastar – if you play your cards right. You'll even have the chance to show off and give them a bit of Buck's 'special'. You'll love that. That'll make your day – that's for sure!"

Angela looked at all the other cats in turn and said reassuringly,

"There'll be no work today. No seeing patients or children. Auntie Dawn will be here shortly to look after you until we return. Then we'll tell you just what we've been up to."

Angela detected a particularly anxious Lily.

"Don't worry Lily. I'll be bringing your darling hubby back safe and sound….. although you might have to make an appointment to speak to him after this!"

The door bell rang. The chauffeur driven limo had arrived!

CHAPTER ONE

Funny how love can be

Angela Tillsworthy was not blessed with an easy childhood. The relationship between Millie, her even tempered mother and Oliver, her austere and self-centred father was fraught with a mixture of resignation and resentment. The real bone of contention lay with Priscilla, Millie's daughter by her first marriage. Priscilla was two years older than Angela, but she was never able to totally accept Oliver as her new father, any more than Oliver, although he tried hard, felt able to genuinely accept Priscilla as a daughter.

In spite of the tension and differences this situation caused, Millie and Oliver did their level best to treat both girls equally and certainly, with regard to education, both were to benefit by going to the same schools.

Although Angela and Priscilla were totally different in so many ways they were good friends, with sisterly love being apparent on numerous occasions.

Oliver's parents were Victorian through and through, which resulted in Oliver being very set in his ways and believing happiness and success in life could only be achieved by hard work, dedication and doing things yourself using your own initiative. He found it hard and was certainly considerably out of his depth, bringing up two girls and eventually having to deal with short skirts, lipstick and boyfriends. He really wished he had had a son with whom he could have so much more easily related to. He would have enjoyed man to man talks and imparted his own particular interests, views and goals in life, hoping his son might one day follow in his father's footsteps.

Like his father, Oliver was a workaholic, achieving self-made success by having the inspiration of setting up his own company and using his ability and exceptional talent in the world of business and commerce. This took time and dedication and he did not tie the knot until he was thirty-six years old. Through sheer hard work, which was an almost fanatical obsession, at only forty-two years old he became well-off financially, and very secure. However, his self-centred attitude towards life, and his work in particular, was to cause some serious friction amongst the family with Millie, his long suffering wife, justifiably complaining of the lack of leisure time spent with her and the girls.

"You're married to that bloody business, not me," Millie would complain bitterly.

Having been a successful Bank Manager for some time, Oliver's pleasure and obsession in life was now the challenge of doing business deals all over the world in conjunction with his two business partners, ex-bank customers, in the buying and selling of companies which entailed transactions involving millions of pounds. It was somewhat ironic that he met Millie when she had made an appointment to see him to negotiate a bank loan! The initial attraction was obviously there, as he deliberately went out of his way to make sure he personally had secured it for her, which was not his normal way of doing things. Although surprised, he was not particularly concerned to discover that Millie had been married before and was now divorced, but he was a little taken aback to realise that part of the package was the taking on of someone else's child, namely Priscilla, who was then two years old.

Initially, Millie was relieved, pleased and proud, having escaped the traumas of a rather dodgy marriage, that through her new husband's clever business acumen she had, in fact, found herself landing on both feet, feeling financially secure and living in a very nice three bedroom mortgage-free residence, situated on the periphery of Gerrards Cross, a very much up-market area in the county of Buckinghamshire. She was, of course also extremely happy for Priscilla, especially as Oliver had offered to do his level best to accept her. Although treated somewhat like completing the terms and conditions of a business agreement, Oliver was more than relieved when Millie told him she was pregnant.

Millie gave birth to a little girl and they named her Angela. Millie and Oliver were relieved to find that Priscilla had accepted the new arrival the moment she saw her, and Millie really relished the many precious moments when Priscilla, in her own special way, showed she truly loved and cared for Angela.

Oliver was glad that the whole business, as far as he was concerned, was over and done with and he inwardly congratulated himself, regarding the whole thing as being a 'job well done'. He could now relax and get on with what made him really happy; playing games in the world of finance where stakes were high and rewards even higher!

For the following few years, family life for the Tillsworthy clan settled into an acceptable and uneventful routine, but Angela and Priscilla were growing up fast. Millie was gradually finding herself becoming more and more frustrated with a life filled with loneliness, especially as the two girls were now going to school. This was solely due to Oliver's business deals slowly but surely becoming more and more internationally orientated, necessitating him being off on business trips around the world and away from home for weeks and sometimes months at a time.

The house in Gerrards Cross was blessed with a three quarter of an acre garden. It was a bit of a mess, but it had great potential and it became Millie's saving grace. She started to put all her energy into it and found she really loved it. It was hard work but creatively rewarding and it wasn't too long before it didn't really bother her that Oliver was away. She also discovered that Angela was fascinated by what she was doing and in a sweet, childlike way wanted to do something herself. Millie got the idea of giving Angela her own flower bed and she got a great kick out of helping Angela to create it. She loved colour, so Millie treated both girls to a trip to the local garden centre, where Angela picked the flowers and colours she liked. Priscilla had no desire to get involved with any 'hands on' participation with gardening, but admired the result from a distance. Millie had noticed that Priscilla loved to read 'girlie' magazines and so she asked Oliver if she could get an attractive wooden summer house that she had seen in the garden centre and erect it in a corner of the garden, where Priscilla could read quietly to her heart's content. Oliver had no objection at all and told Millie that if it made her happy she could spend whatever she wanted on the garden.

Millie didn't have to think twice about that offer and acted upon it immediately in case Oliver changed his mind, which he had the habit of doing rather too often. Apart from the summer house, she had a small and attractive stone courtyard with an old-fashioned well built on one side of the house. She created a stream which ran the entire width of the garden and this was enhanced by the addition of three small but quaint wooden bridges placed across it at various intervals. An impressive stone archway with a wrought iron gate became the entrance to the house, which she named Odd Acres, and she artistically designed an appropriate looking name plate. There were four beautiful grass lawns, all of which Millie painstakingly nurtured and tended to. The garden overall was kept in an impeccable state, with Millie lovingly devoting many hours to it. Angela became equally as conscientious about the garden and gardening, helping her mother at every opportunity. What Millie and Angela had finally created was unquestionably a visual work of art, but what it had done above all else was to significantly upgrade the value of the property. Oliver was beside himself with joy on discovering this and congratulated Millie a thousand times, saying what she had achieved was almost as good as the success of one of his business deals, and not only that, it was almost an incentive for him not to go away so much but to stay at home and enjoy it all!

During their teenage years, being in the same school together proved not to be such a good idea as it was first thought, since Angela and Priscilla began to drift apart. Priscilla, being the elder sister, began to feel over-shadowed by Angela's academic ability. Angela was quite plain looking but had an amazing natural charm, and like Oliver she was good at mathematics, which was to provide her with a commendable business strategy later on in her life. She also took part in a school play and found that she became desperate to learn to act. Having seen Angela perform, Millie managed to persuade Oliver to let her join a local theatre group. She had a natural talent and by the time she was eighteen and leaving school she had been offered a leading role in a well known play, but dressed as a man! The acclaim she received did not go unnoticed by the local press, who especially commented on her natural ability as an actress with a positive future. The leading article on the *Entertainment for You* page in the local paper read, 'Tillsie's talent shines like the star she is!' This was the very first time the endearing name of Tillsie had appeared, but unbeknown to Angela at the time it was to reappear later on in her life, contributing much to the success of a completely different sort of role.

Millie was so thrilled and proud of her daughter's achievements that even Oliver could not turn a blind eye to the fact that Angela had mastered something incredibly commendable and, what's more, totally on her own initiative.

Understandably, life was a lot different and a lot harder for Priscilla, especially being two years older than Angela and being a half sister. She was pleased at Angela's success, but inwardly she was naturally a little jealous too. Commendably she never showed it. She was average at everything, but outstanding at nothing. Certainly at times she felt lonely and insecure and the relationship with Oliver didn't help. She decided the only way to deal with this was to make herself feel and look more attractive. She had both the figure and the facial features to create a nearly perfect marriage between clothes and make up. She loved looking older than she was and she looked quite stunning. Millie didn't like her doing it, but sympathised with her predicament, and to keep the peace if nothing else, Millie put aside a good proportion of her house keeping money to enable her to do this. Oliver was not at all amused and made it plainly obvious. On leaving school, it wasn't long before Priscilla formed an unhealthy relationship with two or three teenage girls about her own age, who found themselves in a similar situation. Unhealthy because they were all totally infatuated with the world of fashion, the opposite sex and seemingly all the trimmings that went with it! Millie could find no answer to Priscilla's new way of life, and Oliver had given up trying to persuade her that she needed to find a job and do something sensible with her life, instead of looking and behaving 'like a cheap tart' as he put it!

Priscilla could never understand why Angela would never go out with her and her friends just to party and have a good time.

"I don't understand you, Angela. Why can't you come out with me one night? We'll go to a club, meet some guys and just chill out." She would say, somewhat frustrated.

"I just don't want to, Priscilla. I have my leisure hours cut out with the theatre group and that's my life," Angela answered.

"You're such a bore Angela," Priscilla retorted.

CHAPTER TWO

A Matter of Life or Death

It was so sudden and so unexpected. There was no warning at all on that fateful day in June.

Oliver had phoned Millie late that afternoon in a panic, asking her to bring over a file he had forgotten to take to the office that morning. He had pointed out that it was a matter of life and death that he got the file by 5.30, since it would close a sale with a great deal of money at stake and the client was coming in to pick it up. It was 4.45 and Priscilla had asked Millie if she could cadge a lift to the station, as she had to meet a friend early that evening. Angela had left earlier as she was rehearsing for a new play which was to open shortly.

It was raining hard and Millie was driving faster than usual, bent on getting to Oliver's office by 5.30. She never saw the car that hit them. For a moment that seemed like an eternity no one, out of shock, did anything. But then a passer-by called for an ambulance and thankfully it came within a few minutes.

When Millie had not arrived at Oliver's office by 5.30 with his client agitatedly waiting, he was beside himself with anger, but this turned into worry when he could get no reply from Millie. After thirty minutes he called Angela and told her his concern, after which they agreed they should stop what they were doing and go home immediately. They both got back to the house about the same time, but there was no message and no note of any kind had been left. They were on the point of calling the police when the police arrived. They informed them there had been an accident and that both Millie and Priscilla had been taken to hospital, but their condition was as yet unknown.

On the way to the hospital Angela and Oliver did not say one word to each other, since inwardly they feared the worst. On arrival the senior doctor gently informed them that Millie had died, but had not suffered unduly as she had never regained consciousness. Oliver was as white as a sheet and looked as though he was about to have a heart attack. In his head were his last words to Millie that it was *a matter of life or death* that she got to his office by 5.30. Angela, thankfully not aware of this, broke down and cried her heart out. The doctor endeavoured to lessen the grief by informing them that Priscilla was in a coma, but apart from that had miraculously survived with only a fractured left leg. They were treating her accordingly, but had no idea how she was going to respond as it was too early.

Angela insisted on seeing her mother, but Oliver was in far too much distress and could not in any way face doing so. Once she had seen for herself that, in spite of everything, there was the look of peace on her mother's face she felt a little calmer. She then insisted on seeing Priscilla and as she lovingly looked at her and held her hand she prayed, and how she prayed, for her safe and speedy recovery.

Suddenly the world seemed to be on Angela's shoulders and once more she prayed, but this time for God to give her the strength to handle the loss of her mother as well as coping with caring for Oliver and eventually Priscilla, who at this moment did not know her mother had died. Sadly, Oliver was noticeably a broken man, who stared constantly into space most of the time. Through sheer perseverance, Angela persuaded him to go to the office, to occupy his mind if nothing else. His two business partners were extremely sympathetic and helped to lessen the blow in as many ways as they possibly could.

Vicki

Vicki Brown was a fully trained nurse with specialised qualifications directed to the care of patients who needed constant twenty-four hour monitoring. Priscilla was naturally diagnosed as being one of these and Vicki had been signed exclusively to her care. Angela respected her enormously and Vicki had kept her promise of giving

Angela a daily update on Priscilla's progress. Angela was also grateful that Vicki had agreed that she should be the one to tell Priscilla of her mother's death as she alone would know when Priscilla would be mentally and physically capable of accepting such traumatic news. She also advised Angela to go ahead with the funeral arrangements and the funeral itself, since Priscilla would not be in any condition mentally or physically to cope with that.

Thankfully it was not too long before Priscilla was out of the coma and realised just how much she owed Vicki, who in turn simply said that she was only doing her job. They soon found they had a natural bond between them and became firm friends. The day Vicki had selected to tell Priscilla that her mother had died in the accident and that the funeral had already taken place was the most difficult thing of all to do, but eventually with Vicki's astute mental therapy Priscilla managed to accept it. Angela was indeed indebted to Vicki for this and welcomed her sister back into the real world, but had to tell her that Oliver was unfortunately in a bad way. However, she would try to persuade him to come and visit.

"Come on Dad, why don't you come to the hospital with me one day? Priscilla would love to see you."

Angela detected bitterness and guilt in his voice.

"I'm frightened to face her. It was my bloody stupid fault for asking Millie to go to the office in the first place on that day. I'll live with that for the rest of my life."

Once again those dreaded words *'a matter of life or death'* came into his head.

"It was an accident and nobody's fault except for the guy who hit her. You will have to put up with Priscilla until she comes to terms with it, which, given time, I am sure she will," Angela answered philosophically.

Oliver, with some commendable courage, did eventually take Angela's advice and went with her to the hospital. Priscilla, now feeling much better, showed no mercy towards Oliver. She raised her voice with a mixture of grief and anger,

"It was all your bloody fault. You and that bloody office. That was all you effing cared about. Mum's gone all because of you. You are wicked."

Angela responded gently, "Priscilla, life goes on. We cannot undo the past. It's going to be hard for all of us, but we must stick together. It is all we have and mother would want it that way."

There was a moment's pause before Priscilla, with tears in her eyes, looked at both Oliver and Angela and said, "I'm sorry, I couldn't help myself. It's over now."

The day Priscilla was to be discharged from hospital was fast approaching, so she decided that a heart to heart with Vicki was essential.

"Vicki, I want you to know how fantastic you have been and how much I value our friendship. Now my mother has gone I need to build a new life. I should really think about helping Angela to look after Oliver, but there is something else on my mind. I want to do what you do. I want to care for people who are suffering. I want to be a nurse."

Vicki responded without any semblance of surprise.

"Priscilla, you have become a friend, my best friend. Unknowingly you have done a lot for me too, but are you positively, really positively sure it is nursing you want to do? It is often a very thankless job." She paused before continuing, "If it is, I know this hospital is short staffed and I know I could get you on to their training programme. It would mean dedication and a lot of hard work. Apart from that, once you have committed yourself to it there is almost no turning back."

"I don't have to think about it. I am absolutely sure it is the right thing for me to do and will hopefully make me feel I have done something worthwhile with my life."

"Well, I also have a proposition for you. How would you like to move in with me and share my apartment in Haselmere? I used to have a boyfriend sharing with me but he has gone now and there is just me, Lily and a spare bedroom and, besides, I could do with some help with the rent. Lily, by the way, is my little cat. My boyfriend hated her and the feeling was mutual. He accused me of loving the cat more than him. She is as white as the driven snow but strangely has unusual grey markings on her tail and paws."

Then, as an after thought, "Oh my God I hope you like cats."

"We've never had a cat or a dog in our family. Oliver had no time for them. I think cats are very therapeutic animals and Lily sounds adorable. Oh Vicki, I am so excited.

Thank you so much for everything."

Vicki informed Angela of the day Priscilla was to be discharged from hospital and offered to drop her home. Angela then invited Vicki to stay for dinner, which unexpectedly gave Vicki and Priscilla the opportunity of being able to tell Angela and Oliver what they had in mind.

Although initially a little surprised, Angela could only be pleased for them, and Oliver was really happy that Priscilla at last had come to her senses and wanted to follow such an esteemed profession and do something worthwhile with her life. Angela suddenly realised that the responsibility of looking after Oliver was going to rest squarely on her shoulders. Priscilla knew this only too well and inwardly was feeling considerably selfish and guilty in moving to Haselmere so soon.

As time went on, Oliver's health and well being was slowly deteriorating. Angela was well aware of it and noticed that Oliver's hearing and particularly his eyesight were not as good as they used to be. He was now only going to the office two days a week and for the remainder of the time became a recluse, either locking himself in his study at home or staring at the TV all day long.

But one evening over dinner he caught Angela completely unawares.

"Angela, I had a call today from my business partners. They're very concerned about my health, and the business, which has been suffering due to my lack of interest and drive, especially as I have only been going to the office two days a week. Prospective customers have been becoming anxious and existing deals have not been negotiated or completed as they used to be. I have to admit that since Millie died my world has fallen apart and my heart has not been in it. My partners knew that something was seriously not right. They have offered to buy me out if it would help, and if I truly felt there was no other solution. To be honest, I was relieved and I didn't really have to think twice about it. Basically I agreed to the proposition, and whilst I still have some sanity left they will work out some sort of amicable financial agreement over the next few weeks. When a settlement is finally reached my wish is that both you and Priscilla share the money equally. I have no need for it, especially as you, my darling Angela, are now taking care of me so well."

Angela bit her lip as she listened to this, but at the back of her mind she'd had the feeling that something like this would eventually be on the cards. Oliver needed strength and that strength had to come from her. She answered him positively.

"You are talking as if you have written yourself off and it is the end of your life. If this is really what you want I am not going to stop you, but I am going to try to get you to change your way of thinking. I want you to get rid of this ridiculous guilt you are living with and I want you to see a counsellor. I want you to get back to work and be the person you used to be. You cannot let this destroy you, because it is destroying Priscilla and me too. Mum wouldn't want it. If I arrange the counsellor will you do it, for yourself and us?"

"If you can really be bothered, then arrange it. How I wish to God I could change the past," he said with so much hurt, guilt and regret in his voice that it was painfully chilling.

"You can't change the past, but you can build a future. It's not the end of the world. You have got to realise that," Angela responded with conviction.

Oliver remained quite adamant in wanting to sell his share in the company, which the counsellor pointed out to Angela was probably his way of punishing himself. In order to do this and put the buy-out wheels in motion his two business partners found they had no option but to tell Oliver that the client who was waiting in his office for the file on that fateful day of Millie's death did in fact return, but at a later date, and they successfully concluded the business deal that Oliver had initially painstakingly put together. It also turned out to be the company's biggest and most successful deal to date and it was to translate into a considerable amount of money, which his two partners confirmed would be reflected in the final buy out figure which would shortly be forthcoming.

Oliver's reaction to this information was very strange. He seemed to be neither pleased nor upset, but the counsellor had noticed that Oliver was finding it impossible to eliminate the fact that it was his tenacity and hell bent obsession in bringing this particular deal to a successful conclusion that became the catalyst to literally blowing his world apart, fuelled by those unforgettable words instructing Millie to get to the office by 5.30. He could never in a million years have predicted that such a statement was to bring about the reality of such a dreadful tragedy.

In Oliver's mind, all the money in the world could not replace the loss of Millie, so the knowledge of the success of the ultimate deal was of no consequence.

The strain of everything was beginning to tell on Angela. She looked harassed and tired and was beginning to question her own strength in handling what was becoming an intolerable situation. However, there were times when Oliver's mind was still as sharp as a razor. He made Angela call his lawyer to ask him to be prepared to raise the necessary documents to apportion the forthcoming money as he requested and at the same time to re-define his original will. He also asked Angela to invite Priscilla over for dinner so he could spell out his wishes to them both at the same time.

Oliver was genuinely pleased to see Priscilla, especially as she was now well on her way to becoming a fully trained nurse. She looked so mature and grown up that Oliver had a problem in believing it was really her. Priscilla was very concerned and quite frightened at seeing his condition. She opened the conversation.

"Dad, (she had never used that word before, but thought it might be a good piece of psychology) you mean the world to Angela and me and for our mother Millie's sake, if for no one else, you have got to come to terms with the fact that she is no longer with us. She would have wanted you and expected you to take charge of this family. Please try to understand what we are saying."

Oliver deliberately discarded Priscilla's comments, pretending not to hear at all, and then slowly and emphatically told them that the money received from the sale of his share of the business, which would be quite considerable, was to be divided equally between them. As far as 'Odd Acres' was concerned, he wanted the deeds of the property to be transferred into Angela's name. If Angela decided to sell the house then thirty per cent of the monies received after the normal deductions would be paid to Priscilla.

Angela and Priscilla remained rigid and silent whilst everything began to sink in. They were both very embarrassed, since all this was something new and very difficult and different for them to accept and deal with. In the silence of that room Oliver's softly spoken words had only helped to add to the impact and realisation of the devastating loss of their mother and the dreadful guilt that lay with their father. They knew life had to go on, but they also knew with this dramatic change of events they were now going to be rather financially well off. Oliver broke the silence.

"When the money becomes available I advise both of you to invest it immediately. It is virtually equal to my entire career earnings, but it will be your money and I know you will use it carefully and wisely. I am more than happy that both of you should have it."

Angela responded on behalf of them both

"We really don't know how to thank you, but the money is not important when it comes to you and your health. Priscilla and I would much rather have you well and happy and like your old self again." Oliver was quick to answer.

"I hate my old self," he said with considerable anger and changed the subject immediately.

"Priscilla, how long have you got to go before you become fully qualified? And how is the apartment in Haselmere?"

Angela interjected, "And how is the lovely Vicki?"

"The lovely Vicki is lovely and sends her love. I have just a little longer to go before becoming a fully trained nurse and being paid full time, all thanks to Vicki by the way. The apartment is great, small but comfortable and little Lily is fantastic. Vicki thinks we should get another cat to keep her company. She is on her own a lot."

"I have never had time for animals. They can't replace humans and I don't really care for them actually," Oliver said, appearing to be deep in thought. "I think Millie would have loved a cat, or even a dog, but as I couldn't be bothered we never had one. After all, think of the cost and all their nasty little habits, but …. maybe we should have had something."

Angela answered with a smile, "A cat would have been nice. Not much up-keep and you wouldn't have had to waste your precious time in taking it out for walkies!"

Priscilla then said, "Lily is one in a million. Although not a pedigree or anything like that she is quite aloof in her own way. She is always preening herself. She tries and almost succeeds in making herself and us believe she is a 'posh pussy' and one cut above the rest, but she lets herself down by displaying her vulnerability in being too loving and too adorable."

There was a pause and momentary silence.

The two girls simultaneously realised that the conversation was making Oliver feel uncomfortable, bringing up things in the past that possibly should have been done and considered but had been discarded as not being that important.

CHAPTER THREE

True love ways

Angela began to realise that to ignite the fire of life in Oliver again would need more than a miracle. There were the days when she really felt there were signs of progress and improvement, but Oliver would suddenly, with no warning at all, slip back into the depths of despair and depression. Because she so dearly loved her father and in spite of feeling sorry for the unfortunate predicament he was in, her will power and determination to at least improve his quality of life were more important to her at this moment in time than anything else, certainly much more important than his money and sadly more important than her beloved theatre group.

Angela hadn't really noticed how serious it was until the documents concerning the buy-out arrived from the lawyers for Oliver's perusal and signature. He seemed to be having considerable difficulty in reading the contents, even when wearing his normal glasses. A subsequent eye examination, which he reluctantly conceded to, confirmed that Oliver had cataracts in both eyes that needed an operation, which in this day and age was not too much of a problem and could easily be arranged.

Angela had desperately pleaded with Oliver to have this done as it would give him so much more quality of life. Oliver flatly refused to listen, maintaining that he had no intention of going through the trauma and "messing about" of any sort of operation, let alone an eye operation.

Angela inwardly cried a million tears, with all the worry and caring seeming to be so pointless. Having to witness Oliver pathetically feeling the food on his plate with his fingers as he tried to work out what he was eating, seeing the vacant look on his face and the continual staring into space were the saddest things of all.

Oliver's money finally arrived and Angela gave a shocked Priscilla a cheque for fifty per cent of it as Oliver had requested. Although amazed by the huge amount of money that it was, Priscilla was much more concerned and upset to learn that Angela was once again seriously thinking of giving up her theatrical career. However, Angela wanted to make sure she had considered all alternatives before coming to the drastic decision of having to give up the theatre group. She therefore decided to arrange, *without* Oliver's permission, for the attendance of a nurse to come in for a few hours three or four times a week, which would give her some much needed respite and cover some of the time she needed to go to her theatre group.

Exasperated and virtually at the end of her tether, she finally came to the conclusion that she was entitled to a life of her own and that she didn't really care what Oliver thought. He would just have to accept it. Since Oliver was still physically pretty functional she even contemplated the possibilities of a white stick and a guide dog. With a wicked smile on her face she thought, "He and nursie would be able to go out for 'walkies' together. How nice would that be!"

Sadly it wasn't long before another problem began to emerge, when Oliver's hearing decided to 'go off air' with Angela very often having to almost shout before Oliver showed any response at all. Finally he became totally deaf. This forced Angela to make changes she dreaded, but sensibly she continued to retain the nursing care. She eventually had no alternative but to commit Oliver to the confines of a wheelchair. Oliver's deterioration meant that she was no longer in the position of being able to continue with her career and the theatre group. It upset her incredibly to realise that Oliver now had little or no quality of life whatsoever, and the situation was made worse by the fact that Oliver's mind was still very much alive. What he had to cope with daily did not bear thinking about as it could only be described as a living hell.

Angela, for her own sanity, religiously continued to take care of the garden, which had been so much a part of her mother's life and anyway she enjoyed it. For two or three days, whilst tending to the flower beds near the kitchen back door, she felt she was being watched, but never actually saw anybody until she heard a faint meow.

"Hello – you don't look too good. Where have you come from?"

A scruffy but strangely beautiful grey cat was sitting watching her. He was noticeably thin and very much the worse for wear. Angela felt sorry for him.

"Would you like some milk?"

He followed her indoors, started to purr and rub against her legs. He drank the milk in seconds and then sat looking at her, watching her every move, and then he was gone. The following evening he was there again and did exactly the same thing. During the next day Angela discovered that one of the small windows in the summer house had been left open and on the floor in a corner was an old blanket with tell tale signs of someone having made a bed. That night he was back again.

Angela said inquisitively

"It's you again. You've been sleeping in the summer house haven't you?"

Once again she gave him some milk and some leftover food, which he demolished at breakneck speed. He then looked up at her, again watching her every move, and she was wondering what he was going to do next. She deliberately left the kitchen door open, but he followed her into the lounge. As if it had always been home, he found the rather large and beautiful fur rug that was laid in front of the fireplace. He settled himself down, licking his lips contentedly and wiping his face with his paw. Angela momentarily thought 'what a cheek' and was about to remove him when, for some reason, she had second thoughts. On looking at him in more detail Angela could clearly see he was once a very beautiful cat. There was a definite pedigree look about him, although she knew nothing about that subject, having never had a cat before. She figured something pretty awful must have happened to him. Angela opened the conversation:

"So tell me all about it. Where have you come from? What's happened to you? How on earth have you got into this state? You look terrible."

He looked at her wishing more than anything else that she could understand what he was thinking and trying to tell her.

"I have been thrown in the back of a van for nearly two days with no food or water. It was worse than a nightmare and I have never been so frightened in all my life. My home was in Liverpool, where I was born. They were a lovely couple in their seventies and they paid a lot for me and my twin sister because we were classified as being pedigree. Our breed was named British short hair and that's what they wanted. They called us Henry and Henrietta. We hated those names.

It happened so quickly. One minute we were playing in the front garden and the next we were each put into a sack and thrown into the back of a white van filled with hundreds of empty cardboard boxes. We seemed to be driving forever, but even though I realized we had stopped for the night somewhere, we were given no food or water. I know my sister was in deep distress because she was meowing very loudly, but eventually this stopped and there was silence. I felt sick."

Angela stared sympathetically at the cat, wondering just what to do.

"The next day we were driving again and I felt I was suffocating, so I began to gnaw and claw at the sacking and I managed to make it tear. The van pulled into a garage and the driver left his door open. This was my chance. I tried to find my sister but I just couldn't amongst all those boxes. There was an opening in a partition between the driving compartment of the van and where I was so I jumped and ran for my life."

Angela was thinking that perhaps she should call the RSPCA. They might be able to trace his owner.

"I ran and ran and ran and came across your garden and the summer house, which had a window open. There was an old blanket on the floor so I stayed there shaking and wondering what I was going to do next. I felt quite ill thinking about my sister. I always looked after her. I was frightened, hungry and thirsty. I knew I must have looked terrible but I had at least managed to escape.

Angela then had a brainwave. She decided to call Vicki, feeling sure she would know what to do since she already had a cat.

She said with concern in her voice,

"Vicki guess what? I have acquired a cat and although he's in a dreadful state I'm sure he has a semblance of a pedigree. He was sitting by my back door watching me gardening. He looks like he's suffered something awful and is obviously feeling very sorry for himself. He is grey, rather thin and his fur is in a bad way. I have given him some milk, but I just don't know what to do with him. He must belong to somebody."

Vicki answered, quite intrigued,

"I reckon he's been kidnapped, or rather catnapped, and managed to escape. If he is a pedigree he's worth money you know, quite a lot. I reckon you should keep him."

Priscilla, having overheard the conversation, then said to Angela

"Without being unkind, Oliver would never know, and he would be company for you in that big house."

Angela looked at the cat and remarked,

"He is beautiful. I suppose he's a he, but I need to get him cleaned up. I'll think about what you said."

The cat now curled up on the rug but, with those tiger-like eyes wide open, looked intently at Angela, knowing his fate lay firmly in her hands. He thought,

"You know what, I quite like it here. You've been very kind, so I think I'll call this home from now on. It's a nice big comfortable house with plenty of room. You can be my mistress if you like. I won't object to that at all."

Angela made a mental note of what Vicki and Priscilla had said, but her conscience got the better of her and she decided she should at least put an ad in the local paper with a suitably worded description, saying she had found the cat and was hoping to find a much relieved owner. She gave her name, address and phone number and whilst she was waiting for a possible response over the next few days she decided to try to get the cat looking something like she thought he should. Angela got the blanket from the summer house and spread it out on the kitchen floor. She carefully put the cat on the blanket, got some soap and water and on her hands and knees gently washed his fur. She was amazed to find that the cat had no objection to this at all, even arching his back in obvious ecstasy and purring with sheer delight.

"Oh this is seventh, eighth and ninth heaven. I've never had this done to me before. I will do anything for you Angela. I am yours forever and ever and ever."

Angela rubbed him dry with a towel and then brushed him… with Oliver's hair brush! She brushed him methodically for the next two days and his fur started to become silver blue grey in colour with a beautiful sheen. It was also soft and quite thick. He had somehow suddenly become important to her and she inwardly hoped there would be no reply to the ad in the paper. When she had finished the grooming she said,

"You look so much better. You're really quite a big pussy and you're so beautiful. Those tiger-like eyes are just gorgeous. You can stay on the rug in the lounge temporarily until I think of something else. I wonder if anybody will claim you. I hope not."

"I do think about the old couple in Liverpool quite a lot and feel sorry for them, because they will miss us both a great deal. I wonder where my sister really is. I pray for her every night and pray she has not lost all of her nine lives".

It was seven o'clock one evening when there was a knock on the door.

A youngish man with a fresh complexion, in his early thirties, wearing jeans and trainers with a baseball cap turned round the wrong way, was standing at the door. Angela suspected something untoward before she had even opened the door. With a noticeably strong Liverpudlian accent, he said,

"So you've got my cat. I thought he was gone for good. I've come to take him back."

"How do I know he's your cat?" Angela retorted

The cat, hearing raised voices, decided to investigate. He got a shock when he saw who it was and showed his feelings by hissing and snarling.

"You're the one. You kidnapped my sister and me and put us in those dirty horrible sacks in the back of your bloody van for nearly two days. Going to sell us, no doubt! No food! No water! Nothing! We practically starved to death, and what the hell have you done with my sister? Is she alive or have you also found some horrible way of disposing of her?"

"I don't think the cat likes you. Before I let you have him you have to give or show me some definite proof. I want to see the bill of sale and receipt or give me the name and address of the people you bought him from," Angela said emphatically.

"I'll do no such thing. He's my cat. I'll come back and bring the police with me," he said angrily.

"You do that," Angela responded and shut the door.

The cat returned to the rug whilst Angela made herself a cup of coffee and then, sitting next to him, said,

"Well he didn't get you and I don't think he'll be coming back. You know what. I think you should have a name. I am going to call you Buckingham, because it's the name of the beautiful county I live in and it is where we first met. It is a powerful name that commands attention and respect and that is how I see you."

She paused for a minute and then continued,

"Buckingham – I think you and I will be good friends and I want you to feel this is your home, but we are not alone here. There is Oliver, my father, who is sadly in a wheelchair and cannot see or hear. He is sleeping right now. There is a nurse who comes in quite often and there is Priscilla, my sister, who I know will be dying to meet you. She and her friend Vicki love cats, in fact they have a beautiful little white cat of their own called Lily."

*"Buckingham. I'm not sure I like that. It's a bit of a mouth full compared to Henry and will take some getting used to, but the sound of it is quite regal and makes me feel proud."*And then after some *paws* for thought – *"How about Bucks?"*

Priscilla called Angela to find out what had happened with the cat. Angela replied,

"He is settling in quite nicely now, thank you, but we had a near escape with the ad I put in the local paper. Some guy came round and said he had bought him, so I asked for proof, which of course he couldn't come up with. When Buckingham saw him he went berserk."

"Buckingham? That's unusual. Whatever made you think of that? It sounds very up market. Lily wouldn't like that. I'm longing to see him."

"Why don't you and Vicki come round?"

An hour later the door bell rang and Angela knew who it was.

"Bucks, come and meet Priscilla and Vicki."

"What did you just say? I can't believe it. You must have read my mind. You've said it. You've actually said it. I love the sound of Bucks. That really makes me feel good."

As soon as Priscilla and Vicki saw Buckingham, they were virtually speechless for a few moments. They hadn't expected to see such an amazing cat. Vicki gently picked him up and carried him into the lounge, sat down, put him on her lap and started to gently caress him. Buckingham succumbed immediately, purring loudly.

"My goodness. You're a big, beautiful boy."

Buckingham looked at her with eyes filled with pleasurable catitude.

"I have never been picked up like that before. You're so gentle and so loving".

Vicki and Priscilla, virtually in unison, said, "He is gorgeous."

Priscilla then said,

"Now, how's Oliver doing?

Angela answered with real sadness in her eyes,

"He's coping just but there's no quality of life."

Angela found it hard to hold back the tears for a few seconds, whilst Vicki, Priscilla and Buckingham looked helplessly on. Stroking Buckingham affectionately, Vicki said,

"Angela, Buckingham's really concerned. I've never seen a cat look like that. Look at his eyes. I think you could have more than just a good friend here."

Angela gradually composed herself and even managed a smile.

Priscilla then said,

"You know what Angela, I want to do something worthwhile with Oliver's money. Nursing is my life and I have been fully trained for a while now, thanks to Vicki. So we have come up with an idea and we have already started to put the wheels in motion.

Vicki continued,

"We thought we would look for a large house or building somewhere and convert it into a residential care home with facilities that would qualify it as providing what we would call HALE–Home Assisted Living for the Elderly. It is basically envisaged as a home from home for the elderly, but with care staff on hand at all times to deal with the activities of daily living that can be problematic, such as mobility, washing, dressing etc. A resident, rather than being an object of care, would be able to develop a one to one relationship with a carer at the same time as being able to enjoy the company of others, both male and female, in a friendly and homely atmosphere. Vicki and I have worked and cared for old people so much that we strongly feel this would work. Because everyone would virtually be in the same predicament, an environment like this would hopefully give them something to live for, with some real quality of life."

Priscilla intervened,

"The number of residents would depend entirely on the size of the building. There would be plenty of opportunities to socialise and relax as it would have a number of communal areas and hopefully a garden. There would also be planned excursions."

Vicki excitedly continued,

"Priscilla and I would, of course, live there. I intend to put what money I have into it, which would include the money from the sale of my apartment, and we would own it jointly. I have already given the brief to an estate agent friend of mine who is at present looking into suitable and available properties. Unfortunately, it might require us to move to another area, but we believe in the idea so much that we are determined to go ahead and make the dream a reality."

For a few moments Angela was silent, trying to take it all in

"Would there be any conditions to living there?"

Vicki replied,

"Well yes. You have to quite definitely be over sixty years old."

Priscilla interjected,

"And there is the small matter of finance of course. It wouldn't be cheap. We also thought it would be a brilliant idea to have Oliver as its first resident. He would have round the clock care and you, of course, could visit as often as you liked. The greatest thing of all is that it would give you some space and time to make something of

24

your life, other than being a carer for twenty-four hours a day."

Angela responded quite positively

"Well, it's a wonderful idea and I don't see why it shouldn't work if you're careful and sensible. I think you're both mature enough to handle something as responsible as this. Oliver may not agree to the proposition, but if there is anything I can do you know where I am."

And then looking at Buckingham, "I'll have a word with him and see if he's got any bright ideas!"

Lap cat!

Angela felt really pleased for Vicki and Priscilla, but perhaps inwardly a little jealous of them being in a position to look forward to the excitement of a whole new adventure. Her theatre group had been everything to her, but now there was a large hole in her life that needed filling. She was, of course, very pleased that Buckingham had suddenly appeared, since he was quietly making a big difference and she began to realise that she was going out of her way to deliberately spend as much time as possible with him.

Looking after Oliver and his twenty-four hour needs, even with some help from a nurse, was beginning to tell. He couldn't really appreciate the trips out in the wheelchair and she felt so helpless. She could find nothing nor think of anything that would give him something to live for and make both his and her life less of a nightmare.

Incredibly, a miracle was about to happen beyond all comprehension, taking Angela completely by surprise.

It was a Wednesday afternoon and it was raining hard. Oliver was in his wheelchair in the lounge as usual, staring into space. He was obsessed with having a blanket covering his lap and his legs, probably because it made him feel secure, but as Angela looked at him it occurred to her that he still had the sense of feel and touch; after all, she watched him every day pathetically feeling the food on his plate.

The TV was on as always, for Oliver's benefit, but goodness

knows why, as he could neither hear nor see. Buckingham was curled up on the rug, but looking strangely and intently up at Oliver in a way that Angela had never seen before.

"I'm going to give him the surprise of his life. He won't know what's happened and I'll keep my paws crossed and just hope he doesn't die of shock."

Suddenly, with no warning whatsoever, Buckingham leapt onto Oliver's lap. Oliver threw his arms up in the air as if the end of the world had come, whilst Angela screamed as if someone had just attacked her from behind.

"Bucks, what the bloody hell do you think you're doing?"

Plainly incensed, she went to grab hold of Buckingham to get him off Oliver's lap. Buckingham refused to let her do this, sticking his claws into Oliver's blanket. Once over the initial shock, Oliver's reaction was both extraordinary and unbelievable. He actually started stroking Buckingham's fur putting his hands deep into it and gently kneading it. Buckingham responded with a purr as loud but as smooth as the sound of the tick over of a Rolls Royce engine. Absolute **purr**-fection!

"Now that's more like it. That's what I hoped and wanted you to do. I'm going to keep purring because I like what you are doing and I know you like what you are doing. Angela, bless her, was well out of order, but then she wasn't to know my ingenious strategy. Oliver, I'm sorry, but from now on I'm in charge and you're going nowhere without me."

Seeing the sudden change in Oliver, who now had the most extraordinary look of contentment on his face, shocked Angela so much that, perhaps against her better judgement, she decided to leave Buckingham to his own devices. He obviously knew exactly what he was doing, so she asked him:

"Bucks that was a very clever but stupid thing to do. It could have been disastrous. In fact you might have killed Oliver. Where did you get that idea from? You know you've made a rod for your own back now, or rather a lap for your own bum, and now you've made a relationship for yourself with a serious commitment. Do you really think you can handle it, after all, you're only a cat for God's sake?"

Buckingham, having now firmly positioned himself on Oliver's lap, looked at Angela:

"You underestimate my strategy. I've been watching him closely for some time and it was a pre-determined gamble that paid off. He can touch as much as he likes and he can feel as much as he likes and I can purr as much as I like – and as loud as I like and he will feel that too! He will now have, as far as I am concerned, a wonderful quality of life – that he is rightfully entitled to."

It wasn't long before Oliver and Buckingham became inseparable and Angela often had a problem getting Buckingham off Oliver's lap when it came time for Oliver to retire. Buckingham seemed to become very protective, even over protective at times, but Oliver now had something to live for. Those big, beautiful cat's eyes continually caught Angela off guard.

"You know what, Angela, if I couldn't see or hear I think I'd make a reservation in pussycat heaven, that is if they'd have me but then we have nine lives and he has one!"

Angela found herself muttering to herself

"He's just a cat. He's not even a human. He's just a cat – a totally stupid, wonderfully unbelievable cat!"

CHAPTER FOUR

Tillsworthy House

It wasn't too long before Vicki's estate agent friend, knowing what they were looking for, although unusual, came up with some prospective properties to view. It was the third one that seemed to have the potential to accommodate what they had in mind, but it would need a great deal of work and of course a great deal of money. However, upon investigation it would be cheaper than building something totally from scratch. This large, neglected property built in the nineteen thirties was situated on the outskirts of Guildford in Surrey. It was an enormous traditional six bedroom house including servants' quarters, built in ornamental grey stone with a daunting entrance dominated by two huge Romanesque stone columns. It had almost an acre of land, with a driveway leading to the house, being at least three hundred yards long with surprisingly well-preserved period stone statues spaced out at intervals on each side of it.

As the story goes, the property belonged to a much respected but assumed, Lord and Lady Wilkinson. They had bought the house apparently outright and had established themselves in the community as very nice people. But it was later discovered that the Lord was in fact somewhat of a rogue, whose real name was William Wilkins, alias Willie Wilkins, who had graduated with full honours into the art of professional burglary. Both he and his wife, through boredom more than anything else, became totally addicted to gambling, which was eventually to be their undoing. Having enjoyed a luxurious lifestyle for some time, good luck turned to bad with the Lord and his Lady's 'dodgy deals' catching up with them and giving them eventually no alternative but to flee the country. The house became neglected and was allowed to fall into disrepair until The State managed to acquire it and put it up for sale.

Priscilla and Vicki were fascinated with its history and viewed it two or three times before finally making up their minds. They decided that it had the potential, and more, for accommodating what they envisaged, so they did the deal and set about finding a suitable builder and architect. They both had positive ideas about its design, and although it was a bit of a tennis match between them and the architects, they finally came to amicable agreements on everything, as numerous ideas came up for consideration. The house was unusual in having three floors, but for what they had in mind this was considered to be an asset. For obvious reasons there would have to be a lift installed and the interior of the house would have to be virtually gutted. It would be totally re-designed, but would retain the magnificent staircase, which provided a powerful centre piece to the whole interior. The house, originally named Wilkinson Manor, would be re-named Tillsworthy House. On completion it would accommodate fifteen fully functional residential care rooms or suites. They would all be fitted with en suite bathrooms and toilets, but the rooms themselves would not be furnished, the idea being that the residents would bring their own furniture and personal effects, which would give them the feeling of having something that was part of their lives and totally personal to them. The entire downstairs area would be open plan, incorporating various facilities and providing the ultimate in relaxation.

What had been the servants' quarters would be converted into a luxurious two bedroom apartment for Vicki and Priscilla. It was hoped the job would be completed within six months, during which time an advertising and marketing campaign would have to be seriously thought about and put in place. The accountants were a little concerned about the, understandably, emotional side of things getting in the way of running the venture as a profitable business, especially as both Priscilla and Vicki were totally inexperienced. However, as both their track records were exemplary as far as professional care and nursing were concerned, they assured the accountants that this was a lifelong commitment. They would not let the fact that they felt a little sad that only those fortunate enough to be substantially financially well off, would be able to afford the luxury of the benefits that something like this home offered, affect that commitment.

It was indeed an exciting time for Priscilla and Vicki as they watched in awe as Tillsworthy House grew and changed incredibly as each day went by. When the interior furnishings started to arrive, it began to look and feel rather like a five star country hotel, but there was a subtle difference in that its overall features were less austere and business-like. The interior colour scheme was a blend of soft pinks and greens shared between carpets, curtains and cushions, giving a feeling of tranquillity, finesse and comfort. In spite of the sumptuous settees and chairs scattered around and the Olde Worlde book cases, coffee tables and dining furniture, there was no attempt at deliberately creating opulence. As you entered the building through two rather beautiful glass doors that had the name Tillsworthy House etched in them, you felt it was really a home from home for those fortunate enough to be in a position to enjoy it. The most impressive feature of the whole downstairs area was that there was absolutely nothing that was symmetrical. Even though there was a specific dining area, a specific TV viewing area, a tea and coffee lounge and an unobtrusive reception desk, there were interesting and unusual nooks and crannies everywhere.

At first it was hard to take everything in, but without a doubt the staircase was a breathtaking feature. It was about three feet wide and covered in a thick, pastel green carpet. The beautiful wooden banister and slats had been restored and curved like a snake winding its way up to the next floor. Two wooden eagles perched on top of a majestic wooden column on each side of the first step signified the beginning of the staircase. Amazingly, the whole feature was repeated on the next floor going up to the third floor.

Since the day of completion was getting closer, it was now imperative to think about residents and to assemble an experienced and caring staff. Although the actual opening date could not yet be fixed, Priscilla and Vicki decided to put the wheels of advertising and marketing into motion. They agreed that word of mouth and a website were initially the best ways of attracting attention.

There was, however, an unforeseen element of luck coming their way. The local paper had got wind of the sale of Wilkinson Manor through obvious connections with the local council. Mainly due to the intriguing and fascinating history behind the place, and the fact that it had at long last found a buyer and that it was going to be turned into something commendably unusual and beneficial to the community, they decided to run an article promoting the venture and strongly supporting it. Photographs were taken and Priscilla and Vicki were interviewed, which provided them with the ideal opportunity of saying what they intended to do and offer, and that they were at present looking for residents and staff. The response to this, to the website which was now up and running, and by word of mouth, was staggering.

Tillsworthy House and HALE (Home Assisted Living for the Elderly) were now about to become reality. An attractive and distinctive notice board was accordingly positioned prominently to one side of the front entrance.

Priscilla and Vicki personally replied to all the enquiries and decided there should be a viewing period of one month before the official opening. Priscilla agreed to take on the job of interviewing prospective residents, whilst Vicki had her time cut out dealing with staff recruitment.

More important than anything else was the offer they had made to Angela regarding Oliver. He would have the honour of being the first resident and they subsequently 'ear marked' a suitable suite next to their apartment so they would then be able to keep a constant eye on him.

By the end of the four weeks they had reservations on all but two of the suites. Priscilla had to carefully evaluate every prospective resident to confirm their likes and dislikes, their financial situation and above all what caring or nursing facilities they would require. Vicki also had her hands full with the huge number of applications for employment. She had to be ultra selective, especially as far as caring and nursing were concerned, and particular attention had to be given to food, meals and cooking.

I could eat you!

With their 'baby' just about to be born, Priscilla and Vicki knew they owed much to Angela who, from a distance, had saved the day on more than one occasion. First of all, without any hesitation whatsoever, she came to their rescue financially, with an interest free loan when an unpredictable bout of bad weather had put a stop to any work being done for seven weeks. Priscilla had become genuinely depressed and worried that they had bitten off more than they could chew with the enormity of the project. But there was a forgotten lifeline. Angela informed the girls that she had now seriously made up her mind to sell 'Odd Acres' and that Priscilla was entitled to thirty per cent of the sale. The relief and gratitude on Priscilla and Vicki's faces was a sight for sore eyes and made Angela feel very happy.

Every day Priscilla and Vicki were up at the crack of dawn making the trip to Tillsworthy House and not getting back until late evening. They could not afford to miss one day, but as a result Angela was being sadly very neglected, so one night they decided to invite her over to dinner.

On arrival Angela spied Lily in her basket, went over to her and said affectionately,

"Oh Lily, you're such an adorable little 'pussikins'. You're gorgeous. I could eat you."

"Someone's paying some attention to me at last. I've been ignored, neglected and left on my own for hours and hours. I don't know what Priscilla and Vicki are up to but it is certainly not cat business. I am so lonely that I have seriously been considering leaving and finding a new home somewhere."

Lily gave Angela a rather sad and forlorn look. Angela responded, "Lily you don't look at all happy."

Over dinner, conversation turned to the excitement of the now amazing progress of Tillsworthy House and the prospect that Oliver would soon be able to move there.

Priscilla asked,

"Angela, how is Oliver doing these days?

Angela replied with a smile

"Well, Buckingham is his life and his life is Buckingham. What that cat did was totally out of this world. I shall never ever get over it. Where I go Buckingham goes and where Buckingham goes Oliver goes. Buckingham has changed my life forever. Oliver moving to Tillsworthy House is a great idea and very good for me, but Buckingham is going to be a pain in the bum because they are totally inseparable. However, there is one thing I want to say. I want you to bill me monthly for Oliver's living and care expenses. In that respect I insist he is treated as any other resident. You are not running a charity."

Vicki responded,

"Well, we can certainly do that, but Oliver is family and should have preferential treatment."

Angela was adamant.

"I don't agree at all and I will be very upset if you don't agree with my request. I don't want to hear any more about it, until you send me the invoice that is."

Vicki continued,

"Angela, how would you feel, and I know it's an imposition and a bit of a cheek, if Buckingham had some cat company in the form of Lily. Lily is unavoidably being left on her own for hours and hours due to Priscilla and I having to be at Tillsworthy House every day. We are very worried about her, in fact we are thinking about a cattery."

Angela's response surprised both the girls

"A cattery! Never! Oh I'd love to have Lily. Of course I'll have her. She's so cute and adorable, and Buckingham, well he'll go totally berserk, but he'll just have to grin and bear it."

Angela paused in thought for a moment and then sighed rather heavily.

"God knows what I've let myself in for."

Priscilla commented

"He should be so lucky. It's not everybody that gets a female thrown at his feet without having to do a thing."

Lily's ears pricked up

"A female thrown at his feet! Whose feet, for God's sake? That's not going to be me. I do not intend being thrown anywhere – not if I can help it. I'll be gone before that happens."

A classic touch

Angela had never bothered with a car since she believed having one was more trouble and money than it was worth, even though Millie, bless her, had insisted on teaching Priscilla and Angela to drive. She was now thinking very differently and strongly believed it could add a whole new dimension to her present way of life.

Oliver owned a beautifully maintained midnight blue Jaguar XJ6, which was his pride and joy and at present was forcibly mothballed in the garage. As it was far too big for her to contemplate driving it herself, and since Oliver was in no state to give an opinion on the matter she decided, needless to say with some reservation, to sell it and concentrate on finding something small and reliable.

Angela never had much time for modern things. She loved the

world of oak beams and everything that went with them. A car was the same. She would much rather own an 'old banger' or even a classic car than anything else. She remembered that there was someone in the theatre group who bought and sold classic cars. Through various contacts she managed to track him down and, as luck would have it, he had one, so he said 'just the jobbie'.

She looked sensational and there was only twenty-three thousand miles on the clock and not a mark on her. The black Morris Minor Traveller, with its part wooden body, was, for Angela, love at first sight. It was more than she had imagined and she could get Oliver's wheelchair quite easily in the back. As she proudly, if somewhat nervously, drove back to Odd Acres she felt she had the world at her feet and a whole new adventure was about to begin.

Getting Oliver into the car for the first time in his condition turned out to be somewhat of a feat. Angela had to painstakingly make him *feel* what she wanted him to do, hoping he would realise he was getting in and sitting in the seat of a car. Buckingham's reaction was at first very strange. He seemed to be scared.

"Oh God, it's like that van, but then it's not, because it has windows and it is not white and there are no boxes in the back either. I suppose I shall have to purr and bear it."

Angela briefly thought of putting Buckingham in a cat box, but then decided to leave him on Oliver's lap, which was the best solution for both of them. She had decided a ride in her new toy and a trip to the local superstore would be fun.

She knew Oliver would have a problem with wondering where he was so she tried to get him to feel things as she pushed the wheelchair down the aisles of the store with a

store trolley designed to attach to the front of it, and at the same time hoping no one was going say anything about the 'cat on the lap'. Buckingham was relishing every minute of this new adventure, discovering a new found fame in being the centre of attention that was consumed with adulation. Angela was stopped and asked a million times if he was for sale and how much she wanted for him. Buckingham was highly amused and soon saw them coming. He was not however about to allow curiosity to kill the cat.

"Here comes another one. Don't even think about it. There's no way you

can afford me because I am classified as priceless. I am not on the shelf yet and I am not for sale. Besides, if you got me you would have to have him too (he gave Oliver a furtive glance)

and Angela would never in a million years agree to that. I do sign autographs by the way, if that helps. Perhaps you'd like to start a fan club?

Lily

The day came when Angela proudly drove over to Haselmere to collect little Lily. Priscilla and Vicky were more than impressed with the car and both agreed that it was 'very Angela'.

Sadly the tears, goodbyes and assurances of love from Vicki especially, couldn't calm little Lily's trauma at wondering what on earth was in store for her.

*"Why are they doing this to me? I thought I had the **purr**fect life for a cat. Obviously Vicki doesn't love me anymore and wants me to live somewhere else. I'm very upset and hurt."*

Angela tried in vain to pacify her on the drive back to Odd Acres. Her constant crying was upsetting and distressing, but perhaps worse for Angela was the thought of how Buckingham would react to this unexpected package that was coming his way.

"Why am I so scared of Buckingham?" Angela kept on asking herself.

As Angela opened the door of the house she was saying over and over again, "It's all right Lily. Just try to keep calm. There's a good girl. It's all right. It's all right."

She put the box on the kitchen floor and went into the lounge to check on Oliver, and of course Bucks. If looks could kill, Angela was well and truly dead. Buckingham was throwing a wobbly.

"Who the hell is making all that noise? You've brought some horrible kind of creature back with you haven't you? I can smell it and it's not nice."

Angela looked at Buckingham and, with a touch of sarcasm, said,

"Bucks, it's your lucky day. We've got a beautiful young lady out there called Lily. She will be staying with us, so I want you to show me how much of a gentleman you actually are."

Buckingham voiced his disapproval accordingly.

"I don't want some nasty little female invading my space. Why should I

have to put up with that? I don't know where she's been or who she's been sleeping with. She's certainly not coming anywhere near me. You know Angela, you've been really unfair doing this behind my back. Quite frankly I want nothing to do with her and I don't intend being something I don't feel like being. I am referring to the word 'gentleman'."

Angela went into the kitchen, retrieved a protesting Lily, took her into the lounge and showed her to Buckingham. Serious dislike was very apparent. Oliver went into minor shock as Buckingham arched his back, barred his teeth and growled.

"Surely that thing's not a cat. It's more like a white rabbit. Just keep her away from me".

Lily returned the compliment with an appropriate hissing noise.

"I'm not putting up with him. He thinks he's God's gift. Well I think he's a 'catastrophe.' He's a disgrace to the world of cats and it's painfully obvious he wouldn't know how to treat a lady anyway."

With that Lily jumped out of Angela's arms, ran into the kitchen and hid in a corner.

Angela looked at Buckingham exasperated and, somewhat annoyed, said,

"Bucks. That was not called for and it was selfish. Apart from anything else you've upset Oliver and that, you know, is a no no."

Asking God to give her strength Angela then went to put food and milk for Lily in the kitchen next to Buckingham's dishes, but for almost two days neither Lily nor Buckingham would go near them. She also put a blanket in a corner for Lily as a temporary measure until she found a better place for her to sleep, preferably away from Buckingham.

For some time Lily cowered in the corner of the kitchen, but eventually cautiously ventured out and began to explore the house room by room, deliberately avoiding the lounge area and Buckingham. Suitably reprimanded by Angela, Buckingham was back in his rightful place on Oliver's lap, but he knew exactly where Lily was and what she was up to every minute of the day and night.

Angela didn't really approve of animals climbing all over furniture, but she reluctantly decided to coax Lily to settle down in one of the armchairs, which she eventually did, much to Buckingham's disapproval. Sometime later when she went to check on her she found that Buckingham, obviously not to be outdone, had decided to commandeer the other armchair once Oliver had gone to bed.

"You're not getting away with having your own chair. I'm having the other one. Not only that, I can keep a closer eye on you there, especially at night, than on the rug on the floor where I usually sleep."

Lily mentally responded,

"Having to forcibly tolerate being with you at all is bad enough and now having to look at you all day long and having you next to me all night long as well is even worse, so I am going to persuade myself that you don't exist and that you're just not there at all."

Angela had to concede that a chair each was fair. Buckingham had made very sure of that, but cat's eye contact between them, filled with absolute mistrust, was abundantly clear. Angela was getting rather fed up with it, to say the least, but decided not to interfere. They would just have to work things out for themselves. In time they'd find their own way of dealing with it.

It was plainly obvious, however, that Buckingham's mind was working overtime.

"Why did Angela have to ruin everything and spoil a quiet and peaceful life? I have ingeniously sorted Oliver out and this is the thanks I get. It's bloody well unfair but she (looking at Lily) *won't be getting away with anything as far as I'm concerned. Little does she know it, but she's in for the time of her life!"*

CHAPTER FIVE

I'm impressed.

Vicki had no problem in finding a buyer for the apartment, and the two girls were glad to make the move to Tillsworthy House for good, and be able to be on hand twenty- four hours a day. There was an incredible amount to organise and they made the rule that no resident could physically move in until the opening date. However, in view of Oliver's unusual condition, and for the sake of his welfare, they agreed with Angela that he should get settled in a week prior to the opening. They also thought it a good idea to allow Buckingham to stay for that week, after which Angela could bring him over whenever she liked, or perhaps to be more exact whenever Buckingham demanded it!

The day Angela had been dreading had arrived when she felt she could wait no longer in telling Buckingham that Oliver was going to a new home for good and that she was in just as much of a state about it.

"Bucks, you have to understand that the move to Tillsworthy House is for Oliver's sake as I just cannot look after him and his needs any more. With you and Lily as well it is killing me. He will have his own room, or suite, and Priscilla and Vicki will take very good care of him, and you will love it because there'll be lots of other people there too. Vicki and Priscilla have also agreed to allow you to stay with Oliver for the first week, after which I will take you over there two or three times a week for a couple of hours or so. I am also thinking about moving so both of us can be nearer to Oliver. You see how I always think of you too!"

Buckingham looked like he understood, but had he?

"She could have at least discussed all this with me beforehand, instead of organising such drastic changes in my life. Anyway, I am not sure I approve.

She gives with one hand and takes away with the other. First she dumps Lily on me and now she's taking Oliver away and moving herself. Well at least that annoying little white thing won't be bothering me for a week!"

Remembering Vicki's words, Angela said,

"You know what Bucks, you're a very lucky boy to have found someone who puts up with you and loves you as much as I do. You'd do well to remember that, and don't forget that I'm entitled to a life too. You go where I go. Understand?"

Angela was naturally very harassed the day that she had to take Oliver over to Tillsworthy House. Everything seemed so final and Oliver didn't really have any idea what was actually happening to him. Even though Buckingham made sure he was glued to Oliver's lap, he had also decided to exercise his vocal chords in a way Angela had not heard before, imparting his distinct disapproval with what was going on. This only resulted in Angela becoming even more distraught, bringing her almost to the end of her tether.

She said, unusually angry,

"Bucks you're bloody lucky you're not in a box. For God's sake just shut up and put your seat belt on."

Even though somewhat of a pointless exercise, Angela, as thoughtful as ever, selected some of Oliver's most personal things, particularly those dear to both Millie and himself, and moved them over to Tillsworthy House. Priscilla was particularly pleased about that for both her sake and her sister's since it kept the memory of Millie alive and closer to them.

Oliver's suite, as they all were on the first floor, was finished in pale blue, the second floor being in pastel green. They were all tastefully complimented with fitted carpets and matching curtains with a touch of Olde Worlde charm. Although the bathroom had a semblance of hotel about it, it was beautifully done and very functional. The shame of it all was that Oliver could not see it to appreciate it. Buckingham, on the other hand, seemed to have taken exceptional notice of his new surroundings. For a short while Oliver's lap had been replaced by Oliver's bed. Angela was really surprised at that and on Vicki and Priscilla's initial guided tour of the house, Buckingham investigated every single nook and cranny. The look on his face was extraordinary. What on earth was he thinking?

"I'm impressed. I am really impressed. It's almost a cat's paradise and you've done all this for me? I'm really looking forward to watching television in the TV lounge, having a coffee in the coffee lounge, checking out new books in the library lounge and just making friends, lots of friends. You've been so thoughtful about everything and it's certainly more than seventh heaven. It won't take me long before they all realise who owns the cat's whiskers round here."

He looked up at the three girls

"Oh don't worry, Oliver will always be my first concern. Why don't you invite Lily over here then maybe she could get lost!"

The wickedness in Buckingham's eyes did not go undetected, but was there a hidden truth behind that remark?

Troy

Angela was pleased to learn that, after a couple of days, Oliver, painstakingly aided by Buckingham, had settled in quite nicely. Although Angela missed them both terribly it was an enormous weight off her shoulders and she could now concentrate on herself. She realised Lily was once more on her own, but it was very noticeable that she really enjoyed it, probably because Buckingham was not on her case every single moment of the day and night. Fear and trepidation were no longer evident as she made herself more at home as each day went by.

Angela immediately put Odd Acres up for sale, placing it in the hands of a reputable local estate agent. She was quite adamant that her new home had to be within easy reach of Tillsworthy Hous, which meant Surrey and the Guildford area. She scoured the local papers to get an idea of what was available and prices. She and her beloved Morris Minor Traveller came to realise just how beautiful Surrey was, and even historic Guildford itself became quite a consideration in her mind. Apart from its own special charm it was complimented by many big name stores interspersed haphazardly throughout the main street. Having shops like House of Fraser was a major plus. However, she knew in her heart of hearts that it was the countryside that she yearned for. Almost by chance she came across an area which had a number of unusually quaint villages with names just as unusual. One of these was Troy, which she immediately fell in love with, but the initial fascination could well have been the name. It was different, to say the least, but how on earth did a quaint and very historic looking English village get christened with that? She simply had to find out. It was also a welcome piece of luck to discover that Tillsworthy House was only a short drive away, which if all went well was totally perfect.

Angela parked the car in front of All Saints church and then decided that a walk would be the best way to look around Troy. It was noticeably quiet with hardly a soul in sight, but then it was the middle of the week and midday. Obviously drinking time. The village centre was defined by an unusually beautiful fountain which incorporated a replica of the famous Mannekin Pis. The pub next door to it was named The Wooden Horse which was rather amusingly apt. As she walked, the more she saw, the more she liked. The cottages, however, were very English. They were scattered about with no symmetry at all, but they were all extremely picturesque, dressed up in a multitude of colours, giving the feeling that they were trying to out do one another in the way they looked.

Angela had always had a soft spot for churches and on arriving back at the car she could not resist having a quick look inside All Saints, especially as the building itself was so outstandingly beautiful. She was looking at the pulpit when a voice behind her said,

"You're admiring our little church then. You must be a visitor. Allow me to introduce myself. I am the Reverend Bradley Smith and this is my little corner of the world."

"My name's Angela, Angela Tillsworthy, and probably like everyone else I have fallen madly in love. I am not really sight-seeing but am looking for somewhere in this vicinity to live and this is truly paradise, but the name sounds as if it's come out of a school history book!

"Have you noticed how quiet it is? At this time of day everyone is over there." Bradley pointed to the Wooden Horse. "So why don't you let me buy you a drink and you can meet some of the residents and probably Denzil Whitehead, the landlord. He's a real character, virtually the life and soul of this village and a truly lovely, lovely man. What he doesn't know about Troy is not worth knowing!"

How could she refuse, chatted up by a Reverend no less!

The Wooden Horse was definitely the place to be and without a doubt Troy's Central Office of Information, as Angela was soon to find out. It was very well equipped to handle virtually any problem or information in connection with the village and its surrounding area. It was obvious that the Reverend Bradley Smith was exceptionally well respected, so much so that anyone he introduced was automatically greeted with the same deference. Angela started to feel rather important and rather honoured to be in his company.

Denzil Whitehead had truly perfected the habit of happening to be there just at the right moment. He was indeed a character of some dimension, especially in the totally off- beat way in which he looked and dressed. The handlebar moustache and the striking, or was it clashing, colour co-ordination of his orange and green attire could be described as a visual piece of art, depending on how one regarded it of course.

"Denzil I would like you to meet Angela Tillsworthy and I know it won't surprise you in the least to know that, like everybody else, she's fallen for our village and has, dare I say, thoughts of living here. She would also love to know how it got such a romantic name! You're the only one to put her straight on such matters. Diplomacy has always been your forte!"

"Bradley, you're too kind."

Denzil looked Angela straight in the eye.

"The name is simple, the rest is not. There was nothing in this area around the early part of nineteen hundred until a wealthy gentleman by the name of William Troy fell in love with the beauty of the area and decided to build a cottage. This is now a tourist attraction and is situated at the far end of the village. Soon word got around and others followed. It was agreed by everybody that the name of the village should rightfully and respectfully be registered as Troy. There was, of course, no pub but it wasn't long before

William Troy built this illustrious and important building, calling it The Wooden Horse.

The local council then intervened and amazingly sanctioned the construction of that beautiful fountain with the exact replica of Mannekin Pis. The rest, as they say, is history. Eventually the two shops followed and people moved to the area, being allowed to only build cottages, and they appeared all over the place. Today the council has stopped giving planning permission for any more building in this area and Bradley will confirm that funerals here are a rare occurrence."

Bradley and Denzil looked at Angela, lost for words.

Angela was not that upset, after all no one in their right mind would want to move from Paradise. Denzil then suddenly spoke

"Bradley, that lady who lives on her own up the hill above the church, wasn't she talking about her daughter wanting her to move to Cornwall? She didn't like her mother being on her own at her age and having to walk up that hill and all that stuff."

"You're right. I'd forgotten about her. Adele. Adele McKenzie, that's her name. She did mention it to me in church the other week, but I didn't take too much notice."

He turned to Angela and said

"I'll go up there tomorrow with an excuse of some kind. God will tell me what to say and if you can come to the vicarage around three I will give you her answer, but don't in any way pin your hopes on it. Frustrated estate agents say it a million times a month that Troy is totally impregnable to a prospective buyer, which is good in one way but sad in another."

Angela answered gratefully.

"Thank you so much. You've both been so kind."

Before leaving, the Reverend and Denzil introduced Angela to a number of the regulars who were curious but gave the impression of being very protective and proud of where they lived and where they drank. Angela felt they didn't much like the thought of anyone new invading their patch anyway, but quickly burying that thought she said she looked forward to seeing them all again.

Angela met the Reverend at three o'clock the next day at the vicarage as arranged.

Of course it was just as quaint as the church itself and very comfortably furnished. Over a welcome cup of tea Bradley seemed to be anxious to let Angela know that he had never been married except to the church and that he really enjoyed living on his own.

However, on the matter in question he had apparently given Angela such a glowing reference that Adele really had no choice but to say she would be pleased at least to meet her if the Reverend cared to arrange it.

"So Angela, at least she is prepared to meet you, and who knows what might come out of it? The rest is down to you," The Reverend said encouragingly and then, as an after thought,

"Oh and please call me Bradley from now on."

Adele

From the first time they met, Angela and Adele had a rapport and really liked each other. Angela discovered that Adele had a soft spot for cats and at one time had three of them. But one day two of them just vanished into thin air and the other one died naturally of old age or probably a broken heart. She didn't want to replace them. Once Angela had briefly told Adele the story of her life, especially the antics of Buckingham and Oliver, and more recently Lily, she seemed only too pleased to show Angela around the cottage. She apologised that although the internal décor was perfectly fine everything desperately needed a good spring clean, but she was just not able to cope with it, which was one of the reasons why her daughter wanted her to move to Cornwall. The other big reason was the walk from the village to the cottage or vice versa, which was unavoidable since she was not eligible to hold a driving licence.

The lounge, incorporating a cute dining alcove, was impressive with oak beams (Angela's particular weakness) and a sensational stone gothic-looking fireplace. A beautiful centre light fitting enhanced with delicate pink shades and single matching fittings around the walls completed a picture that gave the room a wonderful feeling of peace and comfort. The use of chintz was something Angela also liked immensely.

There were three bedrooms, which were arranged in a slightly unusual way. The master bedroom together with the third and smallest bedroom, used at present as a storage room, were upstairs in the barn part of the cottage with access via five well used stone steps. The second bedroom was on the ground floor. The master bedroom, with a double bed and fitted wardrobes with sliding doors, was delicate and feminine with everything depicted in white and pastel green. Floral patterned curtains and wallpaper gave it an embracing Olde Worlde charm which Angela adored. The second bedroom, also with fitted wardrobes, was attractively furnished in walnut veneer and had a single bed in it with matching headboard. The cottage had not so long ago been decorated inside and out so there was virtually nothing to do except a considerable amount of cleaning. The musty smell had not gone unnoticed. Adele was quite prepared to leave carpets and curtains and even fixtures and fittings. The kitchen was a dream, unusually big with oak panelled fitted cupboards and drawers and a beautiful flagstone floor. The cats would be pleased with this; they wouldn't have to eat next to each other.

Angela was somewhat overwhelmed.

"Adele you must be so proud of it and I can really appreciate why the decision to move must be awfully difficult for you."

"Realistically, my daughter is right, and by staying I might do myself some terrible injury, so I am going to have to let it go. The one other thing I have not mentioned is the garden. Well the front garden, as there isn't a back one. That is one big patio, but the view is breathtaking. You can see over Surrey for miles. The front desperately needs attention. I just haven't been able to do anything with it at all so it looks terrible. I am really ashamed of it."

"That's no problem Adele, because I simply adore gardening. I find it incredibly relaxing. Even Buckingham likes gardening, especially digging, if you know what I mean!"

They agreed a price and a moving-in date which was mutually convenient to them both, even though as yet Angela had not sold Odd Acres. She knew she had no alternative but to take a calculated gamble in this respect as this was a one in a million opportunity.

With business out of the way, Bradley once again became the

topic of conversation.

"You know Angela, that man is a darling. He'd put himself out to help the whole world if he could and nothing is ever too much trouble for him. The whole village loves him, but he has no one to help him, that is except Harry. He's that gorgeous big black cat with a white patch under his chin. You must have seen him. He weighs about thirty pounds, but he keeps Troy safe at night. He loves the responsibility of guard duty and amazingly he does much towards the *purr*vention of crime in our beautiful village. He's a lovely boy, a truly super cat."

"That's extremely interesting. Bradley never said a word about a cat. I wonder why? Poor old Bucks, how is he ever going to deal with that as well? He's already got a big hate problem with Lily."

"Well, you never know. Harry and Buckingham might become the best of friends."

As Angela prepared to leave she asked Adele to stay in touch and added that in a few months time, after she had got settled in, Adele should come back to check out the garden and of course her nice but naughty cats!

It wasn't long before the estate agent started to ring Angela wanting to make appointments for people to view Odd Acres. It became necessary for Angela to be available for viewings, which made it difficult to make trips to Tillsworthy House. Buckingham was even more upset, having his nose put out of joint. However, against his better judgement, Buckingham condescended to try to speak to Lily civilly on the subject.

"You know what Lily, something tells me we are not going to be in this house much longer, but we're still going to have to be together, the thought of which does not please me at all. Strange people are coming and going and since Angela has not even taken me to see Oliver this week I am trying very hard, and I might add against my will, to put up with you."

Lily replied sarcastically,

"Well it's a two way street. I also have to put up with you and you can't have everything your own way all the time. There are other things going on in the world besides you and your life."

Buckingham replied disdainfully,

"I knew I couldn't expect you to understand, after all you've never lived in a house. You're just a little flat lady".

Over the next two weeks people came and went and two firm offers for the sale of Odd Acres were put on the table. The first died at the eleventh hour. It was a cash sale but at the last minute it fell through. Sometimes at the final crunch it can be heart breaking to find people have not in fact been telling the whole truth. Angela wasn't worried, since she had time and money on her side. The deal with the cottage in Troy was well on its way to completion, with contracts due to be exchanged in two weeks time, which meant she could move in any time after that.

Angela loved Odd Acres, after all her mother had really made it her own with the unselfish love and hard work she had put into it. Angela wanted the new owners to appreciate that and because she was in an enviable financial position she could afford to be fussy. The estate agent got the message and one weekend sent round a young couple with two small daughters to view the property. Whilst Mum and Dad were being shown round by Angela and the estate agent the two girls were exploring the garden when they came across Lily. They were immediately mesmerised by her whiteness and her cuteness and they managed to stroke her with a gentleness that Lily couldn't resist. Lily arched her back and purred loudly. Lily was to enjoy fifteen minutes of ecstasy and adulation before the girls were called into the house.

"Mummy, Mummy, we want that cat. That beautiful white cat. We love her and she loves us."

Unbeknown to anyone else, Buckingham had witnessed it all.

"You can have her. She's not as beautiful as she looks. It's all show. There's nothing of her. Like all females she's selfish and I'll be pleased when she's gone. It wouldn't bother me that much not to see her again."

Angela liked the family and they loved the house and they made an offer which Angela finally accepted. However, Angela had no hesitation in turning down the very attractive offer for Lily, in spite of Buckingham's hope of getting rid of her. The disappointment on the two children's faces was a bit upsetting; they so desperately wanted her.

As Adele had furnished the cottage so beautifully and tastefully, Angela had made an offer to buy most of the furniture. However, there was one item at Odd Acres of her own that she was quite adamant about keeping and that was the chintz three piece suite. Apart from having memories of her mother, how could she forget that Buckingham and Lily had now claimed the two armchairs as being theirs? God forbid they should be denied having those! It would definitely be inviting a cat attack of some magnitude on top of everything else!

The move went without a hitch (kind of) except that Buckingham freaked out at the sight of cardboard boxes. Obviously his memory was working overtime and what with having to tolerate Lily as well he was not in a condescending frame of mind. Angela finally had no option but to put them, or to be more exact, shove them into separate cat boxes on the back seat of the car.

With a distinct tone of exasperation in her voice, she as good as shouted,

"Now for God's sake you two just stop it! I wish you didn't bloody well hate each other so much. It would make my life so much easier. You've got to travel together now so you'll damn well have to put up with going like this."

Buckingham couldn't contain himself :

"How can she be so blind not to see that this relationship is quite definitely a non starter? Now I am going to be lumbered with you somewhere else. You'd better be sure Lily, I'll be watching your every move morning noon and night!

Lily replied with ideas of a female cat attack, but being separated, dispelled any thought of it.

"Buckingham you're so bloody spiteful. You seem to have a big chip on your shoulder. Just because you happen to be a pedigree, ooh la la, doesn't make you any better or any different from me, and talking to yourself is a distinct sign of madness. You've even forgotten how to purr for the right reason. Have you ever thought about Angela and all she does for us both? We are going to have a new home so you could at least consider some sort of cat chivalry, instead of being a disgrace to our breed. Remember I am on your

case too and you had better not get any funny ideas about anything."

Buckingham, feeling his manhood was being threatened, replied,
"Funny ideas! You must be joking. You really think I could fancy a piece of white fluff like you. You're too delicate to be taken seriously!"

CHAPTER SIX

King Cat

The move to the cottage in Troy was the talk of the village, but Angela found being on her own was sometimes more of a disadvantage than she first thought. However, money talks and she soon found she had plenty of willing hands.

She was sad to leave Odd Acres, as it had some unforgettable memories. More important than anything else was her discovery of the inspirational portrait of her mother, which Oliver had unbelievably painted himself. Thankfully he had actually managed to finish it. As she gazed at it in disbelief she said out loud,

"Mother, I love you! You are going in the lounge in your rightful place of honour above the fireplace."

Bradley, of course, was delighted that Angela had managed to acquire the cottage and that she had virtually become his neighbour. He made sure that she knew that if she wanted any help at any time, all she had to do was call.

After just a few days, Buckingham and Lily had found their bearings around the cottage almost as though they had always been there. One evening Angela found them curled up in their respective arm chairs in the lounge, so she decided it was time to have a chat about sleeping arrangements.

"Sorry to disturb you two but from now on these arm chairs are not to be used as beds. You can use them in the day, but your bedroom will be the spare bedroom and your sleeping quarters will be the double bed in that room. Sorry it's not king size but cats size it certainly is, and it's big enough for you not to know you're both on it. I have covered it with cushions and blankets for your additional comfort and pleasure. Your toilet facilities are also in there. Try to keep it clean. Bucks, from now on you are in charge of that room. Do I make myself clear?"

Both cats gave Angela that disinterested or 'leave us alone' look. To institute this, for the next three or four nights Angela had to physically pick them up and put them on the bed. They finally got the message and Buckingham, looking at Lily, responded accordingly.

"I never thought the time would come when I would be forcibly put in the same bed with you. So you know, I am sleeping in the corner at the top on the blue blanket. I suggest you sleep at the bottom as far away from me as possible. Thank God the bed's big enough for you to get lost!"

Lily, lying at the bottom of the bed, responded quite firmly, but a little sarcastically,

"I'm as upset as you are about it. Having to sleep with you, even at this distance, is not far enough and you are destroying my beauty sleep. Out of despair more than anything else we should both try really hard to at least speak civilly to each other. Of course that would be rather difficult for you, since it is obviously not in your nature. There are times when I feel Angela could be more considerate and this is certainly one of them!"

Priscilla and Vicki simply adored the cottage, and on visiting for the first time were extremely pleased to see that Lily appeared to have adjusted extremely well having had to suffer three different homes over such a short period of time. However, the friction between her and Buckingham was plainly obvious and finding a resolution was becoming totally impossible.

Angela remarked, with a big sigh,

"They can't tolerate each other and even seem to hate each other. I am really at the end of my tether with it and I am at a loss to know what to do any more. You know Vicki, it had occurred to me that Lily is rightfully yours and if my memory serves me correctly she was only on loan to me. Would you not like, or be able to, have her back?

Vicki answered positively, but with a hint of embarrassment,

"I really feel bad about the situation and I fully sympathise with you, but Tillsworthy House has literally taken over my life, leaving me little or no time for anything else. I really feel little Lily would become more confused and insecure than she is now if she were to move again. Angela, I am truly grateful for the time you have had her but I feel, in spite of Buckingham, she enjoys being with you and feels she does actually have somewhere she can now call home. Your lovely new home might make a difference to both of them given time, but if you feel that there is no feasible solution then of course it is only fair that I should have her back."

Priscilla intervened:

"Tell you what Angela, after Buckingham's week here on his own is over and the official opening of Tillsworthy House is done with, bring Lily with you when Buckingham comes over for his weekly assignment duty and we'll have her for an hour or so. Maybe Vicki and I can sort her out."

Angela replied with a big sigh,

"Well truthfully I would hate to have to part with Lily. I have got to love her very much and want her to be happy and feel she has a proper home, but Buckingham's attitude towards her is insufferable. I tell you I couldn't put up with that! It seems a good suggestion and with the way things are at present anything at all's worth a try."

The official opening of Tillsworthy House was deliberately a laid back and quiet affair. Free food and drink was readily available all day. All the rooms had been accounted for and the residents had managed to make their moves in quietly and efficiently, mainly due to the mammoth effort by Vicki and her team of staff, who went out of their way, and often beyond the call of duty, to organise the entire proceedings. The nursing staff in particular had their work cut out, but knowing beforehand the individual caring needs required by each resident was a godsend. The event made the front page of the local newspaper and the praise showered upon Priscilla and Vicki was overwhelming, but totally justified. In fact, Tillsworthy House felt as if it had already been established for some considerable time, with its programme of Home Assisted Living for the Elderly having already achieved envied recognition. It was really only a matter of time before it became nationally acclaimed.

During their week together prior to the opening, Buckingham

had remained on Oliver's lap for practically the entire time. Once the residents had moved in Priscilla positioned Oliver in a suitable place in the TV lounge each day, which ultimately became recognised as 'Oliver's spot' and of course no one dared to commandeer it any more than they dared to question Oliver and Buckingham being an 'item'. However, for all other residents there was a house rule of 'no pets allowed' although they were allowed to visit for a short stay. The lounge, being a favourite place for residents and friends to congregate, to relax and generally be looked after or to just 'chill out', provided Buckingham with the golden opportunity to impress everyone. It also provided him with the perfect opportunity to showcase his natural talent for playing King Cat in various unmentionable ways and acquiring more than a fair share of adulation in the process.

The time eventually came when Angela had to tell Buckingham that his holiday was about to come to an end. Vicki and Priscilla assured Angela that they would keep a special eye on Oliver, as he would obviously be seriously upset.

Angela, with a lump in her throat and supported by Priscilla and Vicki, looked at Buckingham on Oliver's lap before picking him up and said,

"Bucks, we're going home now, but next time we come here we are bringing Lily with us. That'll make your day! You had better sort yourself out with her before that time otherwise I shall have to do something I might regret – like leaving you at home!"

Buckingham had an idea what she was saying by her tone of voice, so he replied accordingly:

"You have given me a week on my own with Oliver for which I am truly grateful, especially as I have had inexplicable joy in not having to tolerate that white creature, but now it's back to the same old thing and you want to bring her to Tillsworthy House as well! That's really taking the p…! Sharing the same home is practically intolerable with no thought for my feelings, so to my way of thinking the only way forward is for you to keep her out of my sight as much and for as long as possible."

Angela knew what Buckingham was thinking and decided on a suitable parting shot.

"Bucks, if you are not prepared to change your attitude towards

Lily I shall be forced to send you away to a *very special place*, for some cat counselling amongst other things, and I can assure you that you won't like it, not in any way shape or form. Do you understand?"

Buckingham and Oliver's week together at Tillsworthy House was the perfect dream as far as Angela was concerned as it enabled her to concentrate on enjoying her new home and arranging it as she envisaged. Lily too was in seventh heaven and she almost couldn't cope with it. However, Buckingham's return brought them both down to earth quite dramatically with a very unusual and noticeable change in attitude between them. Somehow they had managed to agree to adopt the silent treatment and terminate any communication between themselves whatsoever, in addition to deliberately ignoring each other in every possible way. This made Angela's daily life even more confusing as she didn't know how to cope with it and she couldn't decide which was worse. It certainly presented a new nightmare. At least she now had perfect peace, but with an atmosphere that would suit an Eskimo!

The drive to Tillsworthy House to establish Buckingham's first normal assignment with Oliver, after spending every day of the previous week with him, was to remain in silence. It was very strange, but to be safe Angela decided to put Buckingham and Lily in separate boxes. Funnily enough they didn't object at all, since they were refusing to communicate. On arrival Buckingham couldn't wait to find Oliver. Angela, Vicki and Priscilla were quite happy to leave them to their own devices. Meanwhile, Lily took to following Priscilla and Vicki around wherever they went. Being so small and completely white she was often thought to have disappeared, when she was in fact there all the time but just not noticed.

Suite five was occupied by Sinead and Margaret O'Grady, two outgoing, charming Irish ladies who were twin sisters. However, they dressed quite differently with Margaret always looking impeccably smart. One unforgettable day, whilst Margaret was on the loo thinking about nothing in particular, she noticed to her horror a little furry white creature sitting in the corner watching her every move. Being somewhat shocked to say the least, she complained to the Management, who apologised profusely and said they would come and remove the offending creature immediately. This was easier said than done. Lily would have none of it and wanted to stay with Margaret for some weird and wonderful reason. Margaret, who had just turned sixty with two unhappy marriages behind her, was apparently a professional artist, who had had some considerable success in her younger years sketching caricatures for magazines and newspapers. In spite of her delicate health she was truly a lovely lady with an obvious heart of gold.

In view of what had happened, Vicki felt they owed Margaret a personal apology and invited her for coffee in the apartment. Priscilla, Vicki and Angela wanted to assure her that it was most unusual for Lily to act like that, although it might be that the bizarre relationship with Buckingham could be the *cat*alyst behind some strange thinking. Whilst this conversation was taking place Lily knew she was the subject of discussion and reacted by sitting on her haunches between Margaret's legs and looking up at her without ever taking her eyes off her.

Margaret remarked,

"I haven't had such adulation since I won the Daily Mirror award for best cartoon strip, oh, many years ago. I am quite overwhelmed."

"Well, if it bothers you we'll keep Lily confined to the flat when she's here," Vicki said.

"No, no, don't you do that. Just let her be," Margaret said emphatically.

Lily must have had some dramatic effect on Margaret because she kept asking, even pleading, with Priscilla and Vicki to tell her how Lily was and when she was going to see her again.

"Oh Vicki, please ask Angela to bring her again. Even though she caught me in a most unladylike and uncompromising position, I would love to see that little girl again. She makes me laugh. I love her to death."

Angela desperately needed a break. Buckingham, Lily and the move had all caught up with her and she was feeling physically and mentally drained. She decided to chill out for a week and sort the garden out.

With the help of a local landscaping company she established a grass lawn running the whole width of the front of the house with a length of about fifteen feet. This was then split in the middle by a block paved pathway leading to the front door. The lawn was then enclosed with an attractive Cotswold stone wall running all the way round it, and flower beds were incorporated to provide and establish some colour. She then had two wrought iron arches made to her design, the smaller one for the side of the house giving access to the rear and the larger one giving access to the front door. The cottage had never had a name, but with inspiration, and bearing the cats in mind, she came up with Cozy Cats Cottage. The more she thought about it, and having said it to herself over and over again, the more she liked the sound of it. She thought it was catchy and memorable and the look of the cottage justified it, so she had it incorporated into the wrought iron front arch.

Cozy Cats Cottage plc

Angela knew she was blessed with having two cats with a **cat**itude problem. She also knew that cats were fast becoming an obsession with her and she started to read anything and everything about them. She bought books, magazines, encyclopaedias and books and more books on the habits, health and temperaments of these fascinating creatures. She had come to the conclusion that cats, more than any other creature, were exceptionally therapeutic. She had seen it for herself in witnessing what Buckingham had physically and mentally managed to achieve in giving Oliver something worth living for, even though it was only demonstrated by feel and touch alone.

The more Angela thought about it, the more convinced she became that she had come up with an unusual yet brilliant idea. Whilst Vicki and Priscilla had successfully set up Home Assisted Living for the Elderly, Angela's idea was to create an additional caring facility also for the elderly, but which would also embrace the lonely and the physically and mentally handicapped, and in certain cases even children, by selectively administering the natural therapeutic powers of the cat and using them to their greatest advantage.

She envisaged forming a company, calling it by the inspired name of Cozy Cats Cottage, with the addition of plc, which in this case would stand for *pussy loving care!* Buckingham and Lily would make the ideal first employees since Buckingham's relationship with Oliver was well established and Lily's relationship with Margaret looked like it might prove to be something mutually compatible.

Angela realised that the onus of responsibility lay with her to marry the right furry creature with the right client. Compatibility was the key issue and a wrong partnership could easily turn out to be considerably *cat*astrophic. A meeting with Priscilla and Vicki would be the next obvious thing to do.

Having had the benefit of a week to herself, with the new garden now looking out of this world and her mind being fuelled by the excitement of telling Priscilla and Vicki about her prospective new venture, Angela demanded some immediate cat response.

"Come on you two, chop chop, we're going over to Tillsworthy House. Oliver and Margaret are dying to see you."

Buckingham and Lily sheepishly appeared.

"Christ almighty Angela, you've been off for a week, which has prevented Oliver from seeing me, and now you want me to come running when you call. Well, I might just not be quite ready to come now. I couldn't care less about her and Margaret. They're not important to me."

As Buckingham seemed reluctant to move himself, Angela, with positive anger in her voice, almost shouted,

"Bucks, you're totally selfish. I might even consider never taking you to Tillsworthy House again. I know it would be Oliver's loss, but then it might be for the better, and for God's sake have some consideration for Lily and Margaret too for that matter. And what's more, it's time you two started communicating with each other. The atmosphere you are causing in this house is intolerable."

Lily decided this was the moment to break the silence and so, whilst on their way from the back seat of the car, she quite sarcastically said,

"Well, Sir Buckingham, having your own way doesn't always work does

it? You should be careful in case you lose some of those high and mighty whiskers one day, when you least expect it. Remember too that I am now equal to you because I have Margaret and I know she loves me. I reckon you had better be a little more careful with your attitude towards me from now on. After all, you never know, you might even need me."

Buckingham replied,

"Lily. Needing you would be the last thing on my mind, today or any day."

Within minutes of arriving at Tillsworthy House, Buckingham was off like a 'cat out of hell' to the TV lounge where he knew he would find Oliver. The look on Oliver's face on feeling Buckingham's plentiful fur coat was once again a sight for sore eyes. No words could describe it. Joy and disbelief were etched on the faces of all who had witnessed this miraculous scenario. There was not one person in that room without a smile of admiration on their face.

Vicki suggested Priscilla and Angela organise some coffee whilst she took little Lily down to Margaret in Suite Five. Sinead came to the door, but Lily decided to totally ignore her. Sinead, naturally a little put out, called Margaret and as soon as they saw each other nothing else in the world seemed to matter. They were all over each other.

Margaret, somewhat shaken by the extraordinary outburst of affection by both herself and Lily, apologetically said,

"I'm sorry Vicki, I feel so stupid acting like this over a cat, but I never realised how much I missed her. It's all so very strange. Please thank Angela for me. Lily has unknowingly given me back something in my life that I thought had gone forever."

Vicki answered,

"Well it's obvious the feeling's mutual. I'll leave her with you for a couple of hours. Angela or I will come down and get her, or you can bring her up to the flat."

On the way back, Vicki thought to herself

"Talk about love at first sight. Oliver and Buckingham were much the same.

There's method in the madness of that, I'm sure."

As they listened to Angela's almost uncontrollable excitement, but mixed with some words of sanity, Priscilla and Vicki thought the whole idea of Cozy Cats Cottage plc was totally hilarious, especially the plc bit! However, they totally agreed that Angela's observations concerning the therapeutic power of the cat in relation to the human race were totally right. The whole thing reminded them of the time they were telling Angela about Tillsworthy House and HALE. Now the roles were reversed.

The business needed to start with something positive and it was of course staring them right in the face. Buckingham and Oliver and now Margaret and Lily were positive proof of credible relationships with proven success which Angela had actually already realised. But Vicki and Priscilla were quick to point out that from their own bitter experiences with Tillsworthy House it was easy to be blinded by the emotional aspect of the whole thing. Buckingham and Lily had to be the company's first two employees and the first two cats to go out on assignment, after which Angela must without fail invoice Tillsworthy House for Buckingham's services and likewise for Lily, but on behalf of the company as opposed to herself.

Angela thoughtfully interjected,

"Margaret might not agree to that, since it was Lily who actually made the first and persistent move."

Vicki responded,

"I assure you Angela, Margaret will agree. She would give the world for Lily right now."

Angela then firmly said,

"I am really thrilled and pleased with what we have discussed, but my intention is that any money made out of this venture will go to charit, in fact to a particular charity. In conjunction with the RSPCA I intend to set up the TTPCC. The Tillsworthy Trust for the Prevention of Cruelty to Cats. To my mind, something like this is desperately needed to protect this amazing animal."

Priscilla answered,

"That is really commendable, especially as it plugs our name but it's still a business you're running Angela. What about vet fees, medical expenses, food, insurance etc? They all have to be accounted for. How many 'cat employees' does Cozy Cats Cottage intend to have? Remember you would carry the ultimate responsibility for getting the cat to the venue at the agreed time, picked up at the agreed time and dealing with any other problems that might unexpectedly arise."

Angela seemed to be not in the least deterred and said,

"Well, Oliver was the business brain and hopefully it runs in the family, both with you and me. You totally believed in Tillsworthy House, as I totally believe in Cozy Cats Cottage. It will not fail, of that I am sure."

It was not long before the first two payments made out to Cozy Cats Cottage plc from Tillsworthy House had come through. Angela was relieved and thrilled and was now spending considerable time in her office making positive plans for the company's future. She felt a few words in Buckingham's ear would not go amiss.

"Bucks, Cozy Cats Cottage is now a company and you are a company employee, but I have decided to give you the honour of becoming the first Managing Director, which means that from now on you will be responsible for the general welfare of the other company employees, the only one of which at present, you might be sorry to hear, is Lily. You have got to treat her as from now with that respect. You have been acting long enough as a chauvinistic male cat with an attitude problem, which is not befitting someone who holds the position of a Managing Director. Perhaps now you will consider making some serious changes to your daily attitude and set an example, otherwise I might have to consider taking the title from you and giving it to someone else"– she paused "like Lily. How would you like to work for a female Managing Director?"

Angela knew that would hurt. She waited for Buckingham's reaction.

"Finally you have recognised my natural ability as a born leader. It has taken you some time, but at least you have acknowledged this fact by giving me the position of Managing Director. You talk about respect, but such a position commands respect, a great deal of respect, and before I can lower myself to being nice and polite to Lily she has to show me some of this and

that she really means it. I really can't tolerate some jumped up little female telling me what to do. Meanwhile, you have my word that I shall obey and carry out your instructions as far as company business is concerned without complaint, and I shall feel proud of carrying the name of Managing Director of Cozy Cats Cottage plc."

Harry

Angela felt a little guilty that she had not really thanked Bradley properly for being so instrumental in her acquisition of Cozy Cats Cottage, so after church one Sunday morning she invited Bradley to come over for afternoon tea; after all, wasn't that the normal thing to do as far as vicars were concerned?

On Bradley's arrival she first took him on a guided tour of the cottage and its surrounds, as she had changed one or two things since Adele had left. Being a keen gardener himself, he was particularly impressed with what Angela had done with the garden, as his memory of it was that it had suffered considerably from unavoidable neglect. He singled out the lawns, the block paved pathway and in particular the wrought iron arch with Cozy Cats Cottage incorporated into it. Bradley had never seen the view from the rear of the cottage and was somewhat taken aback by the sheer drop from the patio directly into woodland. He was however amazed at being able to see so incredibly far over some of England's most glorious countryside.

Buckingham and Lily were conspicuously visible, stretched out on their respective arm chairs, so it wasn't long before conversation turned to furry creatures.

Bradley said,

"I omitted to tell you Angela that I have a cat. He's totally black except for a round white fur patch under his chin. He's sort of Persian at first sight, but with short hair and big yellowish soulful eyes. He weighs practically thirty two pounds, so he's quite a big boy. He's fifteen years old and belonged to one of our parishioners. When they died I offered to take care of him. We've been together for five years now and I love him to bits. If it is 'catfully' possible, there is little that is too much trouble for him."

Angela, totally fascinated, said with a smile,

"He sounds a godsend. Does he have a name?"

Bradley answered, sort of proudly,

"His name is Harry. It wasn't my choice but it suits him. He protects me, the church and the environment with his life, but although his size is certainly intimidating he's quite harmless and a real softie. The village community have incredible respect for him."

Buckingham, as usual, had eyes and ears everywhere and always picked up on conversation around him, especially if it was about cats.

"Harry. That's a stupid name. That's as bad as Henry, the name I used to have."

Angela smiled and said,

"I wonder if Bucks would like him or view him as competition. It would be funny if they did meet."

"Competition? I doubt it, but maybe we could palm him off with Lily!"

Bradley replied,

"Well it is not out of the realms of possibility, because Harry has a habit of *cat*walking several times a day and especially at night. He classifies it as guard duty, but I don't think he's ever attempted to wander this far."

Angela answered, pointing to Buckingham,

"It might be good for him to have some competition. His whole world is centred around Oliver or sleeping on that chair. Buckingham has little interest in anything or anyone else, but now he has a problem with Lily stealing some of his thunder. I think he's jealous, but he would never admit it."

"Jealous is the last thing I am. She has nothing to offer except being an annoying little female who invades my space. Harry might be a pleasant relief!"

Lily had also been listening

"There you go again. Lord of the Manor, King of the Castle. Doing your number, thinking you rule the world. Remember we are both working now. I have as much to offer as you. You just might have bitten off more than you can chew this time around."

Angela, continuing the conversation with nervous excitement, told Bradley all about her idea for Cozy Cats Cottage plc, what it meant and what she intended doing, pointing out that Buckingham and Lily were the first employees to have been sent out on assignment.

Bradley was speechless, but had to admit that it was an extremely clever idea, and on thinking about it, an obvious idea with great potential. Giving any income to charity to help fight cruelty to any animal was highly commendable. He then said,

"Unfortunately Harry is already committed to looking after the church and me, otherwise I would suggest him. He'd be an ideal candidate."

Angela answered teasingly,

"Oh that's very sweet of you Bradley. He might have been able to put a smile on Lily's face!"

"Well I don't know about that, because there could be no 'rumpy pumpies' going on between Harry and Lily, because Harry has been 'seen to.' You should see about Buckingham and Lily in that respect if you haven't already."

Buckingham and Lily seemed to be rather horrified by this conversation.

"Rumpy pumpy? Harry has been 'seen to'? What does that mean? No one had better tamper with my tackle. I'm not playing ball games, not for anyone. What say you Lily?"

This was the first time Buckingham had ever asked for Lily's opinion or participation in a conversation

*"Bucks, in your case they call it **cat**stration and I wouldn't wish that on anyone not even you. No one's going to interfere with my personal particulars either. Oh and by the way, that goes for you too if you know what I mean, and I think you do."*

Angela answered, a little concerned, looking at Buckingham first and then Lily.

"I haven't had time to think about that. It hadn't even occurred to me actually. I'll have to get in touch with the local vet. I should make his acquaintance anyway. He could be a rather important person in one or two people's lives."

Bradley got ready to leave, but before doing so went over to Buckingham and gently stroked him. As he sank his fingers into Buckingham's fur, Buckingham purred loudly and stretched himself out fully enabling Bradley to stroke his whole body.

He then said,

"Buckingham your coat is amazing, so beautifully soft. No wonder Oliver likes doing that. Harry is blessed with the same too. You are a very lucky boy."

Buckingham responded,

"Oh I like you. You must come and do that again. It would seem that Harry's a lucky boy too!"

"And you Lily? You're so cute and adorable. Any guy would be honoured to make your acquaintance."

Buckingham had to answer that,

"You don't know what she's really like. She's a wolf in cat's clothing."

Bradley thanked Angela for her hospitality and looked forward to seeing her again soon. He then said,

"The vet's name is Mike Cass and you'll find him opposite Popinn. You know, the shop where the post office is. He's a charming guy and he adores cats. They are his favourite patients, which will be good for you and them!"

Harry unquestionably thought the world of Bradley and for him Bradley could never be or do anything wrong. He respected him, obeyed him and loved him and felt very proud of being given the position of guarding the church and its surrounds. For Harry this was a full time job and, unlike Buckingham, he was not a lap cat, but Bradley did allow him to sleep at the bottom of his bed. Harry was often out late, sometimes all night, fulfilling his *cat walk*ing duty! He never seemed to relax and there always seemed to be something on his mind.

"My job is quite nerve racking and often frightening, but I can see in the dark which gives me a surprising advantage. I caught two of them once kissing and cuddling on one of the grave stones. I thought that was a bit disrespectful and Bradley certainly would not have approved. I was practically at their feet when I hissed really loudl, just at the wrong moment, or rather the right moment if you know what I mean. They ran for their lives, frantically trying to adjust things at the same time. Having such power certainly makes my day, but loneliness is my biggest problem. I really wish I had a friend or someone to talk to. I have never ventured up to the cottage but I have been giving it some serious thought now that Bradley has told me that

two of my kind have recently moved in. I think its time to investigate and introduce myself."

Harry made up his mind to go and one evening found the courage to go up to the cottage. He cautiously made his way through the woodland then over the grass lawn at the front of the house. He looked through all the windows and ended up by the large French window at the back of the house. The blind had been drawn but there was a gap big enough for him to see through. Because she was white he saw Lily quite plainly, curled up on the arm chair. Their eyes met and once Lily had got over the initial shock of seeing Harry, she *paws*ed for thought wondering what to do next. Investigation seemed to be the obvious move and so she made her way through the cat flap to the back, where she confronted Harry face to face. Growls and hisses followed, with her tail going from side to side as fast as a car's windscreen wiper. Harry didn't move, deciding to wait until Lily had decided to calm down.

"Typical female, always jumps to the wrong conclusion and never trusts anybody."

Lily did eventually calm down and realised Harry was not as much of a threat as she first thought.

"I think you are really rather nice and I feel I owe you an apology for my rather hasty and uncalled for behaviour."

Understandably all this commotion outside had roused Buckingham, who had to go and see what all the fuss was about. He was surprised to find Lily and Harry having what appeared to be an intimate conversation with each other. Buckingham announced his presence with a suitable growl, as if to say, *"Do you know who I am, 'cos if you don't you're about to find out. You're tempting fate coming up here. This is my patch, so beware!"*

Harry looked at him straight in the eye and, without flinching, said quite calmly.

"I don't know what you're upset about. I have no dishonourable intentions towards your girlfriend, beautiful though she is, or re-arranging your patch. I only want to be friends with both of you, but if that doesn't suit you, so be it."

Buckingham was quick to respond,

"Girlfriend! Never. We're just good friends, as they say."

Harry didn't really know how to take that remark and Lily

decided to ignore it, but strangely from that moment the three of them had unknowingly established a strong bond of friendship. Funnily enough, Buckingham didn't completely trust Lily, whom he thought at times seemed to be a little over friendly with Harry. Strangely, Buckingham didn't really know why he felt that concerned about it.

Harry had achieved what he thought initially was the impossible. Having not one but two new friends and seeing them practically every day provided him with a much more interesting and enjoyable life. He even took them on a guided tour of the church surrounds.

Bradley and Angela had suspected that something was going on between the three of them, but on investigation they were satisfied that it all seemed to be quite harmless and above board. Buckingham, however, made sure he had the last word on the matter.

"It's all right Angela, we're all just good friends, even though Lily's a bit mad and unpredictable at times. She's only being typically female. Harry might also be a bit of a dark horse and trying to put it about a bit, but at the moment everything's fine."

CHAPTER SEVEN

Love and affection

It wasn't long before weekly chores settled into a pre-determined routine for Angela, which was fine providing there were no unforeseen problems. However, there were certain emotional changes in relationships going on right in front of her eyes, which she had failed to recognise since they had never entered her mind.

Buckingham and Lily were carrying out their respective assignments as conscientious employees of Cozy Cats Cottage plc in a very cool and professional manner, with no love lost between them. Wherever Oliver went Buckingham went and wherever Margaret went Lily went. However, Margaret had suddenly taken it upon herself to ensure that she was spending as much time as possible with Oliver and of course hoping that Oliver would eventually reciprocate. Always with Lily at her feet she would make herself comfortable in an armchair in the TV lounge next to Oliver's wheelchair. Buckingham at first did not approve too much of this and made Lily aware of his feelings.

"Lily, it now seems to me that Margaret has deliberately gone out of her way to come down here everyday to give Oliver some additional company. I don't like that because she is stealing my thunder, but on the other hand, if she makes Oliver happy by doing this then I will have to go along with it. Unfortunately I also have to suffer looking at you all the time, since Margaret won't let you out of her sight for one minute. In view of this one-sided situation, for me that is, I suppose I shall have to try to behave like a gentleman or ignore you altogether but then that would upset Margaret and probably Oliver as well."

Lily replied,

"The word gentleman is not a word in your vocabulary is it? And you certainly don't know the meaning of it, but I shall wait and see if in time you can learn to treat a lady like a lady. If you could achieve this, which I doubt, then you never know just how much of a nice lady I could really be, and trust me I am quite capable of making you feel a very happy gentleman."

Buckingham looked at Lily a little confused, whilst trying to work out what she had actually meant by that remark.

It was very obvious that Margaret was intentionally becoming closer to Oliver day by day. Sadly, conversation, of course, was with herself, asking and answering her own questions. Eventually Margaret became more confident and started to hold Oliver's hand, at times gently caressing it. Remarkably there was a positive response.

This had not gone unnoticed by Buckingham.

"Lily, do you see what's going on? She's holding his hand now."

Lily answered

"Well that's ok as long it's nothing else!"

One day, just after Angela had picked both Buckingham and Lily up to go home, Sinead was anxious to have a quiet word with her sister Margaret.

"Margaret, I don't mean to interfere, but aren't you getting rather affectionate, and even intimate with Oliver? I mean all this holding hands business and Lily looking at you as if she were worshipping some sort of Goddess. I've even caught you kissing Oliver on his lips."

Margaret, a little taken aback and upset with Sinead's remarks, said,

"Well, he showed no objection to that, and Sinead if I didn't know you better I'd think I'd detected a touch of jealousy by your remarks. I assure you my motives are totally honourable and I must admit I feel very affectionate towards Oliver. Buckingham's implicit loyalty and special kind of therapy has produced a miraculous achievement in helping Oliver to have some sort of quality of life, but he also needs the affection of a female."

Sinead replied,

"Oh and I suppose you think you can fulfil that?"

Margaret responded, trying to restrain herself from showing anger,

"Well, I don't know about that. He can't see or hear but he can certainly feel and he does positively respond, so I am only too happy to give him affection by touch, of which there is no ulterior motive, I assure you."

Sinead answered with just a hint of sarcasm

"Well, I hope he gets to appreciate it."

Lost and Found

It was a perfectly normal afternoon, which made it all the more difficult to understand how something so dramatic could have possibly happened, and so totally unnoticed. Oliver, Buckingham, Margaret and Lily were all having their usual afternoon siesta when Sinead had joined them and was apparently quietly reading the daily paper. Suddenly the silence was broken when she frantically exclaimed,

"Margaret, wake up wake up. Lily's disappeared! One minute she was by your feet sleeping the next she was gone."

Margaret looked aghast and exclaimed,

"Oh my God what's happened to her? Lily, Lily, where are you?"

Buckingham instinctively knew something was wrong and even Oliver could sense something was amiss. In no time at all the word was out and all the residents and nursing staff on duty started a search, calling her name over and over again. Sinead, looking harassed and worried, hurried to the flat to tell Angela and the two girls what had happened. Shocked and fearing the worst, Priscilla, Vicki and Angela joined the search checking room by room. Strangely, Buckingham's reaction was as frantic as everyone else and he started to look methodically in places where only cats could hide. Angela had the intuition to follow Buckingham, because he might very well pick up on Lily's scent, being so familiar with it. Buckingham led Angela everywhere, meowing continuously, obviously hoping Lily would hear. They finally arrived at the laundry room, which was situated at the farthest end of the ground floor. The door was shut but Buckingham was going out of his mind walking round and round in circles and frantically clawing the door. Angela realized that Lily must be in there. She opened the door and to her horror found Lily actually inside one of the washing machines. She was meowing with considerable distress, at the same time as trying to claw the glass door. The huge relief of them all seeing each other was clearly written on their faces. Angela gently took Lily in her arms and, whilst talking to her and stroking her at the same time, made her way back to the TV lounge. As she hugged and kissed Lily with tears running down her cheeks, Margaret was speechless, being completely overtaken with emotion. Buckingham, looking considerably the worse for wear, might just as well have been through a similar ordeal.

"God Lily, how did that happen to you and who could have done such a cruel thing? In spite of everything between us, I was really worried about you and I could never forgive myself if anything had happened to you. Like it or not we have become part of each others' lives."

There was silence in the TV room whilst Angela announced that Buckingham had found Lily in the laundry room inside a washing machine which, thank goodness, had not been switched on, otherwise Lily's nine lives would have been washed away rather quickly all at once. She thanked everyone for their help and concern, and vowed that both she and Vicki would move heaven and earth to find the culprit who had the nerve to carry out such a cruel deed.

Lily, once again curled up at Margaret's feet, but this time between her legs, looked at Buckingham with obvious gratitude:

"Bucks, it all happened so quickly I don't know who took me there. One minute I was in a bag and next I was inside the washing machine. I was so scared. I thought the machine was going to start and I was in for the final wash of my life. Bucks, I really owe you one. I know it was you who found me and you who brought Angela to me. Now you are truly my King Cat and I will never forget what you did"

Buckingham responded accordingly,

"Think nothing of it. It was no big deal. Thought I might miss you being around, that's all."

During the course of the subsequent week, Priscilla and Vicki systematically interrogated everyone, both residents and staff alike, but not one shred of evidence was found with respect to Lily's ordeal. Then one evening there was a knock on the flat door. Vicki answered it.

"Sinead! You look terrible. What on earth's the matter?"

Sinead was obviously extremely upset and she was shaking considerably.

She said,

"I can't live with myself any longer. I have to confess I was the one who kidnapped Lily. I did it whilst they were sleeping and I did it out of jealousy. I did it on the spur of the moment and I did it to hurt Margaret. All my life she has had everything. As a child she was the favoured twin. At school she was top of the class and I was bottom of the same class. She was great at athletics and she went on to win awards for cartoons and this that and the other. And now she has Lily worshipping the ground she walks on and Oliver..I know I was wrong, very wrong and I wish I had never done it."

Priscilla, trying to come to terms with the shock of what Sinead had done, then said,

"Sinead, that was so wicked, so very wicked. Lily was frightened to death and thank God you had the good sense not to switch the bloody machine on. You have not only hurt Margaret but every person in this house, and especially Buckingham, who actually found Lily in the end. You owe everyone a personal apology, but that would not be a good idea because with the disgust that people feel you might find yourself making a visit to the hospital. However, as you have had the courage to confess and to deeply regret for what you've done and as you will have to live with your conscience for the rest of your life, Vicki and I (Priscilla looked to Vicki for presumed support) have decided that it would be in the best interests of Margaret and also in your safest interests if we did not say a word to anyone. We will let the matter pass, but consider yourself very lucky."

Vicki continued,

"One thing more, Sinead, and you may be shocked to hear it. In your estimation Margaret has had everything in her life and you have had nothing, but there is one thing she has which you are very fortunate not to have ...."

Vicki paused for a moment.

"......she is terminally ill."

A Thing Called Love

Angela had not forgotten Bradley's advice regarding Buckingham and Lily seeing the vet. She had just not had the time to get round to it, but the appointment with Mike Cass had now been made and the day for that appointment had arrived. Angela was really scared to tell them and even more scared to tell them the real truth, as she knew she would have had World War Three and a major *cat attack* on her hands if she had.

She had no option but to put them in separate cat boxes and suffer the subsequent protest. By the noises they were making as they drove to the vet she knew they were voicing their objections in no uncertain manner

"What is Angela up to now? It's been so sudden and hush hush. I'm not ill or anything, in fact you know better than anyone that I'm on particularly good form at the moment making **you** *happy. Would you not agree Lily?"*

Lily replied with a kind of matter of fact admiration in her voice,

"Bucks, you've got a great big willy and I love every centimetre of it."

Buckingham responded with pride in his voice

"Well Lily, I'm glad to be of service and I assure you I will always be glad to rise to the occasion. So they had better not bloody well start playing about with the love of your life, not at this exciting stage of our relationship anyway."

Angela left them with Mike and waited for the phone call, which came three hours later. He said,

"First of all Angela they are two very beautiful cats, exceptionally beautiful in fact, and I believe with above average intelligence. Buckingham doesn't know yet what's happened to him and will not be at all pleased when he does, but he'll adjust in time. Lily, on the other hand, I can't do anything about."

"Why ever not?" Angela asked, somewhat puzzled. Mike emphatically replied,

"Because she's four weeks pregnant!"

Angela, truly shocked, wondered just who was *the cat that had got the cream!* She immediately called Priscilla and Vicki, who both thought it was extremely funny.

"It can only be Bucks or Harry."

Angela replied,

"It's definitely not Harry. According to Bradley he's not physically capable and hasn't been for five years. Bucks is not now, of course, but the dirty deed is done and if it is him then all I can say is that he has certainly gone out with a bang!"

Vicki laughed and then said,

"Well Angela, the good thing is that it would seem all the intolerance and even hatred between them is a thing of the past and that Buckingham and Lily are now an item. We should all look forward with excitement to whatever little Lily is going to bring into this world."

Buckingham was no fool. There was nothing physically wrong with him so he knew the visit to Mike Cass was for no ordinary reason. Consequently he was shocked and annoyed to discover that he had lost an important part of his male ego. Finding the courage to tell Lily was even worse, especially with how he now felt about her.

Lily listened sympathetically but then clearly with love in her eyes said,

"Bucks, I am as upset as you are about the whole thing but your last performance was out of this world."

Angela suspected that Buckingham knew he was going to be a Dad and Lily quite definitely knew she was pregnant, but Buckingham had a nagging problem on his mind that he felt had to be sorted out once and for all. He suspected that Harry or Lily were up to something because he had caught them seeming to be rather too friendly on more than one occasion. At the opportune moment, Buckingham approached Harry and with a mixture of calculated anger and obvious jealousy said,

"*Harry what the bloody hell have you been up to with Lily? She's pregnant, and recently I have noticed you two have been far too lovey dovey. Are you playing games with her?*"

Harry replied very calmly, looking him straight in the eye.

"I adore and love Lily very much, but purely as a friend. It is all very innocent and you have nothing to worry about. I cannot play games with her because they took my bloody balls away five years ago!"

And then he said

"You know what Bucks, you are going to be a Dad, so I'm telling you as your friend that you should stop these stupid head games right now. You have got to act your age and start showing some responsibility for your recent moments of pleasure, because Lily is going to need all the help she can get with what she is going to have to cope with very soon. Show Lily that you really care. Show her some true love."

Buckingham replied, rather ashamed at his recent outburst.

"I'm sorry Harry. I was well out of order. I regret what I said and hope you'll forgive me. I know you're really a true friend."

One evening Angela noticed Harry staring through the French window, obviously looking for Buckingham and Lily. She became concerned when she noticed that neither Buckingham nor Lily were in their chairs. She checked the bedroom and found them curled up together on the bed with a paw round each other's neck. She was so emotionally overcome with what she saw that she immediately found her camera and captured the magic moment. She then went to the French window and said.

"Harry, they're all right but they are both asleep. I'll tell them you called – all right darling?" Harry was satisfied and went back home.

Angela, whilst having her morning cup of tea, gave some thought to Lily's pregnancy. She had recently noticed that Lily had started rolling on the kitchen floor and rubbing herself up against furniture and she remembered that she had heard Lily make a rather unusually high pitched cry one particular night, but she never thought any more about it. She smiled to herself at the thought that it might well have been at that moment that Bucks had surpassed himself!

Buckingham and Lily continued to work consistently, with Angela taking them regularly to Tillsworthy House, but she knew the time was getting near for Lily to give birth. She told Margaret of the forthcoming event and she was thrilled to pieces. She in turn told Oliver by squeezing his hand and praising Buckingham for being such a clever boy. Vicki found it hard to believe that Lily would be capable of delivering anything at all, being so small, but nature always finds a way.

It was a Sunday evening when Lily made it obvious that she wanted her favourite armchair to be the place to bring her new life or lives into the world. Angela decided to gently place Lily on a towel in a cardboard box, which she put on the armchair. Priscilla and Vicki, who had come over especially, were there to witness the birth. Buckingham didn't really know what to do with himself, so Angela put him on Priscilla's lap. After a while the head of the first kitten appeared and then shortly after, the second head appeared. Ensuring there were no more to come, Angela helped to make Lily more comfortable allowing her to lick, caress and shower affection on both of her offspring.

Vicki broke the silence:

"Lily, what a performance! You've produced a little boy, practically a baby Bucks replica, but with some of mother's flecks of white… incredible… and a little girl who is as white and pure as you are, except for, believe it or not, a few flecks of grey. She's such a little Miss Pretty!"

Angela picked up on that remark immediately and excitedly said

"That's her name, Vicki. She has to be called Miss Pretty."

Priscilla quietly responded,

"That's really sweet Angela, but what about baby Bucks? Poor old Dad here looks like he's seen a ghost."

*"I don't believe what I've just seen. Look what I've managed to do! Well I suppose Lily's done a bit too. Another white ball of fluff has just entered the world, but with a subtle difference. Those little bits of grey are a **Buckingham trade mark,** so I am well pleased, and for sure there's no mistaking **my** participation in the matter. It really is amazing. I am so bloody clever!"*

Lily looked relieved, tired but content. She looked at Buckingham and said playfully,

"Trust you to take all the credit. All you've done is watch me struggle and suffer to produce these two little miracles. My Dad used to say that if a job's worth doing it's worth getting someone else to do it and I have to say Bucks, that you did do a damn good job. I'm proud of them and …well I'm pretty pleased with myself too."

Buckingham answered teasingly,

"*Well, I actually wanted two boys, but I suppose one of each will have to do!*"

There was silence for a couple of minutes as everyone, looking at baby Bucks, was deep in thought thinking about names. Then Angela suddenly said,

"How about Dexter? He was, in fact, the theatre group cat and a real cutie, but one night he mysteriously disappeared. It would be a great memento for me if we agreed to call this little one by that name. Priscilla and Vicki said they had no objection, and in fact they said he looked like a Dexter. They all looked at Mum and Dad for approval.

Buckingham was not at all happy, in fact he thought his son's name should have been Benson for one very good reason.

"*On behalf of myself and Management I would like to say that in our opinion the words and names that only really matter begin with the letter B, for example… big, Buckingham, best, Buckingham, beautiful, Buckingham, bright, Buckingham and of course Benson. That should be his name.*"

Mum responded,

"*Life isn't all about what you want Bucks, even though I love you. God knows why. I think Dexter's a great name and that's what Management wants! I know another word that begins with B that might shut you up, so be careful!*"

The three girls decided the occasion called for a large glass to be raised to congratulate the happy couple on a job well done. From that moment on Miss Pretty and Dexter officially became two additional new residents of Cozy Cats Cottage and two additional new employees of Cozy Cats Cottage plc!

The company had no objection to Buckingham and Lily having maternity leave, but Buckingham was dying to get back to Tillsworthy House as soon as possible so he could personally give Margaret, Oliver and everyone else the good news. After a week at home playing Dad, Angela agreed to take Buckingham over to Tillsworthy House, but insisted that Lily now being a Mum must get her priorities in perspective and stay and tend to the needs of her offspring, even though she was desperate to see and tell Margaret.

As Angela walked into the TV lounge, Buckingham immediately ran and jumped up on Oliver's lap and the look on Oliver's face was as if the gates of heaven had opened. Angela looked at Margaret and with two fingers whispered,

"Two. A boy and a girl – Dexter and Miss Pretty. Wait till you see them. They are something else!"

Money Money Money

Since Millie had died and Oliver had sadly retreated into a world of loneliness and despair, Angela, for the sake of her own sanity more than anything else, had developed a natural business acumen. Initially thanks to Oliver, Angela had invested the money she had received wisely and managed to live reasonably well off the interest accrued, having also taken into account the monthly payment to Tillsworthy House for Oliver's upkeep. Happily, the sale of Odd Acres had more than paid for her new home.

Cozy Cats Cottage plc was in its infancy, being a non profit making venture with monies going to charity, specifically for the prevention of cruelty to cats. Buckingham and Lily were now firmly established as earning employees. Angela's prime concern was now to concentrate on Miss Pretty and Dexter and to find them suitable assignments even though they were still very much kittens. Their first introduction to Margaret and Oliver was a memorable occasion.

Margaret, understanding perfectly, had waited patiently for some time for this day to come and she was not in any way to be disappointed. On seeing them she was, in fact, ecstatic and couldn't get over the fact that Miss Pretty was the double, in size too, of Lily, except for the grey specks which were proudly donated by kind permission of Buckingham. Dexter, on the other hand, was the double of Buckingham, but with a Lily white trade mark right under his chin, which was hardly visible but it was there. He also had small Buckingham trade marks on his tail and on just two of his paws. Otherwise he was totally grey, very cute, cuddly and beautiful. Margaret asked Angela if she could have a photograph of them both to put beside her bedside. Angela really wanted Oliver to realise what had happened so she endeavoured to persuade Oliver to feel Dexter and Miss Pretty for himself, but he appeared to be very confused, especially as Dexter and Miss Pretty were too restless, being unsure of what was wanted of them. Buckingham, having witnessed this little scenario, seemed to be just a little disappointed.

Princess Alicia Hospice

One afternoon at Tillsworthy House when Miss Pretty and Dexter were with Vicki and Priscilla, and Lily and Buckingham were with Margaret and Oliver, Angela spied Sinead sitting by herself in the TV lounge. Angela went over to her and said,

"Sinead, are you all right sitting there all by yourself?"

Sinead smiled and said,

"Well, I like my own company really, but it is in a way punishment for the unforgivable thing I did to poor Lily, even though it was some time ago and, as you rightly said, I am having to live with that every day of my life. Looking at my sister now I would not have believed it had I not witnessed it for myself, but I realise that the bond, or is it love, that exists between Margaret and Oliver is very real, and by the expression on Oliver's face, at times I feel he knows that what is going on is much more than just affection. It's also uncanny that Buckingham and Lily are in a similar situation. It's all rather intriguing and lovely and I am genuinely pleased for all of them.

Angela responded:

"Well, I never realised that the relationship between my father and Margaret was that serious, but I am pleased for them and it can only be for the good in that they are discovering some true quality of life and finding ways to overcome their handicaps, especially Oliver. I am really glad you told me Sinead. I'll go and get us a cup of coffee."

Having made the cup of coffee, Angela continued,

"Sinead, did you get to see Dexter and Miss Pretty?"

"I certainly did, but I didn't know their names till now. Very cute and very unusual. They suit them well. Lily's a clever girl."

Sinead paused and then said,

"Ironically Angela, I have a friend, Vanessa Middleton, who comes over here a couple of times a week and she works for the Princess Alicia Hospice, you know, the home for the terminally ill not far away. The Hospice used to have a cat, well a kitten actually, which belonged to one of the patients and that little pussy apparently brought a lot of happiness to a lot of people. He was even on the staff notice board as an employee, but the patient died and the kitten was taken away by a member of the family. It occurred to me that the Hospice might consider having another one. Miss Pretty would be ideal. The therapeutic power of the animal's so amazing isn't it as we have witnessed with Oliver and Margaret. Shall I have a word with my friend?"

Angela, quite fascinated by all this, replied,

"I'd love you to. I am looking for an assignment for both the kittens, as they are now old enough, and Miss Pretty's docile temperament would be perfect for something like that."

Thanks to Sinead, who said it was the least she could do, Angela had a meeting with the powers that be at the Hospice, and in view of the previous surprising success, they were delighted with the idea of another kitten, providing Angela was prepared to supervise Miss Pretty for the whole time she was there.

A fee was agreed and it wasn't long before Miss Pretty also found herself having the honour of being on the staff notice board, but sadly with no accompanying photograph. Her presence in and around the Hospice had made a great deal of noticeable difference to many of the patients and their daily lives, and also to the staff, and in some cases she had even contributed to bringing high blood pressures down.

Vanessa Middleton had, in fact, phoned Angela congratulating her on Miss Pretty's achievements and how much of an outstanding success she had become. She also indicated that she would be phoning Angela to arrange a professional photo shoot for Miss Pretty as she needed a photograph for the notice board, but she also had other ideas in mind.

Angela could not resist imparting one or two thoughts to

Buckingham and Lily in relation to their daughter.

"You two have produced an amazing young lady in Miss Pretty. She is wowing everyone at the Hospice and now they want her to do a professional photo shoot, so God knows what will come out of that. She'll be signing autographs all over the place."

Before Buckingham and Lily had a chance to say anything to their daughter, Miss Pretty could not contain her excitement

"You know Mum and Dad, I love my work at The Hospice. I love making people laugh and bringing smiles to faces that have little or nothing left to live for. Angela is wonderful and takes care of me, making me feel as if I were a piece of priceless jewellery. I like to think everyone is pleased with me. They have now made me an official member of staff and promised that my photo will be on the staff notice board very soon."

Buckingham, in his usual matter of fact manner, replied,

"You realise you are working for two companies. They should be damned grateful to have you there. Since I was the one who made the most significant contribution to bringing you into this world I thought I might have at least received a personal message of thanks from Management. Still we are very very proud of you."

Lily emphatically replied,

"To bring some happiness into the lives of those who have so little to live for is a truly wonderful gift and you have that Miss Pretty. You will never be taken for granted or forgotten by anybody, not ever. Your Dad might be a chauvinistic old sod at times, but he wouldn't allow it and nor would I. We love you too much."

Special need

Bradley was a good friend and there was little that Angela did not confide in him. He was thrilled to know that Miss Pretty was working for such a good cause and earning money for charity at the same time. Then one day he suddenly asked about Dexter.

"You may not realise it Angela, but what you are doing with the cats has not gone unnoticed by many of my parishioners. They actually can't get over it. I think it's the idea of the whole thing that really gets to them. Have you ever thought about children? Well, a day care to be exact. One of my dearest and oldest parishioner's daughters, Fiona, runs a day care centre, but for children with special needs. Seeing what you have done, she now believes a 'special need' could well be a kitten."

Angela acknowledged,

"That sounds interesting."

Bradley continued,

"Basically, from what she has seen and heard, she is intrigued by the therapeutic power of animals. She thinks her children could really benefit from the presence of a kitten, providing it was supervised properly. Her kids could learn about feeding it, respecting and playing with it. They would receive an injection of unexpected pleasure which, for them would be a gift from heaven. A fee of some kind would be no problem and she knows it would be going to charity."

Angela replied, nodding her head in agreement.

"You know Bradley, that is really worth considering. It's quite brilliant in fact, but would there be a problem with health and safety, with parents worrying about their kids, particularly in their condition, getting scratched or something like that?"

Bradley replied with pride in his voice,

"Well, I'm a good calling card. They trust me implicitly and if I say its OK then I know that will be good enough. Probably a number of them have cats at home anyway, but a lot of responsibility lies with you and Dexter. Hopefully he will get to realise how important he is and if he is anything like his father that shouldn't be too much of a problem! I'm sure he'll put on a good show!"

Angela replied thoughtfully, almost as if talking to herself

"His claws might be a problem, but I think it'll be all right. I'll keep an eye on him. Perhaps Fiona would like to call me and in the meantime I'll have a chat with Dexter."

The way things were going, Cozy Cats Cottage plc was growing rather rapidly and now that Angela had Dexter working at the nursery with Fiona she was faced with the trauma of planning a workable schedule with regard to days and times.

The problem was Dexter and Miss Pretty needing her to be with them the whole time, but there was no way of avoiding that. Once again, with the help of Priscilla and Vicki she managed to avoid anything too *catastrophic*.

Dexter at first was very much in two minds about his assignment and told his parents how he felt

"Children! Why me?! Miss Pretty would have been better at that than me. They can be very loving but also very spiteful. However, these children seem to be different. If nothing else they'll learn to respect animals and especially cats since we are of course more important than all the rest of them put together. I'll give the kids my mind and my body and see what they do with them!"

Lily responded,

"Well darling, I think you might get a nice surprise. Not only will you be helping the children in more ways than one, you might even find it fun. It all depends on how you are prepared to look at it!"

Dexter and Angela had a pleasant shock. There were about ten little kids in the class, all different ages shapes and sizes, and the minute they saw Dexter the laughter and smiles on their faces said it all. What was really noticeable was how Dexter managed to stimulate every one of them. They were concerned about his welfare, was he hungry or did he want to sleep? They each managed to fondle, stroke or pat him and Dexter couldn't get enough of it. There were one or two moments of tears when one little girl thought she was being ignored and one little boy decided to be a little over zealous by pulling Dexter's tail, but on the whole the day care get-togethers went extraordinarily well. Dexter became part of their lives and all they talked about was his next visit. It wasn't long before the parents had the pleasure of meeting him and showering him with compliments and propositions. He was certainly not short of offers of a new home. In fact one frightening night this became a reality when Amy, a totally besotted young lady in the class, ingeniously hid Dexter in the back of her mother's car when she came to collect her. Her mother only discovered him when she got home and she didn't know whether to laugh or cry. However she did know that it would achieve nothing to apprehend Amy who was, as such, only 'borrowing' Dexter and doing nothing seriously wrong in her mind. Sensibly, she rang the nursery immediately and saved both Fiona and Angela from having a major heart attack. With unspoken reservation Fiona and Angela accepted the reason behind the madness, so to speak, and knowing Dexter would be more than well cared for, suggested that she returned him the following day. Dexter, of course, enjoyed and made the most of every minute of this unexpected diversification, and as for Amy.......well she couldn't believe her luck!

CHAPTER EIGHT

Tyson

The local community of Troy had a love hate relationship with it, calling it 'the mechanical animal' as it never failed to disrupt the calmness and beauty of this picturesque village consistently twice a year. But it brought people, lots of people, to the area and people meant business, lots of business. The two local shops did well, but it was The Wooden Horse that really prospered, and Denzil Whitehead, the proud landlord rubbed his hands together in greedy delight regularly for one week twice a year, loving every minute of it. For him, being in seventh heaven was an understatement!

The Pub was full and there was not a table to be had as far as food was concerned. The reason behind all this commotion was a Funfair which had the right to set itself up in two large fields on the perimeter of the village. It attracted visitors from as far away as Guildford, but the local residents were always glad to see it go at the end of the week so they could clean up the mess that was always left behind, as soon and as quickly as possible. It was commendable to witness such pride by a community for the place in which they lived.

Harry also hated the week of the Fun Fair. It became a relentless invasion of his and Bradley's privacy, and even he couldn't believe the disrespect some people had for the church and its surrounds. However, in spite of this, Bradley offered to take Angela to enjoy the fun of the fair. Another date with the Vicar, whatever next!

The nickname was bestowed upon Angela by a local newspaper in a review of a play she was doing during her days with the theatre group. Denzil Whitehead discovered it and insisted on using it.

Angela had no choice but to accept that it was only meant as an endearing compliment.

One evening, out of the blue, Denzil phoned her.

"Tillsie," he paused on the name "I have a problem which only you can resolve. Would you believe the pub has acquired a cat and I can only think he, I think it's a he, has been abandoned by those funny Fair people. Harry unfortunately has already had a confrontation with him. He has obviously been badly treated and he is hungry and aggressive. My problem is that he desperately wants to get into my kitchen and if he does that I could lose my licence. At the moment, believe it or not, he is actually sitting at the bar on a bar stool. The locals have tried to talk to him, stroke him and even offered to buy him a drink, but he won't have any of it. He hisses, growls and snarls at everything and everybody. I thought I'd get your opinion before considering any other action."

Angela replied,

"I can't tolerate cruelty to animals. I'll come down right now and see what I can do"

Denzil greeted Angela at the door:

"Look at him Tillsie, sitting at the bar like a he's one of us. He is actually rather handsome don't you think? It's that stripy tortoise shell coloured coat that's really beautiful, but it has obviously suffered through sheer neglect. It's a great pity he's so aggressive."

Angela replied, as they made their way towards a table,

"He's terrified Denzil, that's his problem. The hissing and growling is his form of defense. He's been abused, probably kicked, unloved and uncared for. He's almost wild, but I appreciate you can't have him in the pub, not with the possibility of losing your licence. Let me try and talk to him."

Angela got up and cautiously went up to him. He looked at her momentarily before hissing and showing his teeth. She said gently,

"All right, all right. I don't want to hurt you, but I would really love to help you."

Angela tried to get nearer but she could see the mistrust and fear in his eyes. Angela went back to the table, but he didn't take his eyes off her for one second.

"You seem different to the others, and I think you love cats. Those human

monsters at the fair kicked me all the time, hit me with sticks and poured dirty water and garbage over me. They called me every name under the sun and I lived on half eaten hamburgers and discarded waste. Each time the pub doors opened I felt the warmth and the smell of good food. It was too much. I had to come in and take my chance."

Denzil answered with a sigh,

"See what I mean Tillsie. I think I'll have to ring the RSPCA."

Angela answered,

"The TTPCC, that's who you should call Denzil. It stands for The Tillsworthy Trust for the Prevention of Cruelty to Cats. I have set up a charity in conjunction with the RSPCA, but especially with respect to the cruelty of cats."

At that moment and with no warning whatsoever, the cat jumped straight onto Angela's lap. Denzil nearly had a heart attack and so did most of those who had witnessed it. He was speechless for a good two minutes whilst Angela had mental flashes of Buckingham and Oliver.

Denzil stammered,

"That's the most amazing thing I've ever seen. What makes you so special Tillsie? What is it you've got that no one else has? That cat up till now would not allow anyone to go anywhere near it. I've never seen anything like that before"

Angela confidently replied,

"A cat always knows a cat lady. He can probably smell Buckingham, Lily and the two kids for all I know, but now what do I do?"

Denzil replied emphatically,

"You have to keep him. Give the boy a chance."

The cat suddenly began to purr, even allowing Angela to stroke him.

"You know what Denzil, he reminds me of Mike Tyson; aggressive, proud, intimidating but at times quite lovable, so I'm going to call him Tyson and we'll see what happens."

Angela would normally walk to and from the pub to get home, but with this turn of events she had little choice but to drive, but still had a short walk to get the car. To say she was scared to pick Tyson up was an understatement, and her obvious fear not only showed on her face but everyone else's as well, including Denzil's, as they watched in total amazement as she picked the cat up. Angela was very scared he would either bite or scratch her, but he did neither and allowed her to put him under her arm and carry him to the car. She departed with Denzil's voice ringing loud and clear, "Tillsie you're one hell of a cat lady."

Once at the car, Tyson insisted on staying on her lap and remained virtually wedged under the steering wheel. Whilst driving back she was inwardly panicking about what sort of reception was in store for her when she plonked the new arrival on the doorstep with no previous warning at all.

"Tyson, in a minute you are going to meet the rest of the clan. They are not going to like it, but it is not going to help any of us, least of all you, if you are going to be aggressive and threatening.

None of them have harmed you as yet and I want us all to get on together."

"Whatever is in store for me could not possibly be as bad as what I have already been through. The only name I knew was 'cat' or 'that bloody animal'. Some of those fair people were animals themselves, human animals! I wouldn't know whether being called Tyson is a compliment or not, but at least you've bothered to give me a name. Maybe you do care. I shall wait and see what happens and just go with the flow."

As Angela had previously discovered, the kitchen was always initially the safest place to be with a situation such as this. Angela gave Tyson some milk and food and told him she'd be back shortly as she was going to have a word with Buckingham, who was relaxing on his chair in the lounge. However, if looks could kill Angela would definitely have been six feet under.

"You've bloody well done it again. You've brought another one home. What is it this time? Is it male or female? Not that that makes any difference to me. You've taken any future prospects away from me anyway! It's all right, it's all right, don't worry I still love Lily."

"Bucks. Tyson is in the kitchen. I've rescued him from the pub and he is in a dreadful state. He has been severely abused and mistreated. Remember what happened to you, so be kind to him – please."

Buckingham gave her an exasperated stare,

"I didn't think you were serious when you said you might be adding more staff to Cozy Cats Cottage plc. You made me the Managing Director, or have you forgotten? You should have sent me a memo about Tyson first. I might very well not have approved, but in view of his predicament I will try to remain cool, calm and collected. However, I cannot speak for the rest of the family. We might have to hold an official company meeting on the subject."

On returning to the kitchen, Angela discovered Tyson had had his food and his milk but was too afraid to leave the room. Instead he sat in a corner, all the while never taking his eyes off the door. Buckingham on the other hand had decided to see what all the fuss was about concerning this supposed new employee. He was greeted with growls and hisses as Tyson indicated his disapproval. Buckingham's strategy in answer to that was to lie down at the entrance to the kitchen and remain there, never taking his eyes off Tyson.

Angela, standing at the door and suitably mesmerized by the situation, had no inkling of what the outcome of this impasse between Tyson and Buckingham might be. A few words with Buckingham might be an idea.

"So Bucks, just what is your intention now? Are you going to stay there all night?

"No I'm not, but I want Tyson to know who runs the show here and that once out of the kitchen area he will have to file a request before going elsewhere in this house, and as for sleeping with us, well that really is a big problem, and as far my family and I are concerned, that is definitely a no no."

"You can't keep him a prisoner in the kitchen forever. He must be allowed out, but for the time being he'll have to sleep there."

Angela turned to Tyson and said,

"Tyson you will have to stay in the kitchen for now, until Buckingham decides otherwise, which he eventually will. I will find you a basket and a blanket. I'll get you some more milk and put a litter tray in there for you. I assure you that in time Buckingham and the rest of the clan will accept you and you will have a proper home here."

Tyson actually looked up at Angela with a semblance of gratitude whilst Buckingham, never batting an eye-lid, continued his self imposed guard duty at the kitchen door. Tyson curled up in the basket and on the blanket Angela had found him. Whilst not taking his eyes off Buckingham he started thinking to himself

"This is total luxury compared to that bloody fairground, even though Buckingham is trying to keep me prisoner. Just who does he think he is anyway? He'll get fed up in the end and as I don't intend to stay here too long I shall let him know it. Hissing and growling have become second nature to me in showing my feelings. I have sharp claws too because I have had to find every way possible to defend myself from those nasty, spiteful cat attacks. Buckingham might think twice if he saw me in full flow."

When Angela came down the following morning she was shocked to find both Buckingham and Tyson nowhere to be seen. She supposed that Lily had probably told Buckingham not to be stupid and 'to come back to bed! Tyson on the other hand could have suddenly realized he was no longer being watched or attacked or being shouted at, but he was being ignored instead, which was almost as bad, since it was his ego that was being hurt. So with her heart in her mouth she opened the back door and shouted his name. She even went into the garden, but there was no response. She was on the point of phoning Denzil, as she thought he may have made his way back to the pub, but decided to check on the cats' bedroom first. The door was open further than usual and she saw a tail wagging rather frantically and realized it belonged to Tyson! On looking closer she saw Tyson and Buckingham facing each other. Lily, Miss Pretty and Dexter, who were all on the bed and wide awake, were showing their very apparent disapproval of having had their sleep disturbed by this stranger walking into their bedroom from nowhere. Buckingham, strongly asserting his authority, was trying to resolve the situation in a cool, calm business like fashion.

"Tyson you can't just walk into our bedroom like that without our approval, and we don't approve, not one little bit. We don't know you. You have been sleeping and living rough, so we don't know how clean or healthy you are. We know nothing about you, so find somewhere else to go, and as far away from us and this house as possible."

Tyson answered accordingly,

"You know what Bucks, you and your precious family have things too good. Do you know what it is like having no home, no one who loves or cares for you? Not knowing where your next meal is coming from and being kicked and beaten every day of your life? It's a miserable existence, I assure you, and I hate every minute of it, but some- how I'm still alive to tell the story and I am not going to let you or any one else make my life more of a misery than it already is."

There was silence for a minute and then Lily said,

"I have to be grateful for being lucky in having love throughout my life, apart from the memory of being thrown in a washing machine not long ago. Miss Pretty and Dexter were conceived, unbelievably, out of love. Big bad Buckingham saw to that. Didn't you dear? But he will tell you that his life has not been so wonderful and in fact in some ways has been similar to yours Tyson. He was kidnapped and thrown into a van He had no home either. You two have a lot in common and a lot to be thankful for, Angela being one

of the things. You should try to be friends. At least talk to each other."

Buckingham and Tyson exchanged glances, not knowing whether to trust or distrust each other. Tyson decided the best idea was to leave the room with a growl and a hiss and make his way back to the kitchen, followed by Angela.

Angela had a word with him,

"Well did that confrontation in the bedroom resolve anything or are you and Buckingham still as unhappy as ever? I feel some progress was made, because in some ways you are alike, but I have to tell you that I now have another problem. I have to take everyone to work today, which will leave you on your own. I don't want you to walk out of this house because I do love you and you have to believe that. If you are not here when we get back then of course we will all know it has not worked out. It would be a great shame if that happened, so all I can do is to trust you or lock you in the kitchen and I don't really want to do that."

As she was talking to him, Angela bent down and gently stroked him. He started to purr and that was the second time she had heard that.

Angela was indebted to Priscilla and Vicki for offering to look after Dexter while she was out working with Miss Pretty and vice versa. Lily and Buckingham were, of course, no problem since Oliver and Margaret were at Tillsworthy House. When Angela related the saga of Tyson's arrival they both thought it was the funniest, yet saddest thing Angela had got herself into so far.

They both said,

"You will soon have no time to cope with all this. How many more cats are you going to have? What plans have you got for Tyson? That is if he's still there when you get back!"

As Angela was driving her precious cargo back home she could think of nothing else but Tyson and prayed that he would be there. She had a feeling that in spite of everything, everyone in the car was thinking the same, Buckingham especially.

On arrival she let them all out on the loose and then went into the kitchen, but there was no Tyson. Her heart sank, but then she heard the familiar hisses and growls coming from the lounge. Thank God, she thought to herself. As she walked into the lounge Tyson was in Buckingham's chair and that was definitely out of order. Buckingham of course was just a little upset to say the least.

"What the bloody hell do you think you're doing, Tyson? You come into this house from nowhere and as soon as our backs are turned you're taking liberties left, right and centre. That chair is mine and that chair is Lily's, so get off it, now."

Tyson didn't really know what to do, so Angela picked him up and he threatened to turn nasty by showing teeth and claws, so Angela said emphatically,

"Now stop it Tyson. It's not your chair. It belongs to Buckingham and the other one belongs to Lily. I gave them to them some time ago. I know just the place for you."

With that she carried Tyson over to the rug in front of the fireplace and practically threw him on it.

"Now try that. It's very comfortable and was very expensive. From now on that can be your place, if it suits your Lordship."

Tyson was in two minds about it, but finally decided it was the place to be, settled on it and gave Angela a very strange look.

"You must admit it was a good try. I nearly got away with it didn't I? I expected Buckingham to be madder than he was, because I knew it was his chair. I wanted him to be upset, to put him in his place, and although it was a bit mean I have no regrets in doing it. However, on second thoughts I will try to find the time to personally apologise to him."

Buckingham, having witnessed the goings on from his reclaimed chair, looked at Tyson

"You might be interested to know that the rug used to be my place, so you have stolen something from me anyway. You should be so lucky. It's very comfortable. Lily and I have…well we have some fond memories of it too!"

Buckingham 'smiled' and gave Tyson that 'put that in your pipe and smoke it' look.

Tyson Cuddles

It was a Saturday morning and it was a beautiful day. The cats were on a break but the garden was crying out for attention, especially the lawns, which badly needed mowing. Angela's mind was totally filled with thoughts of Buckingham and Tyson, wishing that they would see reason and have the sense to swallow their pride and make it up. It would make life so much easier.

Angela used an electric mower with a long extension lead, which she fed through an open kitchen window into a wall plug in the kitchen. She had almost finished one lawn when she noticed Tyson inspecting the surrounding Cotswold stone wall. She stopped the machine to try to attract his attention, but he was too wrapped up in whatever he was doing. Angela thought he was looking a lot better and his coat was beginning to get a nice sheen to it. As she started the mower again and began to move forward with it to continue cutting the grass, the cable somehow managed to get entwined round her left ankle which, with the forward movement of the machine caused Angela to fall over.

She winced with the pain, knowing she had done something to her ankle and prayed that she had not broken it. She tried to move but the pain was too much. She started to panic inwardly wondering how on earth she was going to get up without help. No one was due at the cottage until the postman on Monday morning!

Tyson noticed her on the ground and heard her crying with the pain. He came over to her and started purring and licking her face, not really realising the condition she was in.

Angela said,

"Tyson that's all very nice, but I need someone to help me. Oh God who can help me?"

Uncannily, Tyson had suddenly realised that Angela was in genuine pain and so had decided to find Buckingham. Persuading Buckingham to take serious notice of what he was trying to say was somewhat difficult, but Tyson persisted:

"Buckingham, I am not messing about. You have got to believe me. Angela has had an accident and fallen over in the garden. She is in pain and needs help. Please understand what I am saying to you. Be nice for once and just follow me."

Buckingham got the message and reluctantly followed Tyson, at the same time saying,

"Tyson your life won't be worth living if you're messing about with me."

With sheer determination, Angela had managed to get herself up into a sitting position. It had crossed her mind that perhaps she could use the mower as a support to help pull herself up, but she was then faced with the problem of getting into the house. Maybe she could try to hop on one leg, using the mower as a support. It was a good idea, but the pain was just too much. After five minutes Tyson and Buckingham appeared and Tyson started licking and purring again as if he was telling Angela not to worry.

Angela looked at them both and said,

"Now what are you two going to do?

Buckingham looked at Tyson and said quite seriously,

"*You were really sensible to call me and you have gone up in my estimation considerably, but we are now going to have to use CCS, which is the Cat Communication System. We've all got one and unknowingly you've already used it. I use it all the time, so you stay here and look after Angela whilst I go and find Harry, who will hopefully then be able to tell Bradley.*"

Not only was Angela amazed that Tyson had managed to communicate with Buckingham, but now realised that Buckingham had got the message and was off to find some human help. She examined her ankle and decided she had not broken it, but had probably badly sprained it.

Tyson meanwhile had sat himself down beside her and, whilst purring loudly, started to lick her ankle as if he knew exactly what Angela had done.

Angela, looking affectionately at him, said,

"Oh Tyson, you're such a good boy. I didn't think you cared that much."

"*Well now you know I do and what's more I think Bucks is an officer and a gentleman. We'll get you out of this mess, you'll see.*"

Buckingham knew Lily would be worried, so he quickly told her what had happened and that he was going to find Harry, who would then hopefully find Bradley. As he made his way down the pathway and through the trees he was relieved to realise that Harry was not that far away, due to his distinctive church-like smell. He came across him sleeping on the front doormat of Bradley's home.

"*Harry wake up! We need your help. Angela has had an accident and fallen over in the garden. She has hurt her ankle and can't get into the house. Can you find Bradley?"*

Harry answered quite startled,

"Oh God Bucks, I'll do my best, but I can't guarantee it because he's usually out at this time seeing one of his parishioners."

Harry immediately went into the house and luckily found Bradley still at his desk writing the evening sermon. He started to purr as loudly as he could, meow and claw his leg, getting more persistent all the time.

"Harry what on earth are you doing? That hurts, that's my leg. You want me to do something or to show me something don't you?"

With that Harry started to walk towards the door, followed by Bradley, who then met Buckingham, who joined in with the same scenario. Bradley was quick to realise that something was amiss and hurriedly made his way up to the cottage, followed by a very impatient Harry and an anxious Buckingham. Of course he found Angela sitting on the ground with Tyson standing guard over her, and said with obvious concern,

"Oh my goodness Angela, what have you done? Here, hold on to me and I'll get you into the house and onto the settee."

Once on the settee, Angela explained in detail what had actually happened and that had it not been through a joint effort by Tyson, Buckingham and Harry she would without a doubt still be lying in the garden. As Bradley tended to Angela's swollen ankle with a cold compress, all three cats were sitting together on the floor intently looking at him. He said with total sincerity,

"Three knights in shining armour. I can't believe what you have just done."

Angela had tears in her eyes.

"Bucks, you deserve a knighthood. Harry you are one in a million and Tyson, you are the biggest surprise of all. Bradley, you haven't officially met Tyson have you? He saved the situation by getting hold of Buckingham in the first place. The whole thing was methodically and intelligently worked out. I can't get over it."

Bradley commented,

"Tyson, that's a descriptive name, but he's quite the opposite. I can't keep up with you Angela and all your cats. What incredible creatures they are. A big compliment to you I might add."

Whilst Bradley continued to tend to Angela, the three knights retired to the kitchen to have some well earned liquid refreshment, which Bradley had found for them.

Having had their drink, all three sat on their haunches looking at each other obviously contemplating on what had just happened. Tyson opened the conversation.

"Bucks I owe you an apology for what I did before and being a rat bag, or rather a cat bag. I feel we are even now and we can be friends and maybe respect each other from now on."

Bucks replied,

"Tyson, what you did has shown me your true self. You are part of our family now. Harry and I couldn't have helped Angela without you. Lily will be proud of you too but we should both be very grateful to Harry for getting hold of Bradley.

Harry answered,

"I did nothing that a true friend wouldn't do. You know what? I think Bradley has a soft spot for Angela, so I think it's 'watch this space' from now on!"

Angela was reluctant, but Bradley insisted on calling Priscilla who, without a second thought, immediately came over to offer whatever help she could.

After Bradley and Harry had made their exit, Priscilla wanted Angela to relate the whole unfortunate saga in explicit detail. Angela was very lucky to have got away with what she did and she knew only too well that this was totally due to her being very fortunate in having access to the unbelievable Cat Communication System, so brilliantly executed by Buckingham, Tyson and Harry.

Priscilla, who had obviously not had the pleasure of meeting Tyson before, was totally intrigued, especially by the name. Amazed by Angela's story, Priscilla commented that after Tyson's performance in the pub and what he had achieved now, it would seem he was a bit of a Jekyll and Hyde. If he wasn't before, he was certainly now a beautiful looking cat with a most unusual mottled coat and indeed a compliment to the others.

That night Angela decided to sleep on the settee, whilst Priscilla slept in Angela's bed. Tyson, funnily enough would not leave Angela's side, even though Buckingham tried to persuade him to sleep in their bedroom. Sometime during the night Tyson climbed on top of Angela and pulled himself up to her neck. He then put his paws on each side of her neck, purring loudly. Angela had no option but to put her hands on him and gently stroke him. She was not too comfortable. He was in fact quite heavy, but eventually they fell asleep like that.

In the morning Angela felt a lot better and was able to slowly and carefully walk on her injured leg. Over coffee she told Priscilla what Tyson had got up to during the night.

"Priscilla, he's almost human. I've decided to change his name to Tyson Cuddles, because that's what he's become. He's not a Tyson any more and amazingly Buckingham now thinks the sun shines out of his you know what."

Priscilla replied,

"Angela it's all another chapter in the saga of Cozy Cats Cottage plc. It's exciting and I'm pleased for you. I'm also pleased your ankle's much better."

CHAPTER NINE

Inside Out

Buckingham, justifiably so, had initially considered Tyson a threat to his carefully nurtured male ego. After all, who knows, Lily might have fancied 'a bit of rough'!

Saving Angela from a very nasty situation and thus gaining huge respect from Buckingham, gave Tyson, for the first time in his life, a real sense of achievement, and for Angela to call him Tyson Cuddles was the ultimate accolade. Primarily due to his past, he was not a homely indoor type of cat but preferred the outdoors, especially at night. Consequently he became very close to Harry, who was always out at night, constantly guarding this and that. Harry slept most of the day, which worked well with Bradley's busy lifestyle organising church business and looking after loyal and respected parishioners.

Harry and Tyson Cuddles always arranged to meet at ten o'clock at night by a certain gravestone. There was a good reason for this. The lady buried there had two cats that she'd idolised, and sadly and almost immediately, both died of a broken heart at losing her. She had requested that when their time came they be buried with or next to her. To meet there, Harry and Tyson Cuddles thought it was a show of respect for their brothers, programmed by the power of the CCS, which seemed to work in weird and wonderful ways, even beyond the land of the living!

It was a clear night and by ten fifteen there was no Harry. This was most unusual, so Tyson Cuddles began to worry, and decided to investigate. The first place he went to was Bradley's front door, where he found Harry whimpering in the corner, sitting in a pool of blood. On looking at him more closely he noticed with horror that his intestines were hanging out. Feeling sick and very concerned he said,

"Oh my God Harry, what have you done? What has happened to you? Who the hell has done this? Oh God Harry, don't die on me. I must find Bradley."

Tyson Cuddles found the cat flap and whilst meowing as loudly as he could he ran from room to room until he found Bradley, who was in the bathroom getting ready for bed. Tyson Cuddles started to go frantic, doing anything to get his attention.

"Tyson Cuddles, what are you doing here? The other day it was Harry and now it's you. Calm down. What are you trying to tell me?"

Bradley followed him to the door and when he saw Harry in the state he was he nearly had a heart attack. Harry was still whimpering loudly.

Bradley, quite frantic, said,

"Harry, hang on. I'm going to call Mike now. I pray he's there"

Thankfully Mike Cass answered the phone. Bradley told him that Harry was at his front door with half his insides hanging out. Mike said he would come round immediately, but not to move him. Mike was there within minutes, gently examined him and put him in a special box. He told Bradley he couldn't see how serious it all was until he had had a proper look at him. He would call back as soon as possible.

Bradley, of course, immediately called Angela, who insisted on coming round. He said Tyson Cuddles was with him and it was he who had told him and shown him what had happened. It was a good job she had not seen Harry in the condition he was.

Angela arrived, made some coffee and sat on the settee with a very distraught Bradley. Tyson Cuddles jumped up on Angela's lap purring, licking and kissing her.

Bradley said, very emotionally,

"Angela, I'm telling you that cat is extraordinary. He's done it again and found help. Totally incredible. He really loves Harry and if Harry doesn't make it…. It just doesn't bear thinking about."

Tyson Cuddles looked up at Angela, then Bradley:

"Harry will make it. He's strong and fit and besides he'd never let anyone down. Have faith, Bradley. You know how to pray more than any of us. But how on earth did such a terrible thing happen to him? What sort of accident could cause that?

The phone rang. Mike Cass had good news. He told Bradley that Harry was a very lucky boy. He had managed somehow to acquire a three inch wound to his stomach

and everything had literally fallen out. He had put it all back and hopefully had not forgotten anything! He had stitched him up, but he needed to stay there for a couple of days to recover. He would keep a close eye on him. He said he had no idea how it could have happened, except that something very sharp had done it, such as a spiked iron railing. Tyson Cuddles certainly deserved a medal, because had it been any longer Harry would not have made it.

Bradley, looking at Tyson Cuddles, turned to Angela and said,

"Do you realise he has helped both of us out of pretty serious situations in a short period of time. It's quite uncanny. It's like he's trying to prove something and wants to make up for his past. Like Harry, he's one in a million. We must look after him."

Angela got up to leave, and looking at Tyson Cuddles, said,

"How you've changed from the first day we met. With what you have recently achieved I am almost tempted to drop the Tyson and just call you Cuddles, but for some reason it just doesn't sound right, so from now on I'm going to call you simply TC. How does that grab you?

TC gave Angela a strange look, but there seemed to be a touch of gratitude about it.

"Tyson Cuddles was bad enough, but there was something about it that just made it acceptable. Cuddles on its own is kind of sissy and Buckingham and Harry would really take the piss. TC's really great. You can't get better than Top Cat and that's definitely one up on Buckingham!"

Bradley smiled and nodded his head in agreement at the name change.

Angela was very concerned for Bradley over Harry's ordeal, but Bradley assured her not to worry and suggested that TC stay with him until Harry returned. TC had made it quite obvious by insisting that he wanted to carry out Harry's guard duty for him.

Two days went by and Harry was back quite fit and well and couldn't understand what all the fuss was about.

Bradley stroked him lovingly and, watched by TC, said,

"Harry, by my reckoning you have only got three lives left and you could have lost them all in one go had it not been for TC. Yes, from now on that's his new name, thanks to Angela. Top Cat, and he deserves it! With what happened you're a very lucky boy, and TC has even done your guard duty, bless him."

Harry, affectionately pushing his head against TC's body, said,

"You always seem to be there just at the right time. You saved my life TC and I owe you. I shall never forget that."

TC replied,

"Harry you owe me nothing. You would have done exactly the same for me. The bond between us is forever."

I love my cat

Priscilla wasn't really shocked at all to hear what Sinead had said about the seriousness of Margaret's relationship with her father. It did, however, give her food for thought, so she decided to have a word with Angela at the first opportunity.

"Did you know that it would appear that Margaret and Oliver are involved in a seriously heavy duty relationship? As if it were a gift from God, Margaret seems to be able to communicate with Oliver in a way and on a plateau that none of us could possibly comprehend or even imagine. I have even witnessed her putting a biro in Oliver's hand with a piece of paper in front of him. He recognised it was a pen by the feel of it, and recognised the paper too. He then actually wrote on the paper, 'I love my cat!'"

Angela was speechless for a moment and then said,

"That is truly amazing. Well, it's wonderful because it is a big step forward but serious. How serious? Not marriage serious, surely?

Priscilla answered,

"Well that word's not been mentioned and I believe only Margaret with her communication skills could extract an answer from Oliver in that respect, and she wouldn't risk that without being sure the answer would be positive. Oliver would surely have to really understand what he would be getting into."

Angela replied,

"If marriage became a serious issue, I really don't think that mother would have any objection, because Margaret is a lovely and completely genuine lady and Millie would be pleased to know that Oliver had found love, caring and happiness in the latter years of his life."

Priscilla added,

"It would actually do him the world of good because Margaret, it seems, is capable of giving Oliver a feeling of independence, which in turn could give him a sense of purpose in life, together with something and somebody that were really worth living for. Of course, we're jumping to conclusions because at present the matter has not been raised, so we should keep it to ourselves and see if anything develops in that direction, or who knows, Margaret might even bring the subject up herself."

Two weeks later Margaret, with her heart in her mouth, and casting fate to the wind, put the question fairly and squarely to Angela and Priscilla.

"I want to marry your father and I know he wants me to be his wife. In view of his condition I know that is hard for you to comprehend. We love each other but we need you to appreciate and understand and to condone it."

She continued, with obvious resentment in her voice,

"Of course if Oliver was not in this unfortunate predicament we could be like any other normal adult couple and be able to make our own decisions about our lives and our future."

Understanding Love

Bradley, with understanding and affection, and looking straight at them with no hesitation in his voice said

"Angela and Priscilla, if the marriage between Margaret and Oliver was not meant to be, then God would find a way of indicating this."

Angela answered, really concerned,

"But Oliver is deaf and blind; how can he possibly answer yes or no to a proposal of marriage?

Bradley assured them,

"They have something special and miraculous between them and you have witnessed that. People with disabilities such as your father's develop an uncanny sixth sense. Margaret quite definitely knows how to reach Oliver and vice versa and, after all, they have been together for some considerable time now. As I have already said, if the proposed marriage is wrong then God will not allow it to happen, but I have an inner- most feeling that this was meant to be."

Angela then said, quite confidently,

"Dear Bradley, Priscilla and I would love you to do the honours and conduct the service, which would have to take place at Tillsworthy House in view of Oliver's condition.

Bradley firmly answered,

"A house of God can be anywhere. That would be no problem and it would certainly be my pleasure to do so."

Angela and Priscilla were more than relieved to hear Bradley's words of wisdom as they could now with relief, confidence and approval tell Margaret that they were delighted to condone her proposal of marriage to Oliver.

It wasn't long before word got out and the news became the talk of Tillsworthy House, especially as it would seem that both the wedding ceremony and the reception were going to be held there. Angela, Priscilla and Vicki, with Margaret and Sinead, agreed that the place and area to do this could only be the ground floor, since it was open plan and could accommodate over two hundred people quite easily and comfortably.

Vicki came up with an important proposition directed specifically to Sinead.

"Sinead, Margaret and Oliver will be husband and wife, so they should without question, have the privilege of a double bedded suite, so if you had no objection, would you consider moving into Oliver's single suite, as this would then allow Oliver to move into the double suite with Margaret. I can arrange for the transfer of personal items etc two days before the wedding day with the help of staff, so that Oliver and Margaret would be in their 'new home' for their wedding night."

Sinead had no objection whatsoever and in fact gave the idea her blessing, saying it was absolutely the right thing to do and very perceptive and ingenious of Vicki to come up with the idea in the first place. Priscilla, Angela and of course a very happy and grateful Margaret were in total agreement.

Margaret, however, was a little emotional and overwhelmed by all that had been said and made a very strange remark.

"You know how Buckingham adores and worships Oliver, with the feeling being mutual, and you know how Lily and I are head over heels about each other, well it occurred to me that it is a great pity that cats can't experience the joy and wonder of getting and being married. If genuine love is there, it's such a great experience and achievement in life."

Angela commented quite casually and barely audibly,

"Well why can't they?"

And then with considerable excitement in her voice,

"Why don't we arrange a cat's wedding and get Buckingham and Lily to take their vows at the same time?"

Margaret couldn't believe what Angela was suggesting and, almost laughing out loud, said,

"That would be hilarious and would probably be a first, although they've more than likely done it in America already."

Priscilla, Vicki and Sinead, almost all said it unison:

"I think we should go for it. It's a brilliant idea."

Angela added,

"I will take care of everything to do with the cats and I will put it to Bradley, who will no doubt think we are completely off the wall, to do the additional honours. I think it could be an amazing adventure, making the occasion one in a million."

And so a double wedding was on the cards.

Buckingham and Lily were in for the surprise of their lives!

Something in the air

When TC returned home he was without question a hero in Angela's eyes. When she told her clan of furry creatures about his exploits with Harry they were just as overwhelmed and, although

Buckingham didn't show it, Angela knew he had some of the wind taken out of his sails by what TC had done. Still, Harry was a friend and TC had saved his life and that was something to be commended, even by Buckingham's standards.

*"Oh, so it's TC now. Well I suppose you have shown a certain 'je ne sais quoi' and caring in your recent adventures as far as Angela and Bradley are concerned. Harry should be bloody grateful too. Well, with **my** approval you now have **my** permission to join us in the bedroom if you feel inclined to. I know how much you love Harry, spending almost every night with him. He's a good man and we love him too. Personally speaking, what you need now is a decent job. Angela needs you to work to support her charity the TTPCC. The prevention of cruelty to cats is very dear to her heart and we really love her for that. Anyway TC, we're all working so why the bloody hell shouldn't you, Top Cat or not?"*

TC, a little taken aback by the implication in Buckingham's remarks, responded with a hint of sarcasm,

"Bucks, do I detect a little jealousy regarding my recent achievement in helping to save a life....for the second time, and the fact that I am not working at the moment, or are you implying that I have never worked in my life? I have, after all had such a cushy number haven't I, with everything thrown at me when and where I don't want it! I would love to work, because I love people, the right sort of people of course, which I suppose I have to say you lot are. I don't doubt that Angela will have something in mind. Unfortunately Bucks, we can't all be a perfect specimen of the cat world like you obviously think you are."

Lily decided it was time to intervene,

"My big bad Bucks will always have the last word won't you dear? But TC, you know he's a real softie, especially where Oliver is concerned, and although he has at times an unfortunate way of showing it, he does love you. There is something quite strange going on at the moment between Oliver and Margaret. They seem a lot closer and Margaret is all over him. There is something in the air, but I can't put my paws on it. She knows what she wants does my mistress, and she'll get it too!"

Buckingham interjected,

"I agree with that and Margaret is very open about it. They are really on top of each other. I don't mean that literally, but who knows that too – only time will tell! The question is, have Angela and Priscilla noticed it? Sinead

and Vicki too for that matter."

TC had his say,

"Angela is no fool and she will find some way of dealing with the problem if indeed there is a problem, but you two should know that more than anyone, because you are with 'the love birds' practically all the time, and just as a passing observation – what about you two?"

Buckingham had to respond

"I'll ignore that remark, but whatever the scenario might be, the Managing Director of Cozy Cats Cottage plc will deal with it and that is straight from the big cat's mouth, and he knows what he's talking about!"

Lily had the last word and, looking at TC, said,

"He'll never change and that's what I love about him."

Serious business

Bradley could not stop laughing; in fact he was almost hysterical when Angela told him what she had in mind. After coming down to earth and looking Angela straight in the eye he said,

"It's a challenge, but I'll do it. I will have to dig deep into the archives of my mind to find some suitable wording for this unusual yet historical occasion. So we have Margaret and Oliver and now Buckingham and Lily."

Angela added emphatically,

"And all the others too! Harry is going to be best man cat, with your approval of course."

Bradley shook his head,

"I don't believe this. It's all too much – way over the top, just way over the top!"

Angela had the final word:

"But great fun and very different, eh Bradley?"

Bradley responded with obvious affection in his voice,

"For you Angela, I guess anything, but God only knows why."

He raised his eyes looking up to heaven and then said, somewhat concerned,

"By the way, are Lily and Buckingham aware of all this?"

Well, Lily and Buckingham didn't have to wait too long before

Angela told them that they were going to get married. At the time they were relaxing in their favourite arm chairs and, believe it or not, whilst she spoke they looked at each other and seemingly pretended to yawn.

Angela, a little exasperated said,

"Don't you two realise what I have just said. It's a serious business and you should be pleased that it was me who thought of the idea. You are going to officially become Mr and Mrs T Cat, T standing for Tillsworthy, of course, which is something to be really proud of, don't you think? The wedding ceremony will take place at Tillsworthy House at the same time as Margaret and Oliver also become Mr and Mrs Tillsworthy. Oh, it will be lots of fun, you'll see."

When Angela had left the room, Buckingham turned to Lily and said,

"*What the hell was she talking about? All that Mr and Mrs business?*"

Lily responded,

"*Being a cat of the world, surely you know Bucks that human beings get married when they fall in love for real. They then have babies, but in the cat world relationships of sincere love **like ours Bucks** are built on **trust and honour**.*

As a consummation of our love we have two wonderful kids in Dexter and Miss Pretty. What Angela was telling us was that Oliver and Margaret are getting married and she wants to arrange a human type wedding for you and me at the same time. I am quite taken aback and honoured. I think it's a wonderful idea and rather sweet, and probably has never been thought of before."

Buckingham replied in a matter of fact way,

"*Of course it would appeal to you. Like all feminine creatures you're a cat woman with romantic ideas. We men are much more concerned with the more important things in life, but I do love you Lily, and Dexter and Miss Pretty are, after all, the proof of just how damned clever I am and just how much I do love you. I will have cat man talks with Harry and TC about this dramatic turn of events, as no doubt they will be affected too. Angela will have conjured up something insane for them, that's for sure.*"

The teamwork and imagination required for this double feature had to be perfection in every way. No detail, however small, could afford to be left unturned.

Vicki and Priscilla had carefully studied the downstairs area, even though they knew every nook and cranny of it. They decided the main focus should be concentrated on the TV lounge as this was the largest unobstructed area. The main wall of this area, which was finished in a gorgeous traditional oak, was adorned with a very beautiful and impressive tapestry full of rich colours. This would provide the perfect background to the main ceremony. There would be a small table placed underneath it draped with a beautiful silk white cloth and this would have a small gold cross with two lit candelabras on each side representing an altar.

Since many of the guests would be residents and nursing staff it was essential that there was as little upheaval as possible regarding seating and eating arrangements. Six of the nursing staff would be on duty in the room on that day to deal with any unforeseen problems and to help those that were immobile. Special guests and those directly associated with the two brides and grooms would be seated at an extended table on the left and adjacent to the tapestry wall.

There would be no set meal, but an award winning buffet would be displayed on a number of trestle tables joined together and set up across the middle of the room, directly facing the tapestry wall. The food would be doubled up on each side of the table to lessen the pain of queuing for any length of time, but food would not appear until the ceremony was over. Seating arrangements throughout the area would remain exactly as on any normal day, with everyone sitting wherever they wished. There was plenty of room for additional guests.

Margaret would not normally need a wheelchair, but on this occasion solely for practicality and especially for Lily's benefit, it was decided, and she agreed, that she would use a wheelchair to accompany Oliver for the service. As such they would then appear to be on an equal footing and this would enable Lily to lie on her lap, since Buckingham would be on Oliver's. The two of them together would look rather impressive. After the service the wheelchairs would provide the opportunity for an easy 'walk about' which would enable everyone to see and meet the two couples. It was of course all a bit 'way over the top,' but everyone was into it and having a damned good time planning it all.

Margaret wanted only one flower for the occasion, that being Lily of the Valley.

She had also indicated her desire to have some gentle background music behind the ceremony and she chose 'Jesu Joy of Man's Desiring' which would be transmitted through the audio system.

Music wise, something slightly different was planned for the actual reception.

When Vicki and Priscilla had started to live together they became totally hooked on soul music and the Motown sound. They were so obsessed with it that they asked a competent friend of theirs if he would make up a tape of some of their best loved tracks, which would include such Artists as Diana Ross and the Supremes, The Four Tops, Mary Wells, The Marvelettes and especially Marvin Gaye's 'How Sweet It Is To Be Loved By You', which was so very right for the occasion.

The Luxury of Being A Dog

The success or failure of the entire cat marriage idea lay firmly on Angela's shoulders. It was her own doing, since she had suggested it in the first place and initially she became very scared, believing that the whole thing was outrageously stupid and would turn out to be one big *cat*astrophe. Thankfully, as she formulated some sort of game plan in her mind the adrenalin started to flow once more.

Vicki and Priscilla were only too pleased to let her use their flat as 'a pussy base' All the cats would be there on the day in question, having been brought over by Angela on the morning of the big day.

Angela had to think very carefully as to how to make the most of this occasion. What she didn't want was for any cat, especially Miss Pretty or Dexter, to run off and disappear amongst the quantity of feet, chairs and tables. It might be almost impossible to find them! Apart from Lily and Buckingham, who would be otherwise occupied, she needed them all to be in one place all the time so she could keep an eye on them. This posed a challenging problem.

Like everyone else, Angela received a daily quota of junk mail, which she immediately threw away after a cursory look through it. Five days before the wedding she had still not found the answer to her immediate problem, but just as she was about to dispose of the day's junk mail she came across a small catalogue entitled The Luxury of Being a Dog. She had no real reason to look through it, but on doing so she found an attractive five panelled gate made in colonial style wood with each panel fitted with closely knitted wooden slats. She was quick to realise that a cat would not be able to get through those. The whole thing was about three foot high and each panel was hinged to the next one enabling the construction to move virtually into whatever configuration was desired. With the designated wedding area in Tillsworthy House in her mind, Angela felt the right place to position it was opposite the head table and adjacent to the tapestry. It could be shaped as if it was part of a hexagon, with the straight side consisting of three panels facing the guests table. Even better was the additional feature of the centre panel acting as a gate which could be opened and closed accordingly.

Angela was both relieved and excited about this, but now she needed the company to supply or produce one in time for the wedding. In addition to this she decided her precious family were also going to have the luxury of three wraparound bolster beds which were like three big cushions with a bolster practically going all the way round them, all of which she had noticed in the catalogue. She even had a mind to stitch their names individually on them!

Angela found the company's show room and offices, which were fortunately situated not too far away. She had to muster her greatest powers of persuasion to plead desperately with a rather difficult 'dog-eared' Sales Manager. When he heard these goodies were needed for cats, and a cats' wedding no less, for some reason or other, he burst out laughing sounding very much like a barking dog! His job must have really got to him, or he just loved it too much! He, in fact, was so overwhelmed by the insanity of the whole thing that he found he had no alternative but to assure her that everything her heart desired would be delivered in time. He terminated the conversation with a parting remark that was tinged with sarcasm, saying that he hoped it would not be raining cats and dogs on the day! Then there was that awful barking dog noise again!

Now that problem had been sorted the cats would now, thank God, be perfectly safe, being all together in one place so anyone could come up and see them in their own time. With regard to the ceremony itself, Angela conjured up the idea that the giving of rings by Oliver and Margaret would, as far as Buckingham and Lily were concerned be replaced by the giving of collars, a blue one for Bucks and a pink one for Lily.

Four weeks of mad and frantic preparation were over and now everything was just about in place for the big day. The downstairs area looked fantastic, subtlety adorned with breathtaking Lily of the Valley. A large banner straddled the front entrance of Tillsworthy House, which read, 'THE BELLS ARE RINGING FOR US AND OUR CATS'.

Apart from the residents and staff, invitations had been sent out to numerous other close friends. Denzil Whitehead, the landlord of The Wooden Horse in Troy volunteered to deal with the photographic honours for the occasion. Local gossip had confirmed that he was very good in this department. Bradley had some special parishioners that he particularly requested to be there. Angela wanted Adele Mckenzie there as it was due to her that she had ultimately acquired her beloved Cozy Cats Cottage. Fiona Robinson and six kids selected from the Children's Day Care Centre where Dexter worked would be there and they would be seated on a table on their own. Vanessa Middleton and the management team from Princess Alicia Hospice, on behalf of Miss Pretty had to be represented. As if this wasn't enough, Vicki and Priscilla had a contingent coming from their hospital in Haselmere and, last but not least, the irreplaceable Mike Cass had to be there, if only to keep an eye on the cats to ensure they didn't drink too much!

Margaret, bless her, felt completely overwhelmed by the surprising deluge of response and interest from so many different sources. The cats had certainly stolen her thunder, but inwardly she was genuinely pleased for them, after all they weren't to know there were so many *cat*aholics about!

CHAPTER TEN

Catswallop!

It obviously couldn't be avoided. Being so 'offbeat' the news of this unusual double wedding had leaked out, attracting the attention of the local radio station. The newscaster, who could hardly contain himself, announced five days before the event that one of the couples getting hitched at Tillsworthy House were in fact two cats by the names of Buckingham and Lily. Laughing hysterically he wondered what on earth they would be wearing for the occasion! The response with phone calls to the station was staggering, as were the number of weird and wonderful congratulation cards arriving from all manner of strange places.

It didn't take long before the highly respected local newspaper had got wind of it. The editor was a small bespectacled person in his mid forties, portraying an unavoidably large ego. He loved dictating from behind a huge desk, as he loved owning and driving a huge car. Basically he was justified in doing so since he owned the bloody paper, but power to him was life itself and ultimately all that mattered. He was very proud of the fact that he had a proven track record of being, without fail, the first to have his fingers on the pulse of all matters, however large or small, connected with the local community. With a flick of his fingers he beckoned a young male and female journalist to his office.

"You two don't know how lucky you are. You've got your first assignment. There's going to be a wedding this coming weekend, but would you believe the happy couple are….(with sarcastic disbelief) two bloody cats which belong to some crazy woman called Angela Tillsworthy. Not only that, with an additional four more mad cats, she is also apparently able to provide some sort of new fangled happiness remedy for the old, afflicted and disabled. It all sounds a load of old *cats*wallop to me (he paused to smile and let that piece of ingenuity sink in), but it won't bloody well go away and with a consistent flow of strange shenanigans it is causing one helluva stir locally. There's more to this than meets the eye, so get yourselves on the case now before the nationals start scratching around and getting their grubby little cat paws into it…if you get my drift!"

There was that familiar 'see how clever I am' look and smile again!

They automatically responded, endeavouring to muster up enthusiasm of some sort. They thanked him as if their lives depended on it, which they did. He had, after all, condescended to give them a crumb from the table!

With this ring

With the big day fast approaching, Margaret voiced her concern to Angela and Priscilla regarding the rings, Oliver and the purchase of them. With everything else going on, this had almost been forgotten. How would Oliver cope with the exchanging of rings? Margaret was particularly emotional about this, but Angela managed to calm her down by telling her that Oliver's biggest asset in his present condition was his acute sense of touch and feel, which was probably nothing she didn't know already. He should easily be able to feel the distinctive shape of a ring and would immediately know what it was. Taking heed of Angela's consoling words, Margaret certainly looked a little less stressed.

Priscilla suggested that it might be rather nice if the four of them took a trip into Guildford, had some lunch, wandered around the shops and sorted out a likely jeweller, which they did, and in fact they ended up with a considerable choice.

An exquisite pair of matching gold wedding rings symbolising a knot caught Margaret's eye in one particular shop. As luck would have it the size of both rings was exactly right. She placed the female ring into Oliver's right hand and watched him closely. He knew almost immediately what it was and attempted to put it on any one of his fingers of his left hand, but it was obviously too small. Margaret then managed to manipulate the third finger of her left hand in his left hand and then, taking his right hand which was holding the ring, she guided it towards her finger.

Oliver really needed little help. He seemed to know what was required of him as he slipped the ring so easily onto Margaret's third finger. It was a magical moment!

Thankfully there was no need to repeat this little scenario, because it would be Margaret who would be doing the honours and placing Oliver's ring on his finger when the time came.

The four of them went home happy and thrilled with what they had achieved.

You could say it was a job well done!

The Big Day

It was 1.00 p.m on Saturday May 13th and Bradley had obviously had a talk with someone 'up there', because it was a glorious May day. There was still an hour to go and people had come from God knows where and they were now virtually obliterating the entrance to Tillsworthy House, hoping to get a glimpse of this extraordinary event and its extraordinary participants. Bradley, on the spur of the moment, having realised the situation and seeing all these people on his arrival, made the announcement of a promise to everyone that they would have the chance of meeting both couples after the ceremony was over.

It was more than a full house on that memorable day. All three bolster beds were in the pen, beautifully inscribed courtesy of Angela, the first with Dexter and Miss Pretty, the second with Buckingham and Lily and the third with TC and Harry. Angela respectfully asked that no one should go near the cats until the service had ended and after the food had been served.

With the obvious omission of Buckingham and Lily, all four cats were strangely quiet lying on their relative beds, naturally wondering what was going to happen next.

TC turned to Harry and said,

"Well it all looks pretty organised to me. Bradley's got his white coat on like he does in church, but why are there so many people here? This is not even a church"

Harry replied with the look of knowledge written all over his face,

"*These people have come, TC, to witness two marriages which are going to take place here in this room, instead of in the church, so this represents a church. I presume it has happened this way because Oliver in his condition cannot get to the church and would feel insecure in unfamiliar surrounding, and Buckingham and Lily would not really be allowed to get married in a proper church anyway*".

TC seemed to hang on to Harry's every word and had observed Dexter and Miss Pretty suddenly taking notice at the mention of their parents' names. TC then said,

"*Why not? A church is a house of God and God loves all creatures great and small, and that includes cats.* "

Harry responded with a smile,

"*That is true, but God obviously wanted and thought it was right for Oliver and Margaret to get married and for Buckingham and Lily to be with them, so Angela had the brilliant idea that it would be wonderful if they also had a marriage made in heaven , all at the same time. Bradley would have loved it to have been in his church in Troy, but I'm telling you TC, God is in this room and with us now.*"

Dexter sat up for a minute and said,

"*So when Miss Pretty and I were born Mum and Dad were not married. Dad always said to me that he must tell me about the birds and the bees and I said I don't want to know about the birds and the bees. I want to know about cats and dogs. For some reason Mum and Dad thought that was very funny.* "

Miss Pretty, with true feeling, added,

"*I am glad Mum and Dad are getting married like human beings do, especially as Dad loves Oliver and Mum loves Margaret. It all seems so right*".

TC looked towards the centre of the room and said,

"*Well it's nearly time. We'll see how right it is in a minute.*"

Priscilla looked at the clock on the hall wall and firmly said,

"Right everybody, chop chop, it's time to leave the flat. Let's go."

The two wheelchairs had been meticulously prepared and adorned with white ribbon, almost as if they were wedding cars!

Margaret and Oliver were comfortably seated, with Buckingham and Lily seemingly lying quietly on their respective laps on two small but beautiful white rugs designed and fitted for the occasion. Lily gave Buckingham a strange look and said,

"Bucks, are you nervous, because quite frankly I am peeing myself."

Buckingham answered outwardly quite firmly, always playing the man of course, but inwardly on this occasion trying to withhold doing something stronger than what Lily was doing.

*"Lily, just go with the flow. You've made a good catch. **I'm going quietly. Try to enjoy the occasion. It won't happen again I assure you not if I have anything to do with it** and remember it's Oliver and Margaret's day too."*

You could hear a pin drop. The whole room was in total silence as the most unusual procession appeared and made its way towards Bradley, who was waiting by the altar. 'Jesu Joy of Man's Desiring' began to be heard, but ever so quietly. The sight and atmosphere was more than strange, but totally breathtaking. Oliver, with Buckingham immaculately groomed and lying on his lap, was dressed in a very smart grey suit with a white carnation in his button hole, whilst Margaret, with a whiter than white Lily, adorned with a white eye catching veil lying on her lap, looked quite stunning in a beautifully embroidered ivory silk two piece, holding a small bouquet of Lily of the Valley in her right hand. The four bridesmaids, namely Priscilla, Angela, Sinead and Vicki, were all dressed in stunning lilac skirts and matching blouses, with each one of them also carrying a bouquet of Lily of the Valley.

Priscilla proudly pushed Oliver, accompanied by Angela, whilst Sinead proudly pushed Margaret, accompanied by Vicki, towards the altar, where they positioned one wheelchair on each side of Bradley, but at an angle of forty five degrees and facing the audience. They all then stood to one side of their respective wheelchairs.

Angela could not resist giving the cats a quick look, putting her finger on her lips as if to say shush.

The anticipation and suspense in the room at this moment was electrifying, made even more poignant by the serenity and beauty of 'Jesu Joy of Man's Desiring', barely audible in the background. Everyone was wondering how on earth Bradley was going to handle one marriage with one person being deaf and blind and the other with the two participants being cats! Bradley was not to be underestimated and this was a challenge that, with the strength of God, he knew he could bring to a happy conclusion. One thing he was positively sure about was that the service had to be as short and to the point as possible. After giving the matter a great deal of thought, Bradley had organised a pre-arranged meeting with Angela, Margaret and Sinead, so they knew exactly what he had in mind and what was required of them.

Margaret got up and gently and carefully placed Lily back on the chair on her white rug and walked over to Oliver, standing next to him.

Bradley asked,

"Who presents this woman to be married?"

Sinead answered,

"I do."

At this point Margaret put her ring into Oliver's right hand, guiding his hand to place the ring on the third finger of her left hand. Directly after this she placed Oliver's ring on the third finger of his left hand. Whilst holding their hands, Bradley blessed the rings, after which the vows were read with Bradley speaking on behalf of Oliver. On conclusion, he turned to both Oliver and Margaret and affectionately said,

"I now pronounce Oliver and Margaret as being man and wife together, in the name of the Father, Son and Holy Ghost. Amen."

Margaret turned to Oliver, giving him an affectionate kiss and, returning to her chair, placed an unusually quiet Lily once again on her lap.

Bradley, then looking at both the cats in turn said,

"We are now going to join two of God's beautiful creatures, Buckingham and Lily in Holy matrimony and at the same time rejoice in the recent birth of their two adorable kittens Dexter and Miss Pretty. We acknowledge this union by the exchange of these collars."

Angela then placed a blue collar round Buckingham's neck, which was met with some disapproval and required a few whispered words from Angela. Vicki meanwhile placed a pink collar round Lily's neck, and amazingly her reaction was totally the reverse. The look of pride was very obvious.

Bradley, full of admiration then said,

"I now pronounce Buckingham and Lily as being man and wife together in the name of Father, Son and Holy Ghost. Amen."

Margaret, as an irresistible gesture, picked Lily up and put her deliberately against Buckingham's cheek. With a begrudging look of embarrassment, he gave Lily a quick lick.

Margaret then proudly returned to her wheelchair, after which both wheelchairs were put side by side in front of the altar with Margaret holding Oliver's hand. The two newly wed couples looked absolutely stunning! Denzil Whitehead, hardly able to contain his excitement, with one camera in his hand and another round his neck, ordered everyone not to move until he had performed his duty and captured this historical moment.

The procession made its way slowly towards the entrance of Tillsworthy House to fulfil Bradley's promise to the people who had waited so patiently outside. They were not disappointed. Margaret and Oliver, who must have inwardly known what was going on, savoured the moment. The excitement was electric as Denzil took more pictures and autographs were signed. So many wanted to stroke Buckingham and Lily, who loved every moment of this overwhelming adulation. Buckingham turned to Lily and said,

"Well Lily, this is quite something. I didn't know I was loved so much by so many. I should seriously think about having my own website as well as the fan club. Long overdue I might add. Perhaps you'd consider running it for me, my love? You shouldn't feel too bad because I have noticed one or two out there who think you've made a good catch. Oliver and Margaret seem to be making the most of it too."

Lily responded, looking at her husband,

"Typical Bucks. Don't forget, and I shall remind you, that you're my husband now, so be careful, as this Management might have a few words to say about things from now on," and quickly changing the subject, *" The service was beautiful. Don't you think so, dahling? "*

Buckingham answered, deliberately mimicking Lily.

"You're quite right my dear. Angela and everyone have excelled themselves," (his voice had become strangely emphatic), *"but I'm telling you that as far as I'm concerned, a wife's rightful place is ten cat lengths behind her husband. She goes where he goes. What do you think about that?"*

Lily gave as good as she got and with deliberation said,

"Well, I think we will have to have a cosy chat about that dear when we get home... maybe in bed if you're lucky. "

Buckingham answered with what can only be described as disappointed excitement.

"That used to be a good idea once upon a time, but now they've stopped me rising to any occasion, but Lily you are a beautiful wife and I am very proud of you... but I'm still in charge!"

Lily muttered,
"Dream on my love."

It was thirty minutes before they all got back inside again, and Vicki and Priscilla said they were going to organise the food and drink and make sure everyone was seated properly. Meanwhile, Angela and Sinead continued the 'walkabout' inside. One person stuck in Angela's mind for some reason or other. Her name was Linda Hart and it was hard to judge her age but she looked so sad sitting all by herself. Funnily enough, Angela knew that Buckingham had noticed her too. Nothing was said.

Whilst Angela and Sinead did a tour of the room there were the first signs of boredom and agitation beginning to show in the pussy pen.

Dexter was the first to voice his feelings

"Why does all this stuff take so long? I'm beginning to get bored and hungry."

Miss Pretty followed suit:

"I'm hungry too, but it's been great for Mum and Dad. Like Margaret and Oliver, they are now officially Mr and Mrs Tillsworthy"

Dexter had to interrupt and, mimicking, said,

"Yea and we're two little Tillsworthys."

TC joined in and, looking sympathetically at Dexter and Miss Pretty, said,

"Well, it looks like we're all bloody well starving. Harry, you've said nothing. What did you think of the service? "

Harry responded in his usual knowledgeable manner:

"I must say I was surprised. I thought the whole thing was going to be a total fiasco and a hilarious mistake, falling flat on its bum, but it didn't. I'm sure I detected a smile on Oliver's face when he had the ring put on his finger, and Bucks and Lily exchanging coloured collars was too much. Knowing Buckingham, that won't be on there for long!"

Angela and Sinead finally arrived at the pussy pen and apologised for the time they had taken. Denzil was there like a shot.

"Sorry it's taken so long. You must be starving. Not long now, just big smiles for Uncle Denzil, Uncle Oliver and Auntie Margaret. Another big smile for Tillsie and Sinead. Say miii.......ce!"

Margaret, with laughter in her eyes could not restrain herself from displaying total disbelief:

"Seeing you all together is an incredible sight. Angela deserves national recognition for what she has done. TC and Harry, I haven't even had the pleasure of making your acquaintance. I've heard so much about you. A couple of '*mouse*keteers', so I hear, nudge nudge, wink wink!"

Angela acknowledged Margaret's compliments with a smile and then said to the four of them,

"Mr Buckingham Tillsworthy and Mrs Lily Tillsworthy are pleased to offer you the pleasure of their company and are pleased to join you, after which, guess what?.... Food glorious food! Then we do the speeches, but after that you will have to be on your best behaviour because every one will want to meet you, shake your paw and take pictures like Uncle Denzil has just done."

Angela then gently removed Lily from Margaret's lap and put her on their named bed and then she did likewise with Buckingham. She then said humorously,

"I know it's a bed and a very special bed and you've just got married, but no funny ideas, not in front of the children, and besides the world can see you!"

Buckingham and Lily looked at each other, then Buckingham said showing a touch of anger,

"*I don't think that's funny. Sometimes she forgets about my feelings. To tell you the truth I'm a little hurt!*"

Lily responded, slightly mockingly,

"*You have a one track mind. There are other things in life besides that. The bed is beautiful and Angela putting our names on it like that is wonderful and it's romantic. You should be grateful she loves us so much.*"

Buckingham commented with a look of defeat on seeing everyone else relaxed with eyes closed,

"*Well, I suppose we'll get fed sometime during the night.*"

With all that they had been through they were understandably 'cat- tired.' They closed their eyes, snuggled up together and Buckingham, bless him, put his paw lovingly round Lily's neck. It was a shame about the food and they had almost given up on it, but then good things are always worth waiting for.

At this point of the occasion, Margaret's wheelchair was removed and she went to sit next to her husband, with his wheelchair being positioned behind but in the middle of the main guest table. Next to Oliver on his left were Priscilla, Angela, then Vicki, then Bradley, then Adele. Next to Margaret on her right were Sinead, then Denzil, then Fiona, then Vanessa and, last but not least, Mike Cass. They made a pretty picture and one which Denzil made sure he didn't miss capturing.

The buffet was wheeled into the centre of the room and Vicki made the appropriate announcement:

"Ladies and Gentlemen the food is here at last. It is a magnificent buffet, so please come up and take what you want. Those of you who cannot get there will be waited on by our conscientious staff. Rest assured the other Mr and Mrs Tillsworthy over there (Vicki pointed towards the cats) their children and friends will be well catered for, so no 'kitty bags' will be necessary! There is also plenty to drink. Just ask. Enjoy!"

The compliments on the buffet were overwhelming, but nothing more than Vicki and Priscilla had expected. They had a great chef who loved cats, in fact eight of them kept him and his wife *with little time for much else,* except creating some sensational and original recipes! They were a great ad for Tillsworthy House and HALE.

It wasn't long before some mouth watering smells wafted into the pussy pen. No more sleeping, it was time to be heard. Six voices almost in harmony demanded immediate attention and they got it. There had never been a cat's chorus like this before and if there had been the equivalent of an animal X- Factor they would certainly have won it! They even managed to practically stop the entire audience from talking and eating, but at last it arrived – silence reigned and it was heads down and eat eat eat. A mixture of chicken, salmon and tuna washed down with milk were the delicacy of the day. They savoured every mouthful of it. With all plates and saucers licked totally clean they retired to their respective beds, giving each other a wash whilst purring loudly. They then contentedly settled down, not caring what else might be in store for them.

Two hours of such culinary delight was more than enough for everyone.

Vicki once more made the announcement.

"Ladies and Gentlemen we are now going to hear a few words from one or two people who have contributed so much of their time and effort to make this occasion such a success for Oliver and Margaret and Buckingham and Lily. First I would like to introduce Bradley, our one in a million Vicar."

Bradley was such a lovely man, so genuine and so caring. He reiterated how the incorrigible Angela had put the whole idea of the cats getting married to him and how ridiculous he thought it was at first. Apparently when he asked God what he should do, God replied, "Go for it Bradley. They have as much right to be married as anybody else." He then praised Margaret for her relentless caring and love for Oliver and although Oliver could not see or hear, both he and Oliver knew the marriage was meant to be and Oliver was now about to *feel* his way into a new life. Bradley then said that before he officially introduced his old long time friend Denzil Whitehead to say a few words he wanted to introduce someone else who was very special to him. Bradley walked over to the pussy pen and lovingly picked up Harry, showing him to the audience.

Bradley whispered in Harry's ear,

"Harry this is your big moment. Make the most of it."

"Ladies and Gentlemen, may I introduce Harry my *other* protector and guardian, the one who keeps me sane throughout the week and the one whom my parishioners adore. He does not have a mean bone in his body and he has the honour of being Buckingham's best man cat."

As Bradley put Harry back in the pussy pen there was a ripple of well meant applause, after which Bradley introduced the illustrious Denzil Whitehead.

Denzil as always the life and soul of any party was dressed in his usual wild attire with handlebar moustache, particularly noticeably well groomed for the occasion. He chose to wear red velvet trousers, black suede shoes, a black shirt and a red tie that had caricatures of black cats all over it, obviously chosen deliberately to honour some of the participants in this event. Angela's amazing foresight in realising the therapeutic power of the cat was the main topic of his very funny speech. He pointed out that Margaret and Oliver would never have fallen for each other had it not been for Buckingham and Lily's hours and hours of devoted love and friendship for them, which resulted in bringing their own love for each other to fruition, and their commitment to each other today. Even their two children, Dexter and Miss Pretty, through Angela's relentless drive to help those less fortunate, were now working with children and the terminally ill at the Princess Alicia Hospice. He reiterated that Tillsie was certainly a force to be reckoned with. She was also much concerned with cruelty to animals and subsequently formed the TTPCC, The Tillsworthy Trust for the Protection of Cruelty to Cats in conjunction with the RSPCA.

Denzil, feeling he had the audience in the palm of his hand and hanging on to his every word, finished by saying, with deliberate sincerity

"As the Landlord of the Wooden Horse in Troy I want every one of you in this room to have a drink on me in wishing dear Oliver and Margaret and Lily and Buckingham good health and good fortune for their future. It's been one helluva day. I've never experienced anything like it and for sure I'm not likely to ever again."

Sinead's contribution as Margaret's sister was to thank everyone for coming and accepting the unusual and possibly bizarre nature of the whole event. It had been a great success, resulting in two adorable and happily married couples. She also wanted to point out that all this would never have happened at all without the amazing contribution by Priscilla and Vicki for this wonderful building named Tillsworthy House. It was a dream which, through, perseverance and care for those less fortunate, had brought about the reality of providing a better living and lifestyle for the elderly, at a price not considered to be outrageous for what you got. Unquestionably Tillsworthy House was value for money and she as yet had never seen an unhappy face from anyone who had the good fortune to live in it.

Angela had the final word of the day.

"On behalf of my father Oliver, my sister Priscilla and my wonderful family over there (she pointed to the cats) I want to thank all of you for making what was initially a ridiculous idea into something worthwhile, beautiful and a lot of fun. To see my father with such a dreadful handicap looking so well and happy is indeed a blessing and worth everything. I'm sure if he could, he would have loved to have imparted a huge thank you to Buckingham especially for completely changing his life, and to Lily and Margaret who have made all that we have seen today become such a worthwhile reality."

She paused and then said,

"Now you may, if you wish, go and shake paws with the little darlings over there. They've had a hard day, but they love adulation. Be warned there are those who I shall not name who think they are doing you the favour and not the other way round."

The evening's atmosphere got an unexpected lift when Vicki and Priscilla's music tape of Soul/Motown music started to get an airing through the excellent speaker system. Denzil found his time was cut out at the pussy pen, where everyone in the world seemed to want their picture taken with the cats or a particular cat. He certainly captured some magical and memorable shots. With such adulation being showered upon them, all their individual characters came alive. Angela was so proud of them because they had brought nothing but pleasure to everyone there. Fiona, with help, managed to bring the six children in her care over to see them, and the look on their faces was just so special.

Bucks decided to have a quiet word in Lily's ear,

"You know what Lily, they're getting all this for free. I usually get paid for doing this sort of thing. Dexter's showing off too and Miss Pretty is making the most of her name. TC and Harry seem a little overwhelmed by it all. They're obviously not geared to handle glitz and glamour like I am. Do I detect a little jealousy perhaps?"

A small voice could be heard

"I want a picture with Buckingham."

Buckingham responded accordingly,

"You see I just can't avoid it. Here I go again. All this celebrity stuff is just too much. I mean it is taking the 'puss' a bit, don't you think!"

There was a break in the photo shoot for a minute whilst Denzil fiddled about with the camera, which gave Harry the chance of having a word in TC's ear.

"All this is 'over the top' for me. I'll be glad to get home to some semblance of sanity. It's been a bloody long day. "

TC answered

"One thing I know, Harry, is that Angela really did well with our beds. They are catastic don't you agree? You'll have to tell Bradley to ask Angela to get one for you. I don't know what she has in mind to do with them after this, but I would rather sleep on this than where I'm sleeping at home now. I would have my very own space, so to speak. Your name is on this bed anyway, so maybe Bradley wouldn't mind if you had a 'sleep over' with me sometimes.

Harry showed his approval

"I'd like that. I'll have a word with Bucks and Lily about the bed and see what could be done in persuading Angela to agree."

It was a long drawn out affair before everyone was satisfied with having their particular memento of this once in a lifetime occasion, courtesy of Denzil Whitehead. He had gone out of his way to please and nothing was ever too much trouble. With his wit and natural sense of humour he had contributed enormously to the success of the occasion. No-one could thank him or praise him enough. Even the cats agreed that he was the cat's whiskers.

By about 10.00 pm that evening the tell-tale signs of tiredness and having had more than their money's worth, were beginning to show. Drink had made its mark on some of the residents and Vicki and Priscilla instructed the staff to check on absolutely everyone, leaving nothing to chance before any one had the idea of retiring for the night.

CHAPTER ELEVEN

Guest of honour

With Angela always trying to play the part of the ultimate perfectionist, with impeccable attention to detail, she found herself with little or no time for anything else other than the planning and organising of her part of the two weddings. The cats were always her responsibility and in addition to everything else she still had to take them to work as usual. Always on her mind was the fact that when she first purchased Cozy Cats Cottage she had insisted on Adele Mckenzie coming to visit her. She felt somewhat guilty about this, but luckily the weddings had provided her with the golden opportunity to ask Adele if she would like to stay for a few days, or even a week. Both of them, of course, were looking forward to this very much. However, the one sacrilegious thing Angela had forgotten was to tell the cats, and worse still to tell them that they would have to vacate their bedroom. Somewhat of a bad move, especially on *the* wedding night!

Finally the madness of the day's marital events at Tillsworthy House seemed to be winding down, with some feeling a little worse for wear. It had certainly been a day to remember. The residents began to slowly retire too, but they were fortunate in only having to negotiate a few stairs or use the lift, and to make the short journey to their respective rooms. Whilst Priscilla, Vicki and Sinead were organising the clearing up Angela and Adele decided to check out the pussy pen and have a quiet word with the family about the next few days.

Seeing their state of tiredness, Angela thought it might turn out to be easier than she first thought.

"Well well, who likes their doggy beds then? Didn't I do well? Always thinking of your comfort of course! The good news is that I have decided you should keep them, but the bad news is that for the next few days they will be put in the lounge at home, with everything else being allocated to the kitchen. Auntie Adele is going to stay with us for a while and you are all going to have a break. None of you will be going to work, so for you Mr and Mrs it's an unexpected honeymoon and you should make the most of it! You see how considerate I am?"

She paused for a moment, then with a big smile, said,

"You all look so dog tired. That's what that mad salesman would have said. And Harry, since you now have your own bed here, I'll even ask Bradley if you could come over for the occasional sleep over."

TC didn't miss that.

"There you go Harry. We didn't even have to ask."

Buckingham never missed anything either and had to put his paw in with the usual caustic remark:

"That's a good idea. It will keep me from marital boredom if the occasion arose, especially if Lily wasn't performing properly!"

Lily, looking at her husband, had to respond to that

"And just what do you mean by that? Bucks, if you continue to play 'Mr hard done by' making me feel a fool in front of everybody else at this early stage of our marital relationship, then I shall have no choice but to consider filing for divorce, so stick that up your furry bum. Now that would be a catastrophe."

Dexter looked at Adele,

"Mum and Dad are fighting already. They're worse than children. Miss Pretty and I don't speak to each other like that. I've made bloody sure she knows who wears the trousers."

Whilst Adele was totally mesmerised, Angela commented,

"Adele, you know that they're talking between themselves. They do it all the time and I know when they're doing it. Buckingham is just being Buckingham, doing his thing and making sure no one manages to get one up on him on anything. He has always been like that, and even marital bliss won't change him!"

Back at the ranch

All five cats just stood and watched aghast as Angela prepared Adele's bedroom, removing all trace of their existence, and even eliminating their smell with the use of some ghastly deodoriser. However, things changed when Angela placed their new bolster beds in an appropriate corner in the lounge and moved their food and toiletries into the kitchen. All this was confirmed with the appropriate thank you purrs and meows. It was finally the end of a very tiring and gruelling day for all concerned. Everyone found their sleeping place and peace and quiet descended like a blanket, eliminating all previous activity.

Adele was thrilled that Angela had not wanted to change any of the interior décor in the cottage at all and remarked that it felt like she had never been away. In fact, she wished that her daughter had not persuaded her to move in the first place, even though she was of course very pleased to find Angela so happy. However, it was the front garden with its lawns and block paved pathway that found Adele completely lost for words. Due to her physical incapacity, Adele regrettably had to concede to leaving it in a dreadful state. The change was unimaginable, and for what Angela had achieved in design and creation, Adele emphatically considered it deserved national recognition. She was particularly enthralled with the wrought iron arch incorporating the name of Cozy Cats Cottage, which majestically dominated the entire frontage.

For all intents and purposes, Adele's stay with Angela was intended to be one of relaxation, but that was not what a certain two little creatures had in mind at all. For what was in store for poor Angela and Adele, changing the name to *Crazy* Cats Cottage would have been much more appropriate. Pent up kitten energy was about to erupt. Dexter and Miss Pretty had decided that since Angela had made the next few days an official break it was the ideal opportunity to let their 'fur' down and do some serious showing off. Adele was just the right person to witness what they had in mind and even admire their pre-planned charade.

It was on the second night, whilst Angela and Adele were deeply engrossed in watching their favourite soap on TV, that the real fun began. TC was out doing his thing with Harry, whilst Buckingham and Lily, having just eaten, were licking and loving each other in their bed, seemingly enjoying a moment of marital bliss. Dexter and Miss Pretty were in the kitchen having also just finished eating, but were now planning to get down to some serious business.

Dexter, looking Miss Pretty straight in the eye, said,

"Right my little sister, you know what we're doing. I'm taking the left one and you're taking the right. We'll see who can stay up there for the longest time, and then it's back here for the second assault."

Miss Pretty responded,

"I'm scared Dex. Angela will go crazy. She won't believe it."

Dexter was quick to reply

"Oh Sis, don't kitten out now. We agreed. We're always working. Let's have some fun and do what little cats do. They need to run wild sometimes."

Miss Pretty answered, not at all convinced,

"And what about Mum and Dad? Oh what the hell, let's do it and get it over with."

Dexter added,

"Remember, we do it twice!"

With two harmonious battle cry meows, Dexter and Miss Pretty flew from the kitchen into the lounge, chasing each other at an incredible speed between the chairs, settee and table, before leaping up into the air and onto the unsuspecting drapes which hung from the ceiling to the floor on each side of the French window. The drapes were drawn, providing the perfect battle field. Dexter, who was obviously that bit stronger, managed to get a little higher than Miss Pretty, who was hanging onto the left curtain. Claws dug into the material but eventually, due to their weight, they began to slip and were not able to hang on for any longer. Meanwhile there was an awful tearing-of-material sound coming from both curtains. Before Angela and Adele could say or do anything, Dexter and Miss Pretty rushed back into the kitchen and did the whole thing over again, only this time they included jumping across Angela and Adele's laps and making the tears in both curtains even more pronounced. Then it was back into the kitchen again, having a good drink of water and acting as if nothing had happened at all.

Once Adele and Angela had got over the initial shock, Adele could not stop laughing, but Angela stormed into the kitchen and verbally let rip.

"What the fucking hell do you two think you're doing? This is supposed to be a week of rest, for God's sake. You've ruined the drapes and almost given me and Adele a heart attack. You don't do that sort of thing in front of guests. If you ever, ever do anything like that again you will be in big, big trouble. I shall get your father and your mother to consider grounding you, giving you a good hiding or a bloody good talking to. They've just got married, or have you forgotten that too? You're totally selfish and inconsiderate, and at your age and with your professional responsibilities you should know better."

Dexter and Miss Pretty continued to pretend to drink their water, ignoring Angela. Dexter whispered in his sister's ear,

"I'm glad we did it. It was great fun and I feel much better for it. Angela will get over it in time. She'll just have to get new curtains. I didn't care for the colour of them anyway."

Miss Pretty whispered back,

"It's Mum and Dad I'm worried about. I wonder if they did mad things like that when they were young."

Dexter emphatically replied,

"I'm sure Dad did, and much worse than that. I think he was a genuine mouseketeer when he was young. He loved a bit of er.. action no matter what it was!"

Angela apologised to Adele for their behaviour, but Adele thought the whole thing was a hoot, making Angela feel worse than she already did. They saw that none of this had gone unnoticed by Buckingham or Lily, who were sitting up in their beds obviously shocked, or were they just amused by what they had witnessed.

Lily remarked,

"I'm a little ashamed that our kids could do such a thing without a bat of an eyelid, especially Miss Pretty. I know I did some outrageous things when I was young, but not so blatantly obvious and in front of guests too. It was all so deliberate. They must have worked it all out beforehand."

Buckingham replied,

*"It was the power of the CCS working again. TC would have agreed with that and I would have done the same. It was clever and well thought out, like father like son, and of course like **me**. Dexter's a genius. Angela will have to get some new drapes. The colour was awful anyway."*

Lily responded,

"Do we give them a talking to like good parents should?"

Buckingham answered,

"Only congratulations on a job well done."

My Hero

It took Angela a while to recover from the madness of that particular night. Thank goodness all was quiet for the following two days and nights. Bradley came over for dinner and was delighted to see Adele again. Harry came over with him too and was allowed to stay the night, which pleased TC no end. Subjects of conversation centred around the day of the weddings, what Adele had been up to in her life now she was living with her daughter, and, last but not least, Dexter and Miss Pretty's latest fiasco, which they all had a good laugh about. One matter of concern that Bradley casually mentioned was that he had to take Harry to the vet, and Mike Cass told him that unfortunately Harry, like so many cats around fifteen years old, had diabetes and needed a daily injection. He was quite all right apart from that and at present it was nothing to be too concerned about. Angela was particularly relieved.

The day before Adele was due to be picked up by her daughter, Angela suggested they should take a walk into the village. They took the cobbled pathway through the woods and met Bradley at the church as previously arranged. Bradley made coffee and after an enjoyable chat they made their way to the Wooden Horse for a pub lunch at the invitation of Denzil Whitehead. As usual Denzil was on top form, always putting on a show for the vicar! The pub happened to be quite full and no one

seemed to miss out on passing on their congratulations for the amazing success of the day of the weddings. Denzil had posted samples of all the pictures he had taken so everyone could order whatever. It looked an incredible display and you just could not fault what he had produced.

By the time they had got home they were pretty worn out, and Adele was not really looking forward too much to going back to Cornwall. She had really enjoyed herself, and what Angela had achieved with the cottage and the cats was well worth waiting to see. She admired the idea of setting up a trust, especially for the prevention of cruelty to cats, but most of all she loved 'Pussy Loving Care' being Angela's interpretation of plc in the name of Cozy Cats Cottage plc. Whilst Adele relaxed and continued to contemplate on the week's activities, Angela was in the kitchen making coffee. Noticing that there were two cats missing, Adele called out to Angela with some concern,

"Angela I see Bucks and Lily but there's no sign of Dexter and Miss Pretty."

Angela answered,

"Oh they're probably hiding behind a chair somewhere."

Suddenly there was a tremendous commotion by the cat flap, incorporating some loud scurrying noises with Dexter running around madly in circles. Amidst all this pandemonium there was a distinct squeaking noise. Adele, frightened out of her wits screamed,

"Oh my God, they've got a mouse and it's alive! They're chasing it everywhere and it's terrified."

Angela was at a loss to know what to do and her mind was racing as to how to save the poor little creature. Buckingham had witnessed the whole scenario and suddenly, with no warning at all, jumped out of his bed and with one quick bite, put an end to its misery. He then casually went back to bed. He turned to Lily and said,

"Needs a real man to deal with something like that. You've got to act quickly. You can't fart around."

With that he turned to Dexter and Miss Pretty, who were looking at him in disbelief, and said,

"A true mousketeer will never play around like that. It's cruel. How would you like that to happen to you? If you must hunt and you catch, then you must kill quickly. I don't want to see that happen ever again, do you hear?"

Lily responded with a touch of sarcasm,

"Oh such strong words… but this time your Dad is right."

Having disposed of the poor little creature accordingly, Angela and Adele endeavoured to settle down for the evening, hoping to God that nothing else was going to happen. Adele remarked that she needed a doctor's prescription to calm her down! The excitement of a different show virtually every night was getting to be too much for an old girl! Angela tried to apologise and said the kittens had never behaved like that ever since they were born. Adele responded accordingly:

"But they're still kittens Angela. They need to express themselves and to show you how clever they are. When they go to work at the hospice or the kids' day care place they have to be on their best behaviour and that is not natural all the time."

Angela replied,

"Well they've certainly expressed themselves during this week with more than just a touch of showing off for *your* benefit."

Adele had the final say

"Angela,you are lucky to have them and they are lucky to have you. You make a great team and I am looking forward to my next visit, that is if you'll still have me."

Once Margaret and Oliver were married, Priscilla, Angela and Vicki knew that certain changes were inevitable. Margaret, rightly so, had pointed out that she needed to spend as much time with Oliver as husband and wife as possible. Consequently, although she inwardly fought against it, she knew that it would be wrong for Buckingham and Lily to continue to spend as much time with them as they had been doing for so long. It needed to be reduced. The three girls were in total agreement, but apart from endeavouring to make Buckingham and Lily understand, Oliver might also not be too happy about it. Angela said she would have a little chat with Buckingham and Lily as soon as possible. However she had noticed that Lily was getting on rather well with Sinead! She who had put her in the wash!

The opportunity arrived one night when 'Mr and Mrs Tillsworthy' were about to retire. Dexter and Miss Pretty were safely out of harm's way, tucked up in bed. Angela lovingly looked directly at Buckingham and Lily and quietly said,

"You are not going to be able to spend as much time with Oliver and Margaret from now on because, like you, they are now married. Your jobs are done. You will still see them, but not so often. Lily, I am quite happy with you spending more time with Sinead. She is lonely and needs your company. Bucks, we are going to have to find another job for you, but I already have a hunch about something that I think could be a solution to the problem. Now go to sleep. Sweet dreams. I'll see you in the morning. Oh, by the way, now that Adele is going home, your beds will go back into your room tomorrow. Sleep tight. I love you."

Heart to Hart

The hunch that Angela had up her sleeve was the memory of the walkabout on the night of the wedding, when she and Buckingham had met Linda Hart for the first time. Both Angela and Buckingham had noticed how unusually sad she was, but nothing was said.

One day the opportunity arose. Having left Lily with Sinead,

Angela took Buckingham with her and found Linda sitting on her own in the TV lounge. Linda smiled at seeing them both again and seemed to welcome the opportunity of having some company. Buckingham settled on Angela's lap as Linda slowly yet deliberately confided in Angela and explained why she was feeling like she did. Angela was always the good listener.

The weddings had brought back memories of Linda's own marriage and mental pictures of her two cats, but sadly they were unhappy memories. Linda, now in her early sixties and having suffered a recent nervous breakdown, was a successful self- made business woman, highly skilled at investigating and solving copyright clearance problems on behalf of book publishers, authors, magazines and national newspapers. She worked from a spacious yet tastefully furnished apartment in Guildford on a freelance basis, being far more financially lucrative, but she discovered rather too late that she had met and married the wrong guy. His name was Dennis and at first he was considerate and loving, which culminated in them having a son who they named Jamie. As a fifth year birthday present they gave Jamie something that he longed for – two adorable little kittens that they named George and Mildred. It was about this time that Linda noticed a definite change in Dennis. With his business becoming difficult and problematic he became very moody, with signs of being extremely jealous of Linda's success. Dennis, a kind of rough diamond was a builder by trade and was physically very capable. Things were to get worse and over the following years Dennis turned to drink and became frighteningly aggressive and violent. Linda, for the sake of Jamie and in fear of both their lives, said and did nothing. Linda strangely believed that she was imagining the whole thing and that the scenario might well have come out of any one of the books or magazines she was involved with. Dennis continued to abuse her over a long period of time and eventually his anger turned to Jamie, who had to live with the daily fear of being physically assaulted. Dennis was also clever, milking Linda of a great deal of her saved income to satisfy both his drinking, and as was also discovered, other needs! Dennis wanted to hurt Jamie because in his warped state of mind he felt that would hurt Linda even more. He figured the way to do that was through the cats. He became excessively cruel towards George and Mildred, so much so that out of desperation Jamie had no choice but to call the RSPCA, who agreed to come round to investigate at a time when Dennis was not present. They of course had seen it all before. Sympathetically, they explained to Jamie that for the animals' welfare they had little choice but to take the cats away and find new homes for them once their health had been restored. The cats, however, were not their only shock when they realised the suffering and agony Linda also had to endure at the hands of this 'control freak'. Before departing they emphasised that they would definitely be contacting the appropriate authority to make them aware of the situation, which would result in hopefully getting immediate help of some kind.

The loss of the cats proved to be the last straw for Jamie and one day, in spite of the pain and distress he was feeling for his mother, he finally could take no more and left home. Dennis, in the meantime, drinking as heavily as ever, did everything in his power to prevent Linda from trying to find Jamie. However, drink was to be Dennis' final downfall when he stupidly attempted to drive and became involved in a serious accident, almost killing a small child. Dennis got his due come-uppance and was put away for a number years, but Linda suffered a serious nervous breakdown. Some unexpected sympathetic help culminated in her moving to Tillsworthy House to endeavour to rebuild her life, get some much needed care and regain some sanity. She was granted an immediate divorce, but Jamie had been missing for seven months with no one so far having heard a word of his whereabouts.

Angela was left speechless, with tears threatening to run down her cheeks. Linda reached for her hand and said,

"Angela, I'm much better now being here. Priscilla and Vicki are adorable and are looking after me really well. I have not talked to anybody like this before, but I felt it was right. Buckingham is a really beautiful boy and looking at him gives me a great deal of comfort. Lily's a lucky lady! I was thrilled to learn about the charity you have set up for the prevention of cruelty to cats. It was long overdue for someone to do something specifically for cats with this problem. It is far greater than any one can imagine and I would dearly love to contribute. It would mean so much to me."

Angela sighed, and feeling almost at a loss as to what to say, looked at Linda.

"Linda you are a remarkable lady and what you have gone through makes me feel almost ashamed. All of us here will do everything we can to make your life worth living again. I will definitely see what we could do in trying to find Jamie."

Then looking at Buckingham she said,

"Buckingham is blessed with a sixth sense and knows what you have been through. He wants to see you smile again and has asked me to say that if you were agreeable he would gladly spend time with you as we have done now. In that way you could contribute to Cozy Cats Cottage plc, the proceeds of which would go to the charity, but you would benefit from it with, I'm sure, true love sitting right beside you. He and Lily come over and spend time with Oliver and Margaret, but not as often as they used to. He could easily see you twice a week."

Linda was overwhelmed with gratitude:

"That would be fantastic. He could tell me all about his family and I would love to tell him about George and Mildred, and of course Jamie. I do miss him terribly and can only pray to God that he's still alive and well. Thank you Angela for being so kind and thoughtful."

At Tillsworthy House, finding what happened to Jamie became the most important mission of the moment.

Only the good die young

Gradually the madness of the last few weeks was disappearing and now that Adele had gone home too, Angela felt that Cozy Cats Cottage had become her own again. The cats were over the moon to have their bedroom back and Dexter and Miss Pretty had settled down and seemed to be quite content to be back at work.

Angela was a born worrier. If she had nothing to worry about she would deliberately go out of her way to find or create something to worry about. At the moment it was TC who was mostly on her mind. Angela had not come up with any ideas for him work-wise, primarily because he loved the outdoors and seemed to spend most of his time with Harry. They were bosom buddies and had no secrets from each other. Harry confided in TC, imparting his innermost fear.

"TC, I have to be honest with you, I am not feeling that well these days. Bradley has to give me an injection every morning for my diabetes. This condition makes me tired and I often feel dizzy. I want you to make me a promise. When my time comes I want you to take care of Bradley however you can and to also take care of my guard duty, which is so important to him and the church."

TC pushed his chin affectionately up against Harry and said,

"I promise you I will do what you ask but you promise me you will not do anything foolish. Tell me how you are feeling. Only He up there knows when it is time and your time is certainly not yet my friend. Remember only the good die young and you're already past that!"

In view of Harry's condition, and Bradley obviously being so worried about him, Angela decided to leave TC alone and allow the two of them to spend as much time as possible together. Angela knew that the day she dreaded would eventually come. Bradley would need all the strength and love he could get and Angela did not have to think twice about giving it.

CHAPTER TWELVE

Excess baggage

Nothing too dramatic happened in Troy, day or night, apart from the continuous stream of sightseers who daily came and went nine months of the year. It was basically an unspoilt, laid back, beautiful but lazy village. Once Denzil Whitehead had closed the doors of The Wooden Horse it was time to turn the village lights out, but the night had only just begun for two priceless members of the community's cat family. They had a job to do and that was to make sure peace and beauty remained in Troy uninterrupted throughout the night. This important responsibility had originally been solely entrusted to Harry, but since TC had emerged as a bosom buddy, Harry had been more than grateful for his company on the many long and lonely nights. As such, TC was very proud to have the honour of being Second in Command. Since TC's arrival on the scene, General Bradley, as Harry affectionately called him was obviously delighted that his H.Q, the beloved church, had the benefit of some unexpected additional security.

Over a period of time there had been one or two small dramas. Harry had virtually caught someone red-handed during one night deliberately destroying some of the General's precious flower beds. This was an act of pure jealousy, but through Harry's clever intervention the General was able to deal with the matter accordingly before the sacrilege of such beauty had gone too far.

Apart from The Wooden Horse, the ornate fountain was the village's centre of attention. Harry and TC loved to sit on its stone surround as it provided an amazing point of observation in all directions.

There was no warning and it was over in seconds. A small yellow car entered the village at high speed about two in the morning. As it passed the fountain the rear door opened and a bundle of something or other was thrown into the road. In seconds the car was gone and even Harry, normally quite calm in any situation, was frozen in total disbelief.

A rather shaken Harry was the first to speak:

"Christ Almighty TC (sorry Bradley), that was a first. Troy has never seen anything like that before. It was so quick."

TC, sounding really concerned, said,

"What on earth is that in the road? It doesn't look good at all and there's a rope wrapped round it."

Harry replied assertively,

"Well, whatever it is we'll have to deal with it, after all that's our job."

They ran to the bundle and gingerly investigated. TC said alarmingly,

"It's a body and its male because he's dressed in a man's casual clothes... that is, what's left of them. He's got blood and bruises all over his face."

Harry, looking very agitated, anxiously said

"Is he alive.....or dead?"

TC went up to his face and licked it. For an instant the eyes flickered.

"He's alive. His eyes moved. We must get help."

Harry, taking immediate control of the situation, then said,

"You stay with him and try and keep him alive. I will find and wake Denzil. I know where his room is in there. Just pray he's left the bloody window open."

Luckily Denzil's window was open and as usual he was snoring loudly. Harry found his ear and meowed constantly at the top of his voice. Denzil got the shock of his life, and seeing Harry just couldn't help himself:

"What the fuck are you doing? You want to give me a heart attack? You're trying to tell me something. Harry this better be good."

When Harry acted in this way, Denzil knew very well that there was something wrong. Trying to put some clothes on at the same time, Denzil followed him out into the street, where he saw TC almost sitting on top of something in the road. Denzil muttered to himself,

"Oh my God, what on earth is this? A body with a rope round it, but TC seems to have kept him alive. Much as he won't like it, I'll have to get Bradley to come over and help me."

Between them, Bradley and Denzil removed the rope and carried the body into the pub, and then decided they should definitely call an ambulance and notify the police. They could now see that the person was alive, so they wrapped a blanket round him and tried to administer some water. Whilst waiting for the arrival of the ambulance, Denzil made some coffee and gave the cats some milk. Shaking his head in disbelief and looking at Harry and TC, who were anxiously waiting for a result, Denzil remarked,

"There's no question that CCS saved this guy's life, but I can only deduce that he must have been thrown out of a car."

Bradley, looking at Harry and TC, answered,

"I think you're right, he was. They must have had a big shock. Harry's seen a few things in this village, but nothing like this. Whoever he is (Bradley nodded in the direction of the body) should be eternally grateful to our dedicated security team and I'm pretty sure he will be when he realises just how lucky he's been. He doesn't look that old to me either."

The ambulance arrived. The paramedics took note of the story, examined the victim and put him in the ambulance. They told Bradley and Denzil which hospital he would be going to and that he was concussed and in shock more than anything else. He would eventually be all right, but good thinking and prompt action had helped to save the day. They were glad the police had been informed as it was important to find out who he was and who had committed the deed.

Denzil apologised to Bradley for the rude awakening and reminded him not to forget to phone Angela in the morning, since she would be thrilled to know that Harry and TC had once again acted beyond the call of duty.

Harry and TC walked out of the pub together with heads held high, to continue what was left of the night's vigil, feeling a touch more than proud with what they had achieved.

By the morning's first light the whole village was buzzing with the excitement of what had happened during the night. Both Bradley and Denzil were inundated with questions. Angela had heard from Bradley, who confirmed that TC and Harry were naturally both 'out of it' in view of what they'd been through. However, something was bothering her and she couldn't quite place what it was. She knew she had to go down to the hospital. The police were already there and having verified who she was Angela was informed that the young man was recovering satisfactorily, but so far an identity had not been ascertained. He had no money and no documentation on him, but strangely two silver discs that looked like name tags were discovered. Angela nearly died when she saw the names of George and Mildred!

Incredibly, Jamie Hart had, as such, been found alive and almost well by none other than two cats!

Jamie Hart was more than reluctant to talk about the particular incident or analyse the last ten months or so of his life, which understandably he wanted to forget as quickly as possible. He knew, thank God, that his father, through his own stupidity, had been justifiably caught, punished and was serving time. He was relieved to know that his mother was safe within the walls of Tillsworthy House and was desperately looking forward to seeing her and to do whatever was necessary to rebuild their relationship. He also knew very well that had it not been for the quick thinking of Harry and TC on that fateful night, he might not even be alive. He was indebted to them forever and he made it a priority to find the time to thank them. George and Mildred would have been very proud to have known them. Before he was due to be released from hospital he found he had friends he never knew he had, who were more than glad to go out of their way to help him.

Denzil Whitehead was always unpredictable, but for some reason he had a soft spot for Jamie and once Angela had told him the Hart life story he not only offered Jamie a job serving behind the bar at The Wooden Horse, but also offered him some decent accommodation. Jamie was more than surprised and without any hesitation accepted the kind offer.

The most important day of all arrived when Jamie, courtesy of Angela, went to see his mother for the first time after what had seemed a lifetime apart. This was also the day of Buckingham's first session with Linda, and Jamie and Buckingham clicked the moment they first met. Jamie thought Angela was amazingly perceptive to assess Buckingham's therapeutic skills in respect to helping his mother in her present mental state. Angela decided it was astute to leave the three of them alone.

Summit Meeting

"So Management's let you out then," Harry said with a smile, looking directly at Buckingham.

Buckingham answered rather indignantly, having settled himself down on the fountain wall next to TC and Harry

"What do you mean? If I want to go out I go out. Lily of the Valley, bless her, has no say in the matter. I decided to find you as we haven't met since the wedding, and news of your exploits via Jamie and Linda, who is my new assignment by the way, is all I hear. Quite boring really, but commendable"

TC said in a matter of fact tone of voice,

"Well if Harry and I hadn't used CCS so efficiently, which you taught me many moons ago if you remember, Jamie might not have made it, and your Linda has a lot to be grateful for. We saw Jamie actually being thrown out of the car and he ended up over there with a rope wrapped round him. We moved him into the pub."

Harry intervened,

"With a little bit of help from Denzil and Bradley, of course. Poor old Denzil nearly died when I screamed in his ear. Did he use some bad language!"

Buckingham had to have the final word and, with tongue in cheek, said,

"Well I suppose you both did the right thing. Good tuition is very important, so I feel I helped in having introduced you to the CCS in the first place. You got a good result, which is all that matters."

At that point in the conversation, the door of The Wooden Horse opened and Jamie appeared, obviously wanting a breath of fresh air. He lit a cigarette and then noticed all three cats sitting on the fountain wall.

"All three of you together – amazing! Well that is a coincidence. Words are not enough, but I have been really desperate to thank each one of you for what you have done in saving my life and my sanity. My mother feels the same, and having you, Buckingham, coming to see her twice a week is just fantastic."

As Jamie stroked each one of them in turn, Buckingham looked at him and proudly spoke up for them all,

"It's all in a day of a cat's life really. Like everyone else, we have jobs to do and we do them damn well. Angela is a great boss. I have two great friends in TC and Harry. Sometimes I have a great wife and life mostly is… just great!"

Swings and Roundabouts

The fair was back in town again. Denzil loved it, rubbing his hands together at the very thought of all that extra money. TC and Harry hated it, especially as it instilled some really bad memories for TC and meant a great deal more vigilance for Harry. Having TC with him at this time especially was a blessing. Bradley had a kind of obsession for the fair and never failed to invite Angela to spend an evening with him there. This was, in actual fact, the third time they had been there together.

It was a Saturday night and it was pleasantly warm. The fair was buzzing as Bradley and Angela, for the first time, walked hand in hand eating ice cream. Angela suddenly noticed a collection of about five cats and presumed them all to be fairground residents, but on a closer look she recognised two of them.

Turning to Bradley with a mixture of horror and shock she said,

"Bradley, that's Dexter and Miss Pretty! What on earth are they doing here? They're not supposed to leave the house at this time of night, and look at Miss Pretty! She's got her tail up in the air!"

Bradley couldn't help laughing and replied,

"Well Angela, she obviously wants a bit of the other. Once again you've forgotten to do it, and I haven't reminded you. Get in touch with Mike tomorrow and get them both down there and get them 'seen too,' unless you want a whole lot more trouble on your doorstep. You can't do anything now. You'll have to let them have their last fling and pray that's all that comes out of it"

Angela replied,

"How did they get out of the house in the first place? That's taking the you know what! How could they do it? I'll phone Mike first thing in the morning."

Bradley commented accordingly,

"Well they obviously knew we were going out to have some fun so they thought…. we want some of that too!"

The shock of seeing Dexter and Miss Pretty luckily hadn't spoilt Bradley and Angela's evening together, just added a little bit of unexpected spice to it. The amazing thing was that by the time Angela had got home Dexter and Miss Pretty were sound asleep as though nothing had happened at all, just like two naughty little children. Angela thought to herself, and said under her breath

"Crafty little devils. You've got a big surprise coming your way tomorrow, so I hope you enjoyed your last night of…. 'fun at the fair'! No more ball games for you young Dexter and its tail down, shop closed and out of business from now on for you Miss Pretty."

First thing the following morning, as promised, Angela took Dexter and Miss Pretty down to Mike Cass before they realised what was happening. Needless to say

Buckingham and Lily were alarmed, but not that surprised.

Buckingham, in father mode, said,

"They're young and should be allowed to enjoy themselves, but I know what Angela's up to now just because they've had a bit of fun. There should be a law banning such barbarism by humans. They should not be allowed to have such control over parts of cats' bodies without their permission first!"

Lily answered in a matter of fact tone of voice,

"Well we're lucky we managed to escape in the nick of time and produce those two naughty children. Dexter and Miss Pretty are nothing to be ashamed of and we really don't have that bad a life without all that."

Buckingham answered, a touch regretfully,

"You might think so, but I miss being a proper man cat. I liked flaunting it about a bit," Buckingham smiled, *"only pretend though Lily, nothing serious."*

Ever since Mike Cass had diagnosed Harry as having diabetes, Bradley, as instructed, had been religiously giving him his morning injection. Bradley had been keeping a close eye on him and for some time he had been fine, but now he had noticed a change. He seemed to be sleeping more and didn't have his usual energy. Worst of all he had moments of being noticeably unstable on his back legs. Bradley forbade him to do his usual guard duty and suggested that he explain this to TC as best he could, saying that TC would quite definitely understand.

They arranged to meet by their favourite grave stone and TC knew exactly what Harry was going to say. Harry felt uncomfortably apologetic.

"TC I'm sure you already realise that my days of guard duty have come to an end. Bradley will not let me do it anymore because my back legs at times have decided not to work and he does not want the risk of anything happening to me without him being there. You are the best friend I have ever had and I shall miss doing the rounds with you so much."

TC, with obvious sadness replied,

"Harry, I will do the guard duty from now on. You have taught me everything there is to know. Just like you, I enjoy it, but it will be different without you. You too are my best friend and from now on we must see each other every day. The others will be sad to hear the news as well, but I am sure Angela and Bradley will let you stay over as often as you like."

Bradley and Angela knew Harry's calling was not far away. They did everything they could to make his daily life as comfortable and as enjoyable as possible, but sadly his quality of life deteriorated quite quickly. His back legs could take no more and he virtually remained in one place unable to move. Angela and Bradley reluctantly agreed with Mike Cass that there was no alternative but to take his pain away.

On that morning, whilst waiting for Mike to arrive at the vicarage, Angela gently lifted Harry in her arms and placed him on Bradley's lap. As they both stroked him, caressed him, loved him, Angela whispered,

"Harry, we all love you so much. You are going to a better place where you will have no pain and you will see us all. Oh God Harry, how we love you."

Bradley with tears in his eyes, said gently

"I will be with you. God will take care of you."

Harry was purring loudly as Mike Cass administered the fatal injection. Bradley said a prayer and in a few seconds it was all over.

Within two hours there was no one in Troy who didn't know about it. News of this nature was front page stuff and travelled like wildfire. Because the response was so unpredictably strong, there was no question in Bradley's mind that part of the following Sunday morning service had to be devoted to Harry.

During the week Angela and Bradley had been inundated with cards and phone calls of sympathy. Angela, endeavouring to be brave and holding back the tears, imparted the news, offering gentle words of support to the rest of the cat family, as did Priscilla, Vicki and Denzil, who had immediately come over. When it came to TC, Denzil had a big problem in trying to restrain his feelings.

All the cats knew what had happened, although it had not affected Dexter and Miss Pretty as much as the others because of their age.

In a quiet moment, whilst they were all in their beds, TC gently voiced his opinion:

"There was no one like him. He could never be replaced and never will be. Taking over the guard duty is really an honour and I had the best tutor in the world. Poor Bradley, I feel so sorry for him"

Lily was visibly upset. Buckingham gave her a lick of consolation and spoke on behalf of them all.

"It is hard for all of us but for you, TC, it must be awful. I would be honoured to spend some time with you on your guard duty round if you'll let me, and if Management condones it of course!"

Buckingham gave his wife that certain look, whilst TC responded accordingly:

"I'd like that Bucks. It would help us all a great deal. I know Angela and Bradley would be really pleased and very grateful."

On that Sunday morning, the church was overflowing beyond its capacity. Harry's popularity with so many people was a sight for sore eyes. Not even Angela and Bradley realised how much he was thought of, and the praise showered upon him for what he had done for the community was beyond belief.

The actual burial was attended by a select few just a few days before. Bradley had had the inspiration and foresight to have a small wooden coffin made and had designated a spot in the graveyard directly facing his front door, so he could see it every morning as he walked out of the vicarage. A small headstone with the following simple words inscribed on it said it all.

To Dear Harry
Such a soldier. Such a friend
Rest in peace forever.
We shall never forget you.

It took a while before Troy got over the shock and got back to some semblance of normality. Harry was the topic of conversation in The Wooden Horse for some time to come, but for Denzil and Jamie he had never gone away and never would. TC had settled himself into a constructive regime with both Bradley and Angela's blessing. He carried out Harry's guard duty with high powered efficiency and made the arrangement of staying alternate nights with Bradley and the family at the cottage. It took Bradley a long time to adjust to life without Harry, but gradually he found himself becoming a lot closer to TC.

CHAPTER THIRTEEN

Sound Advice

Outwardly, Angela always appeared to be so cool, calm and collected, no matter how fraught a situation might be. Running a business which necessitated looking after five working cats that seemed to have never ending, relentless energy and all their individual and often bizarre needs, was extremely demanding, both physically and mentally. Inwardly, but she would never show or admit it, Angela felt like she was on the point of a nervous breakdown, several times in fact, but thank God she never quite got to that point. Bradley, of course, had noticed this too and begged her to slow down. She was somehow locked into a belief that totally consumed her. It was more powerful than anything else she had encountered in her whole life, even more so than her beloved but never forgotten theatre group. The success of Cozy Cats Cottage plc, the TTPCC and promoting the therapeutic power of the cat were seemingly all that mattered to her.

Bradley, however, wisely persuaded her to review the organisation of her current activities in depth, as a compromise of any kind would help to relieve her obvious anxiety. He particularly emphasised that she would be doing no one any favours, especially the cats, if she were to become physically or mentally ill and unable to cope. Angela sensibly heeded Bradley's words and came to the conclusion that a great deal of her stress lay in the amount of driving that was involved in getting her employees to their respective places of work on their designated days and times. The co-ordination of this could be improved. Buckingham and Lily were not a problem, since both of them went to Tillsworthy House twice a week at the same time, but with Dexter and Miss Pretty it was a very different scenario. Their places of work were over thirty minutes apart and one of the conditions was that Angela had to stay with them for the whole of their two hours. After discussion with both the Day Care and the Hospice, a compromise was reached involving alternate days. It was better than nothing, and in the long run worked out to be less tiring and stressful.

Her beloved Morris Minor Traveller was also feeling the strain, showing definite symptoms of tiredness, which were gradually proving to be costly. It was time to make a change, and as luck would have it, the guy who had originally sold the Traveller to her welcomed the opportunity of having his 'baby', as he endearingly called her, back in his life. Meanwhile Angela invested in a new people carrier which, being both comfortable and large, allowed plenty of room for the transportation of her precious and valuable cargo. Having a business-like mind and always thinking of ways to advertise and promote her objectives, she decided to invest in having some 'snazzy' sign-writing done on the sides and back of the vehicle; what else but – Cozy Cats Cottage plc (pussy loving care) the TTPCC (The Tillsworthy Trust for the Prevention of Cruelty to Cats) and last but not least – 'Cats are therapeutic creatures. Be kind to them!'

Comfortably boxed in

Since the beds she had previously acquired from the Dog Company had been met with such unexpected approval from the clan, she decided to approach the company again to verify the feasibility of up-grading the cat boxes, after all moggy transportation could not be that far removed from doggy transportation!

Although he greeted her like a long lost friend, Angela could not get away from the fact that the company's head sales honcho still reminded her of a conceited cocker spaniel.

"You're back again. Oh, how nice to see you," he said smiling sarcastically. "I had heard rumours that the wedding was *cat*astic, if you get what I mean, in fact I understand there was pussy galore!"

He barked stupidly at the ingenuity of that remark. Angela quickly retorted:

"By that rather inappropriate remark, I can only assume that you were referring to the fact that there were a number of cats present at that notorious occasion. They were in fact all my pussies."

He smiled sheepishly, but did not pursue the subject any further, thank goodness.

"So what doggy delight can I tempt you with this time?"

"Well, the beds you supplied were, to use your word, *cat*astic. However, I was wondering about your highest graded dog box. I am looking for something really out of the ordinary, comfort wise, to transport my precious cargoes to and from their places of work."

He gave Angela a look of total disbelief and said curtly,

"Cats don't work. Are you sure your animals aren't dogs?" With that remark he disappeared for a minute and returned with a large box that was virtually a cage, being over two foot in length. With those doleful eyes staring right at her he proudly said, but as always with that underlying hint of sarcasm,

"Now this perfect piece of product is designed for those who have 'the luxury of owning a dog' which is what we are all about. You have come to us with 'the bad luck of owning a cat,' which is not what we are about. However, so you don't go barking up the wrong tree, this beauty of a box, as you can see, is exquisitely fleecy lined to attain maximum comfort for the little darlings. Fortunately, you will easily be able to get two of your um......of those creatures, into this one, which might be rather nice for the newly-weds, in addition to minimising the cost to you. It's also deceptively light to handle and we do do a smaller version."

Angela deliberately took her time in voicing her opinion, having noticed he was panting rather excitedly, waiting for her to answer. She just couldn't resist it, so she said condescendingly, as if patting him on the back,

"You are a good boy. I'll take one of those and two smaller ones. They'll be just *purr*fect."

Stars in her eyes

Angela had completely forgotten about it, so when the phone call came from Vanessa Middleton, the head of administration at The

Princess Alicia Hospice, requesting Miss Pretty's presence at a specially arranged photo-shoot it came as a sudden but exciting surprise. With difficulty on the night before, Angela somehow managed to give Miss Pretty, much to her reluctance and annoyance, a full shampoo and set. Buckingham and Lily showed a mixture of emotions as they sat fascinated by the bathroom door trying to make out exactly what Angela was doing to their precious daughter. At one point during the procedure she looked like a wet snowball, but as her fur dried with some help from Angela and a towel, a star was born. She looked stunning.

Angela turned to an amazed but confused Bucks and Lily:

"Well, what do you think of your daughter now? She looks amazing doesn't she? Tomorrow is her big day. She is making a movie and she is going to knock 'em stone dead."

Vanessa Middleton knew she had made the right decision from the very first moment she had set eyes upon Miss Pretty. She had, in fact, taken a considerable gamble in committing herself to employing a very beautiful little kitten and welcoming her as a member of the hospice nursing team. However, Angela had assured Vanessa that she would take full responsibility if things didn't work out.

The patients, who had already had the pleasure of experiencing Miss Pretty's charms during her first few weeks of employment, were overwhelmingly complimentary. Miss Pretty was a huge hit and Vanessa had now informed Angela that she firmly believed that Miss Pretty should be the hospice's mascot and be associated with all the hospice's future activities, including the honour of having her name and picture on the hospice's headed note paper and of course the infamous notice board! The photo-shoot had to be carefully handled and professionally executed. The occasion itself was a memorable experience for all concerned.

Miss Pretty, for some reason suddenly realising she was the star of the show, decided to be difficult and put on a 'one off' performance of her own. Angela, realising the photographer and Vanessa were becoming a little agitated, felt a quiet but firm word was necessary.

"Miss Pretty, you are not a Superstar yet. You have to calm down and do as they ask and not do what you think you should do. Your Mum and Dad would not be very pleased to witness this. You want them to be proud of you, don't you?"

The tone in Angela's voice did the trick and Miss Pretty suddenly completely changed. To everyone's amazement, she re-choreographed her own show, as if to say

"I'll show you who's the star and you had better believe it. Watch this!"

With that she rolled on the floor, sat on her haunches, flashed her eyes, lay on her back provocatively, giving the photographer the opportunity of some extraordinary, different and amazing images.

Vanessa remarked,

"I've never seen anything like it. She's unbelievable. Madonna, or rather Lady Ga Ga, eat your heart out! I'd like one last shot with this cute pink bow round her neck."

Angela lovingly picked Miss Pretty up and whispered in her ear,

"There's no stopping you is there? You are one in a million my darling, but what you have done today will be seen by a million, I assure you. Vanessa wants one last shot with this little pink bow round your neck."

Angela attached the bow. Miss Pretty, flirting as usual, and seeming to wink with one eye, gave that ever so special look and then it was all over.

One week later Angela was facing a very excited Vanessa.

"You will not believe these pictures Angela."

She laid the pictures out on the desk in front of Angela, who sighed and said just three words:

"Oh my God."

Vanessa continued,

"I am going to use, if you agree, the one with the bow as the main publicity shot in relation to the hospice. We will have a big blow up of that picture in the foyer. It will also be used in connection with everything the hospice does and will be incorporated into all advertising, promotional or marketing activities. I am going to send the other images that tell a story themselves to cat magazines, newspapers and such like. I have also decided that over and above Miss Pretty's employment fee we should come to an additional financial arrangement regarding all this, perhaps even a royalty paid to Cozy Cats Cottage plc. How do you feel about that, Angela?"

Angela, a little stunned by the sudden turn of events replied,

"I am of course thrilled and overwhelmed by the whole thing. However, the ultimate effect on your patients is what really excites me. I think they will have something in their lives to latch onto and I also think it might be a good idea to have individually simple framed pictures of Miss Pretty that I will sign as if they were from her. The patients, especially other than the ones she sees at present could have these by their bedside or hung on the wall. As you know, all the income I receive in connection with my cats goes to charity, so I am more than pleased for any additional finance. I will gladly work something out with you."

Vanessa replied,

"You know what Angela, the picture signing is a brilliant idea. Anything that gives our patients additional quality of life, like taking this little kitten to heart, is the most rewarding thing in the world. Did you know this hospice has three others connected to it? I am going to contact them all with regard to Miss Pretty's amazing achievement. You never know, they might also want to have her as their mascot, especially when they see the pictures. If only she knew just how much of a star she really is!"

Angela then assured Vanessa,

"Well, Miss Pretty and I will continue to make our twice weekly two hour visits as normal and eventually, who knows, we might get through the whole hospice. I know how much she loves her work. She also has a very conscientious brother so there's a little in-house family competition going on too which is always a good thing and helps to keep them on their toes. I think I might even consider entering her into the Britain's Got Talent TV Show. You never know!" And then as an after thought,

"There should be a talent show for animals!"

With love
Miss Pretty ♡

Seth

The downstairs area in Tillsworthy House is spacious and the atmosphere is normally quiet and laid back as the residents shuffle about their daily pastimes seemingly without a care in the world. Members of staff appear and disappear as they go about their numerous tasks associated with looking after the welfare of those in need. Vicki and Priscilla soon became accustomed to dealing with all kinds of unusual and surprising problems, which is to be expected when so many people are living permanently together under one roof. To run a happy ship there has to be a considerable amount of give and take by all concerned. However, there is always that someone who has to rock the boat and his name was Seth Jones. He flatly refused to comply with any rules or regulations of the house and seemed to take particular delight in complaining about anything and everything. Worse still was the fact that this was accompanied by some really bad language, with no respect whatsoever for anyone who had the misfortune of hearing it. Vicki and Priscilla on two or three occasions had to warn him severely to curb his tongue, especially if ladies were present. But the complaints regarding his language and his attitude continued to keep coming, so much so that certain residents made matters quite clear by declaring and threatening that 'either he goes or we go'. This had now become a serious situation for Vicki and Priscilla.

Seth Jones was a man in his early sixties, quite suave, well dressed and good looking and physically fit for his age. It would seem he had no friends as such, no family who could tolerate him apart from Sabrina, an unmarried daughter in her early twenties, and a wife who had left him three years previously due to him already being married to a business. The business, which was something to do with printing, ran into trouble ending up with a serious case of litigation. However, as luck would have it he managed to salvage most of the companies' assets. He then sold everything he could and having had enough of that particular lifestyle decided to descend upon the unsuspecting world of Tillsworthy House. At first Priscilla and Vicki, like so many others, were completely mesmerised by Seth Jones' charm, as were the likes of Linda Hart. One thing that eventually was to emerge was his pet hatred of being organised or told what to do. His persistent use of unsavoury words was worrying, since it was certainly not conducive to the type of person he was. The final straw came when he was sitting in an armchair facing Linda Hart, who had Buckingham on her lap and who was by this time the only person who would put up with being anywhere near him, when he was in one of his foul shouting moods.

"Why should I bloody well have to put with it? I'm told when I can have bloody breakfast, when I can have bloody lunch and when I can have bloody dinner. It's bloody well not right when I'm paying all this 'effing' money to live here."

Linda looked at him totally unmoved and said,

"Well, you could bloody well leave and bloody well live somewhere else and 'effing' well leave us all alone."

There was a momentary silence as Seth, unexpectedly taken aback by Linda's outburst, collected his thoughts before the next tirade. He looked at her straight in the eye and deliberately raised his voice to a considerable number of decibels.

"And I tell you what Linda, I hate cats. Do you hear? I positively hate them, detest them. Look at that monstrosity on your lap. How can you bear to touch it?

It's inhuman and it bloody well should not be allowed to 'effing' well come in here." By now he had clearly 'lost it' and Buckingham, realising that both he and Linda were the subject of the tirade, launched himself into attack mode, making straight for Seth's lap but amazingly *without* claws outstretched. He knew that by catching him totally unawares it would achieve a positive result. Seth screamed and whacked him with his hand, at the same time slinging him off his lap and shouting at the top of his voice,

"Get off me you disgusting grey creature."

By this time a crowd of residents had gathered round to witness this outrageous fiasco. Vicki and Priscilla, totally shocked,were there in seconds. Vicki, appearing not to be in the least bit flustered, spoke calmly and deliberately,

"Seth this is really the last straw. You have gone way too far in upsetting everybody, especially with your disgusting language. We want you to leave, *now*.

Sabrina, your daughter is here to pick you up and we don't want you back here again, *ever*, unless your daughter swears that you have *totally* mended your ways and learnt how to behave as a normal human being again. Any animal would have better manners than you. Goodbye Seth."

Seth Jones had not done much for the good name of Tillsworthy House, but the residents were sympathetic and supportive, standing by Vicki and Priscilla in the hope that the incident and Seth would soon be forgotten. Sadly, it was Linda Hart who had been made the scapegoat and she had suffered more than necessary. Naturally, she couldn't believe that Seth had turned out to be such a Jekyll and Hyde character, since when they had first met he was the perfect gentleman. Once again she was totally indebted to Buckingham for realising the predicament and coming to the rescue just at the right moment. She told him that if he wasn't already spoken for she would gladly marry him!

Three weeks later, with no warning, no phone call and no pre-arrangement Seth Jones and Sabrina were to darken the doors of Tillsworthy House once again. He somehow looked noticeably different as Sabrina discreetly sat him in a corner in the lounge area, whilst she went to look for Vicki and Priscilla. Meanwhile,

Linda Hart was in her favourite spot, and having recovered from the initial shock of seeing Seth, coolly acknowledged him. He returned the acknowledgement but made no attempt to go over to her, even though he had noticed that Buckingham was nowhere to be seen.

Seth was actually feeling far too embarrassed, even scared, to go anywhere without first having support and approval from Vicki and Priscilla. As the residents were also reluctant to go anywhere near him, he knew he was already paying the price for his previous irrational behaviour.

Priscilla returned with Sabrina and, looking directly at Seth, said,

"So you've had the audacity to return. Sabrina has assured me that you have radically changed your ways."

Seth tried to answer, but could only attempt to mouth the words and gesticulate with his hands, since he had unfortunately or (fortunately) lost his voice.

"I've lost my voice for one week now, but I am feeling much better. Sabrina has made me have…."

Sabrina interjected,

"Counselling for anger management. I said I would leave if he didn't agree, so I arranged some one to one counselling for him, which, thank God, he has positively responded to. I am praying the old Seth has gone forever."

Priscilla responded

"Well, Vicki will be pleased to hear that, but I think he should personally apologise to Linda. She has suffered intolerably."

Seth nodded his head in agreement and the three of them made their way across the foyer to where Linda was sitting. Priscilla, with the semblance of a smile informed her that, ironically, Seth had lost his voice, but wished to make amends for his previous unforgiveable behaviour. Once again mouthing the words, gesticulating emphatically and putting his hands together he imparted how sorry he was and how he bitterly regretted saying the things he did. He hoped that she would find it in her heart to forgive him.

Vicki joined them and, turning to Seth, made the following comment,

"That, Seth, is what's called poetic justice. I hope we can now forget the past and everything that went with it."

Seth acknowledged Vicki's comment and then attempted to ask *the* question, inwardly hoping that he had gone for good.

"Where's Buckingham? Is he still here?"

Linda had made a mental note of everything that Seth had attempted to say, but when it came to Buckingham that was something else.

"Seth, I know you understand. I will accept your apology for all the awful things you said to me three weeks ago, but as far as Buckingham is concerned it is down to him. I have no idea if he can forgive you or not, but maybe it doesn't matter to you one way or the other, since for whatever reason, you will always hate cats."

Sabrina, who had said nothing till now decided this was the right moment to explain something that even she did not know until the counsellor had told her what she had discovered.

"Apparently, when my Dad was about ten years old he was given a budgerigar for a Christmas present. He called her Twinkie because she always seemed to wink at him when he spoke to her or when she wanted food. At the same time, his mother doted over a loving and timid little grey and white moggy called Romeo. There was some concern initially as to whether these two would get on together, but they became the best of friends, which was to last four years until the fateful day. Twinkie, as usual, was let out of her cage for her daily hours exercise and for no apparent reason at all Romeo turned on her and swiftly despatched her to 'birdie heaven'. She passed away probably due to shock more than anything else. My Dad was naturally hysterical and totally devastated by grief, which mentally became a permanent fixture for years to come. He subsequently developed a passionate hatred for the sight, sound or anything whatsoever to do with cats of any kind. This hatred was to fester within him every day of his life. However, the counsellor, by gently painting an alternative mental picture, managed to turn my dad's thinking around to accepting the fact that, like human beings, every cat is different and sometimes the reason for their actions can be deep rooted and impossible to understand. Romeo could have done with some cat counselling, but why he did that on that day, no one will ever know."

There was silence. Everyone seemed to be mesmerised by Sabrina's story. As Seth gently squeezed her hand, Buckingham appeared, slowly walking towards them across the foyer floor. Although he knew he was the centre of attention, he took his time, making sure that everybody had seen him. He stopped and slowly sat himself down at Linda's feet and then taking his time, looked at everybody in turn. He focussed his attention on Seth, and seemed to be studying him rather than just looking at him. Seth was becoming noticeably uncomfortable as he endeavoured to mouth some words of apology.

"Buckingham…oh, so you are still here. Can you ever forgive me for those horrible things I said…..and did? I wish I could take it all back."

Obviously Seth could not tell what was going through Buckingham's mind, but by the way he was staring at him he decided to gingerly put his hand on Buckingham's head and gently stroke him. Although Buckingham accepted this gesture, even though with certain mistrust, a lot was going through his mind.

"I wonder if he really means it and he has changed from being a silly old fart. It would be one up to me and the world of cats if he has. If he does anything like it again he won't live long enough to regret it, as far as I'm concerned."

With Seth now appearing to having rejoined the human race as a respectable human being, Sabrina, Vicki and Priscilla decided to make their exit, leaving Seth and Linda to make whatever final amends between them. Buckingham, on the other hand, made for his usual resting place, that being the comfort of Linda's lap, but this time with one eye firmly focused on Seth!

CHAPTER FOURTEEN

Watch this space

Oliver and Margaret appeared to be really happy, made for each other in fact, with Margaret seemingly enjoying every minute of taking care of Oliver's disabilities. They had settled into a rather laid back, simple life, with Buckingham and Lily supplying additional comfort and interest, even though their time was shared between Linda and Sinead. It all seemed to work pretty well, with Angela, Priscilla and Vicki all being more than pleased with the arrangement.

That afternoon it was Sinead's turn to have the pleasure of Lily's company. For some reason Sinead was feeling lonely and so she asked Margaret if she and Oliver would like to have afternoon tea with her in the lounge, and maybe ask Linda if she would like to join them. It was a happy little gathering, but Buckingham and Lily appeared to be rather confused, and obviously not wanting to intentionally upset anyone decided to, as all cats do, jump continuously the whole time between the laps of their respective owners, or clients to be more exact. Buckingham would stay on Oliver's lap for ten minutes and then go and invade Linda's lap for ten minutes and likewise Lily would spend so much time with Margaret and then go to Sinead. It was really best for the sake of peace for all concerned to completely ignore what they were up to.

Margaret turned to Linda and asked,

"Linda, how's that boy of yours doing? What's his name, Jamie, yes that's right. I heard he was nicely settled in with Denzil Whitehead at The Wooden Horse in Troy."

"Well, he is, thank goodness, but he wouldn't be here at all had it not been for the quick thinking of Harry and TC (God bless you Harry). I believe Jamie has now managed to thank them personally, which he was desperate to do. Of course we musn't forget young Buckingham here. His contribution of time with me is totally invaluable. He has given me a new life. He is everything to me, as he must also be to Oliver."

Margaret responded,

"That was a very good move on Angela's part, but have no fear Linda, Oliver hasn't suffered with less of Buckingham's time, because I have managed to fill in for him, except of course I can't lie on Oliver's lap, but he does stroke me at times, making me purr and I'm certainly not complaining at that!"

Sinead, who appeared to have been deep in thought for some time, suddenly sprang to life and, addressing Margaret, excitedly said,

"Margaret you were so damn good at it. You won prizes for it. You have simply got to do it again and you have it all right here. I'm talking about caricatures. You have got to do caricatures of all Angela's cats. They're so charismatic. It would be brilliant and it would be a wonderful legacy, if nothing else. Will you at least think about it?"

Margaret, a little taken aback, responded,

"Sinead, I haven't done any sketch work or animation for years and years. I've probably lost the touch and, besides, you need inspiration and the time."

Sinead was very persistent.

"Well, I'm telling you that you never lose the touch, like you never forget how to.......well you know, you know what I mean, and as for inspiration, you have it here right in front of you. Just look at Buckingham over there, or Lily. It's crying out for you to do it, and as for time, well you'll make the time I'm sure of that."

At that point Linda decided to intervene.

"I know it's none of my business, but Sinead is right. I think you owe it to yourself to at least give it a go. You've won awards for it, for God's sake. You never know Margaret, you might surprise yourself, and the opportunity has never been so right."

Margaret, feeling a little embarrassed by now said,

"You have certainly got my adrenalin going and the challenge is really tempting. I don't know if I can do it, but I will give it a try. Watch this space, as they say."

Margaret did give the idea some serious thought and although she wouldn't admit it, she inwardly became quite excited by the whole thing. Fond memories came flooding back. However, there was a problem in that she only saw Buckingham and Lily twice a week and the rest of the family hardly at all. She needed to study them in detail for some considerable time and in thinking about this it suddenly occurred to her that Denzil would have taken numerous and various photographic shots of all the cats at the wedding. In fact she remembered he had a fantastic display. She decided to phone him and ask him if he could let her have a complete photographic showcase of all the little darlings, having explained to him the method behind the madness. Denzil was only too happy to oblige and thought the whole idea was a masterful piece of ingenuity. He couldn't wait to see the result.

Concern

Angela had been to Tillsworthy House so many times now with Buckingham and Lily that she was quite satisfied in leaving them to find Oliver and Margaret or Linda and Sinead on their own.

On this particular occasion, it being Linda's turn to have the pleasure of his company, Buckingham had found her, as usual, sitting in her favourite spot in her favourite corner of the lounge. She was more than pleased to see him and he settled himself down quite comfortably on her lap. Meanwhile Lily, not finding Sinead in the lounge for some unknown reason, looked up at Buckingham and Linda for a suggestion.

"As you can see, Sinead's not down here, which is unusual for her. I hope she's all right."

Linda looked at Lily and said with concern,

"I haven't seen Sinead all morning. I think you should go up to her room. If her door is shut come back down here and I'll go and see what's happened to her."

Buckingham confirmed that decision

"Go up to her room Lily. She might still be in bed or perhaps she's with Margaret."

Lily got to Sinead's apartment and luckily the door was slightly ajar. She cautiously went in and found that Sinead was, in fact, still in bed. She jumped up onto the bed, started to purr and lick Sinead's face but there was little or no reaction, which Lily knew was not normal at all. She knew she had to find Margaret. She was now a cat on a mission.

Margaret's door was shut, so she sat down and meowed and meowed and meowed for what seemed to be hours and hours. Eventually something must have registered because Margaret finally opened the door.

"Lily, what's the matter? You're supposed to be with Sinead."

Lily demonstrated her obvious anxiety by continuing to meow loudly and running frantically backwards and forwards towards the door.

"You must come and see Sinead. There's something wrong with her."

"It must be Sinead. I had better go and see what's happened, hopefully nothing terrible."

Margaret found Sinead in bed and looking very unwell. She knew she needed a doctor and so she informed Vicki and Priscilla, who were naturally concerned. Lily, bless her, decided to stay with Sinead and settled herself down quite comfortably on her bed. The doctor came, but due to having a problem in trying to specifically diagnose Sinead's condition, he wanted her to have some tests done as soon as possible at the local hospital. This was arranged and carried out accordingly, after which everyone waited in anticipation for the results. Over the next two or three weeks Sinead seemed to improve, even with no definite answer to the problem.

The results of Sinead's test came through, which included x-rays, and she was given a course of antibiotics, much to the relief of all concerned. However, there was a slight grey area in that she was advised to have a check up at the hospital in two months' time.

Socially speaking

It was fairly obvious, and would not be inappropriate to say, that Bradley and Angela were an item, although due to both their work commitments, socially they saw very little of each other. When the odd occasion did arise for them to meet it was doubly pleasurable and enjoyable. Bradley was continually concerned about Angela's health and so the decision to have dinner one night at a rather nice Olde Worlde restaurant in a nearby village was a kind of treat. Following this, they decided to go for a drink at their local, The Wooden Horse of course, where with Denzil's input and a touch of Jamie thrown in they were furnished with even more than they had bargained for in the way of the latest 'off the wall' local gossip. A little later they were honoured with the company of none other than Mike Cass himself and, of course, the conversation immediately turned to furry creatures.

Initially it was TC who dominated the subject of conversation, with due praise being showered upon him by all concerned. He was, after all, discovered by Denzil, given a home by Angela, replaced the loveable and incomparable Harry doing guard duty for Bradley and, last but not least, saving Jamie's life. He had also become very attached to Buckingham, with the feeling being mutual.

Mike Cass turned to Angela and said,

"Luckily, thanks to you, I have been honoured with knowing all your pussies, dare I say and without being rude, intimately. Buckingham in particular is a very beautiful cat. He is, as you know, a pedigree and he is a very fine example of a blue British shorthair. I am proud to have been selected as one of the judges and the vet for the Guildford branch of the British Shorthair Club. They are having a showing very soon and I really think you should enter Buckingham, as the prestige and publicity this would achieve, if nothing else, would be of incomparable help to the recognition and purpose behind Cozy Cats Cottage plc and the TTPCC. It would be a great showcase."

Denzil, as usual, was quick on the up-take.

"What a great idea. Tillsie you've really got to seriously consider it. You know how Buckingham loves playing celebrity. For sure he'd be up for it. A picture session with him would be rather fun"

Bradley interjected.

"Seems good to me. How many entrants would there be and what are the prizes for winning?"

Mike Cass was quick to respond.

"The popularity of the Guildford Club has grown enormously over the last two years, so I think there could be as many as twenty five to thirty or even forty entrants this time and there are numerous categories, depending on age and sex, neutered or not and cats that have never been shown before. I believe there is a 'cat of the show' award, but there is no prize money as such, because the prestige value is the prize, which is indicated by some beautiful rosettes. It's all extremely competitive, so the honour of winning or coming in the first three in any category is enormous and the subsequent publicity is worth its weight in gold and can eventually be amazingly lucrative."

Angela had taken in every word Mike Cass had said, but she looked a little concerned.

"Mike, I obviously know nothing about cat shows or what would be necessary in the preparation or requirements of entering a cat, but what about Buckingham himself? Shouldn't we ask him and see if he approves?"

There was no one who didn't smile at that remark and then Jamie said,

"I have got to know Buckingham pretty well through my mother and he just loves attention. You could even say that he demands and cultivates it. He gets a big kick out of it and something like this would *cat*apult him way above anyone else. He might have a little problem with 'her indoors' though!"

Denzil commented,

"It's one up for Management. Lily should be bloody proud, not jealous, after all she is married to him. At the moment, rumour has it that it is Miss Pretty who has become quite the little movie star and is performing for everyone at the Princess Alicia Hospice."

Mike Cass continued,

"I can understand that. She's irresistibly adorable, but Angela, as far as Buckingham is concerned, I will help you with the preparation, the forms that have to be filled in and everything else. A couple of months ago, at the last show, an extraordinary white British Shorthair was shown for the first time and stole the show with being first in her category. Buckingham could do it. He has as much chance as anyone else and you have nothing to lose, and a lot to possibly gain."

Denzil, looking at Bradley and Angela in turn, could not resist commenting again,

"Tillsie, I can hear Harry calling and he's saying 'go for it'!"

Bradley had the last word:

"Angela, someone else up there is listening and nodding their head too."

For Mike Cass, the whole thing was a bit of fun, but it was also a huge challenge and he wanted Buckingham to win, not only for Angela's sake, but for himself and his practice too. He always regarded the cats he looked after and treated on behalf of their owners, as being his own family and he loved them all dearly. Perhaps it explained why he did not indulge in having a cat himself.

With so much pressure coming from all directions, Angela found herself being caught up in the excitement of the prospect of it all. Mike Cass was as good as his word, familiarising her with all that was required and advising her as to how Buckingham should be handled, although he had surmised that Buckingham was happily blessed with just the right temperament and would no doubt relish the unavoidable adulation.

Foreplay

Armed with four different types of brushes, Angela began Buckingham's nightly beauty treatment. A plan of action was necessary, so she decided the right time was after dinner when everyone had been fed, including herself. The best place to carry out the 'dirty deed' was on the rug in front of the fireplace, which was one of Buckingham's favourite 'after dinner' relaxing spots. Unfortunately, she had completely failed to anticipate the reaction to the whole thing by the other members of the household. On the first night, Buckingham was caught completely off guard, but once Angela had dragged a brush gently down his back he was anybody's! He purred louder than ever before, arching his back in sheer delight. For him the earth had moved a million times! Angela found she was having great pleasure in doing it, whilst at the same time she indulged herself in quietly telling him how stunning he was going to be and how proud he was going to make her feel. Although she was totally engrossed in what she was doing, she had the distinct feeling that four pairs of eyes were watching her every move. She casually looked up and saw Miss Pretty, Dexter, and Lily all sitting on their haunches in a semi-circle with an 'I'd like some of that' look written all over their faces. The exception, however, was TC who seemed to be saying, "How stupid is this!"

Angela could almost hear what they were thinking, but Lily soon made it quite clear that she wanted 'words' with her husband.

"You're a 'jammy' so and so, Bucks. How did you manage to swing that? Talk about the cat that got the cream! Angela keeps muttering something or other all the time. There must be some extraordinary reason why she's going to all this trouble. She never has before, so it can't be all for nothing."

Buckingham replied in his usual 'how great I am' sort of way,

"Well, my darling, she has always known I have something special and now she obviously thinks the time is right for the world to know. I have always had to live with the burden of it, and even you recognised it and couldn't resist. Now she might be putting all my hidden assets to good use. Whatever she's doing, I'm just going to make the most of it whilst it lasts."

Lily shook her head in disbelief and said, with obvious affection,

"Why I love you I'll never know. TC has got you well sussed. Then with deliberate emphasis *What are you trying to prove all the time and who are you trying to fool?"*

Angela could not resist excitedly calling Denzil, asking him if he could spare an hour from the pub to come to the cottage and bring the camera to witness and capture the hysterics of the second night at Buckingham's Beauty Parlour. He agreed without any hesitation whatsoever. In his book it was… for Angela… anything and for Buckingham… how could he say no!

There they were again, all patiently sitting in that semi circle, but Angela had come to a major decision. The only way to deal with this little scenario was to give each one of the little darlings a taste of what Buckingham was getting. Immediately after Buckingham had had his hour or so, Angela firmly grabbed hold of Lily (ladies first, of course) and started with the brushes. The sudden shock and surprise of this was almost too much for her. She meowed and purred all at the same time until she finally came to the conclusion that she was in fact half way to paradise and more! When it came to Miss Pretty, she was very accommodating. She was a bit of an old pro since she had, although memorably reluctantly, allowed Angela to beautify her once before. Dexter, on the other hand, demanded that Angela experiment with the texture of each of the four brushes before deciding which one pleasured him the most. And as for TC, he must have thought the whole thing was 'totally over the top' and walked away in disgust at the crucial moment.

Buckingham settled himself down contentedly on the fur rug, but was again interrupted by TC.

"Bucks, this is all very nice but a bit sissy don't you think? And not very good for guard duty either, or are you opting out of that now that you're being groomed for Gods knows what!"

Buckingham replied in a matter of fact tone of voice,

"TC, I don't know what Angela is actually up to. It's all very strange, but I have to admit I love what she does to me and so far it has been two nights in a row. Meanwhile, you will just have to tolerate the company of a 'poofter'. I still love you sweetie," he mimicked.

Denzil was as good as his word and sat there silently clicking away. He was just as thrilled and as shocked as anyone else taking part in this hilarious pantomime.

He thanked Angela for the unexpected pleasure and would let her see the results accordingly. However he also made a mental note to show Margaret, for obvious reasons, the result of this session before anyone else.

CHAPTER FIFTEEN

It's showtime!

Angela found herself unable to contain the excitement she was feeling about the forthcoming cat show. She had to tell somebody, so of course she couldn't resist mentioning it to Vicki and Priscilla, who were so enthralled by the whole thing that they insisted on hearing all the details. Angela was only too happy to oblige, and since it was being held on a Saturday at the Civic Hall in Guildford, she suggested that they join her to witness Buckingham's big moment. Understandably, they could not both leave Tillsworthy House to look after itself, so Vicki thought it was only right that Priscilla should be there, since she was Angela's sister. Priscilla agreed to meet Angela at the venue on the day.

It was an early morning rise for everyone at Cozy Cats Cottage on that Saturday, although Buckingham was the only one who really needed to be disturbed. Angela actually had one of the recently acquired fur lined doggy boxes prepared for him the night before. She gave him a last quick brush and groom, telling him that 'Britain's Got Talent' was nothing compared to what he'd got!

Poor Buckingham naturally couldn't understand why this was happening to him, but he knew he was not going to Tillsworthy House, because Lily wasn't with him and she was complaining rather loudly. The others too, had the distinct look of anxiousness on their faces.

Angela hated the struggle and effort of putting any of the cats in a cat box, since they never liked it and never seemed to get used to it, even though it was a routine twice weekly occurrence. Out of habit more than anything else Angela couldn't help but talk to herself in the hope of verbally calming them down and herself included.

Determination was necessary, so she gritted her teeth, managed to get Buckingham in the box when he least expected it, put the box on the front seat of the car and prayed that they would be coming back with the sounds of congratulations ringing in their ears! Hopefully it would all be worth it. With her heart in some other place other than where it should be and a tear in her eye she said her goodbyes and headed towards Guildford. Buckingham was exceptionally quiet, whilst Angela endeavoured to talk to him encouragingly most of the journey. Perhaps the fur lined box was a good idea after all.

On entering through four huge glass doors the show's reception area was impressively extensive. The British Shorthair Club had posters and banners set up all over the place, with the central point of attention being focused on the reception desk itself. Although the show actually opened at ten in the morning, the various categories and judging were programmed for the afternoon. Angela had to have Buckingham there by eight o'clock in the morning to be checked in and to have the compulsory physical check-up and various other required formalities that had to be dealt with. Having completed the initial signing in, Mike Cass managed to locate Angela and escort her into the main hall, which was divided into six aisles, with each aisle accommodating about ten trestle tables all joined together.

The aisles were marked accordingly and Mike eventually found Buckingham's spot for the day, denoted by 'Aisle 3, Number 13'. Angela sighed inwardly 'Oh God let's pray it's lucky thirteen.' She complimented herself on getting the doggy-type box, which gave Buckingham so much more room. In fact it was a case of 'one upmanship' already! However, every time she looked at it she heard that aggravating bark of the sales manager's voice ringing in her ears. "What sacrilege, putting one of those things in a dog's box, for God's sake. How demeaning is that?"

Buckingham had a look on his face that Angela had never seen before. Under the circumstances, it was perhaps understandable, as he still didn't know what on earth he was doing there or why Angela had brought him in the first place. Mike assured Angela that he would be perfectly all right, with lots of attention being given to him throughout the day. He would be having his health checks sometime during the morning and the judging would begin around 2.30 pm in the afternoon. He then pointed to the stage at the far end of the room, explaining that the organisers and the powers that be would be sitting up there keeping a watchful eye on the day's proceedings.

Angela, as arranged, met Priscilla at the front entrance and they went for a coffee.

They were surprised to see the amount of people attracted by an event such as this. The foyer was packed, and as they were about to enter the main hall, something rather unusual caught their attention. To the left of the entrance was something that looked almost exactly like any household 'loo'. It was beige in colour and the bowl was filled with granules that apparently never needed changing. There was a large sign above the whole thing that read 'The World's Only Self-Flushing, Self-Washing Cat Toilet'. On examining it further it proclaimed to be the only automatic cat box that flushes waste away and, like a cat, washes itself clean! It looked fantastic and Angela had visions of all the cats lining up to use it first thing in the morning! The only possibly prohibitive aspect of it was the price, but it was certainly worth bearing in mind, especially when cleaning out dirt boxes and constantly sweeping up cat litter would be a thing of the past!

By the time Angela and Priscilla had got back into the main hall, the aisles were filled with rows and rows of cat boxes, all accommodating some proud pet owner's precious creature. As they slowly made their way down the aisles, stopping very frequently to admire and talk to the various inhabitants, they both agreed that Buckingham, bless him, had a lot to compete against, and being a judge at this event was not going to be an enviable position in the least. They frequently checked on Buckingham and found that he had remained very calm, having obviously come to terms with whatever fate lay in store for him. He seemed pleased that Angela had not deserted him, and as he lay there looking very regal indeed, Priscilla remarked on how calm and collected, handsome and well groomed he appeared to be.

A section of the hall was justifiably allocated to the 'moggy' contingent and there were some wonderful specimens on view. TC came to Angela's mind more than once. But of course it was the British shorthair that stole the show and the examples that were on display were justification as to just how beautiful and handsome this breed actually was. A striking collage of red rosettes, signifying previous awards were attached to boxes everywhere. All were clearly marked with the appropriate applicable award, some even having several to their credit.

The star attraction was unquestionably the almost perfect example of a white female British shorthair, with the most incredible orange coloured eyes. Her name, marked accordingly, was Bathsheba. Priscilla and Angela were mesmerised by her beauty, and her name, which could never have been more perfectly chosen, said it all. There was something very unusual and distinctive about her. She looked spectacularly elegant in a restrained kind of way, and the rosette proudly displaying the words 'Cat of the Show' was so obviously well deserved.

Angela and Priscilla thanked their lucky stars that Buckingham was not classified in the same category.

Ye shall now be judged

It would certainly appear that with all the meticulous care that was applied to the task of judging cats against one another and taking into account their various individual assets it was seemingly a much harder job than judging human beings in a similar situation. It was a long drawn out process, with each cat being assessed by three people, namely two judges, one male and one female, and a highly acclaimed professional vet. Each cat was placed on a trolley and literally 'man handled' by each person in turn. Numerous notes were taken during this process, but the amazing thing was that the cats themselves really seemed to enjoy it, or put on a brave face, as there was no way of attempting anything else. Mike Cass, of course, having the honour of being the 'vet of the day' was on a pedestal of some significance. By the look on Buckingham's face when it came to his turn, he could have well been thinking, "Another fine mess you've got me into, Angela!" Even so he didn't seem to be too bothered, even with having to tolerate Angela's persistent whispering of sweet nothings in his ears every few minutes.

The time had arrived. Had all the morning's fuss and bother been worth waiting for? The afternoon's judging, based on the morning's assessment, was now complete and the atmosphere in the room was electric, consumed with an air of intense anticipation. The look of impatient frustration was evident everywhere as the results were finally announced. Suitable applause and 'well dones' accompanied the announcements of the winning places of the first three categories and then........

"On behalf of the British Shorthair Club of Guildford in the neutered cat's category of first time entrants, a well deserved third place goes to Number Thirteen, Buckingham Tillsworthy." Angela and Priscilla, totally speechless, looked at each other in disbelief and then at Bucks. Having composed herself, Angela then walked onto the stage and accepted the presentation of the appropriate rosette, which was beautifully inscribed with Buckingham's name, placing and category. The audience reacted accordingly.

There was no question as to who was the star of the show. Bathsheba had done it again for the second time and deservedly so. No one could touch her. She was apparently, according to Mike Cass, as near perfection as you could get in that breed. Her owner, Dawn Arlen, proudly accepted the very prestigious 'Cat of the Show' award to well deserved applause. Angela and Priscilla could not believe that Bathsheba's perfect beauty was also enhanced with such a great temperament, which was most unusual. She was obviously a cat in a million and everyone knew it. But did Bathsheba?

So that everyone could view the winners and meet the owners in their own time, a series of tables were set up in front of the stage, with adequate space behind them to accommodate the relative owner with the relative cat. It was such an uplifting sight once all the boxes were in their respective places and adorned with the beautiful rosettes, all depicting the name, placing and category of the deserving winner.

It was during this process that a very strange and unpredictable event occurred. It took everyone by surprise, being so sudden and so totally unexpected. While looking for their location, Angela and

Priscilla, with Angela holding Buckingham in his box, bumped into Dawn Arlen holding Bathsheba in her box. The two cats made immediate eye contact and literally went totally berserk, making the most awful and unusual noises. Was it agony or ecstasy? Whatever it was, it was certainly frightening, and continued for some time, even after both cats were finally located in their right places and some distance from each other. People nearby got wind of the commotion, and soon an inquisitive crowd began to gather, hoping to witness the outcome of this unusual occurrence. The organisers were on the scene very quickly and decided that Mike Cass should be found immediately, as the cats might be in distress, and in any case he might be able to throw some light on the matter. Angela and Priscilla found themselves totally helpless in trying to communicate with Buckingham, who seemed to be in some kind of trance. Dawn was also having a similar problem with Bathsheba. Mike Cass was quickly on the scene and after examining both cats, the *cat*erwauling noise had thankfully subsided, but taking the best part of ten minutes to do so. He could find nothing immediately wrong or obvious with either cat, but obviously something had sparked the confrontation. Perhaps it was just an immediate dislike, or perhaps just past love gone wrong! The judges, who had no allegiance one way or the other, were quick to point out that if this incident had happened prior or during the show, both participants would have had to be disqualified! That would have been a sad and embarrassing situation, particularly as the cat club, who had a vested interest in Bathsheba, did not want to lose out on what had become one of their prize adverts!

Whilst driving back home Angela felt a distinct uneasiness in the air, with Buckingham seeming to be in a sullen frame of mind. He was certainly not his usual bouncy self and Angela was worried, especially as he had managed to do so darned well and win an award. She decided to talk to him, hoping somehow to get the matter out of her own head more than anything else.

"Bucks, I don't know why you're in such a mood. You're a winner, for God's sake, even though you came third. If you're jealous of Bathsheba wining 'The Cat of the Show' award then you shouldn't be, because that cat really deserved to win it. She was absolutely gorgeous and anyone else would have had a tough job to compete with her. What you achieved was simply *catastic*. You have held the banner high for Cozy Cats Cottage plc. Your family will be proud of you, so don't greet them as if the end of the world is nigh!"

As soon as they heard Angela's key in the door they were all impatiently walking around her and purring and meowing all at the same time. But it wasn't their safe return that they were concerned about. It was of course food, glorious food. Angela let Bucks out of his box and then started muttering to herself with frustrated annoyance.

"Alright, alright, I'll get your bloody food. Bloody hell!"

As she impatiently prepared it, she continued the muttering, directing it towards all of them with an element of sarcasm thrown in.

"What have you lot been doing all day but sleeping? Do you know what we've been doing? Showing off, that's what. Something that Bucks is very good at, but this time he has actually won an award for doing it, but for some ridiculous reason he has decided to throw a 'wobbly'! I've never seen him looking so down. Lily, you'll have to sort him out. I give up!"

One more day of this 'Buckingham madness' or 'cat behaving badly' was one day too much, so Angela felt she had no option but to voice her concern to Mike Cass. Coincidentally, Dawn Arlen had also been in touch, imparting her frustration with the way Bathsheba had been reacting since the incident at the show. Mike Cass suggested that a DNA test might throw some more light on the matter. He emphasised that it was worth exploring every possible avenue, since he was as fascinated as anyone to find the answer to such unusual behaviour, especially as he had also never witnessed anything like it before.

A week later Mike Cass had the DNA test results and he suggested that Dawn and Angela met at his office. He looked at them in turn, and then trying hard to withhold a smile, said very seriously,

"You won't believe this. The DNA test results show that Buckingham and Bathsheba are related. They are, in fact, twin brother and sister, which clearly explains why they made all that noise and fuss at the show. It must have been an incredible moment for them to have found each other after what was probably some considerable time. I firmly believe that the initial shock and whatever happened to them in the past also had a great deal to do with their understandable initial reaction and subsequent behaviour. In view of the circumstances we should most certainly forgive them. They've obviously been totally devastated since."

Dawn and Angela looked at each other, amazed at what they were hearing. After it had all sunk in, Dawn felt she should explain how Bathsheba had actually come into her life.

Bathsheba

It was an unusual story, centred on Emma, her rather frail eighty year old mother, who lived on her own and who adored cats, or rather one cat in particular. His name was Marmaduke, due to the unusually magnificent colour of his coat. He was in fact a 'drop dead gorgeous moggy' who had survived eighteen unscathed years of a beautiful life and then had passed away quite naturally. Emma had vowed she would never replace him, that was until a certain advert had caught her eye in the local paper, which read, "For just £200, a beautiful white pedigree from Lancashire *desperately* looking for a home." She couldn't resist following this up, and a young man with a strong Liverpudlian accent brought the cat round, but Emma was shocked to find that the cat was in a dreadful state, noticeably very thin and obviously hungry. Emma rightfully demanded to know what had happened to her, but she never received an explanation that made any sense, and apart from that, there was no positive proof of ownership either. In spite of everything, and against her better judgement, Emma just couldn't resist the temptation of acquiring this rather beautiful but sad looking animal. For the next two months, with painstaking love and care she nurtured the cat back to good health. The transformation was nothing short of a miracle. She looked stunning! Fascinated, and on further investigation, she discovered that she was in fact a female white British shorthair. She needed to have a name, but strangely, finding the right one was not that easy.

Amazingly, it was a TV series entitled 'The Fall of the Roman Empire' that finally provided Emma with the inspiration she was looking for. She was enthralled by the spectacle, the pomp and glory of the whole saga, and in particular the romantic sound of such names as Anastasia and Bathsheba. She thought to herself, "Why not? Why not Bathsheba? She looks like a Bathsheba, proud, regal and incredibly beautiful."

To say there was a definite bond and understanding between them would be an understatement. They so obviously loved each other, and Dawn swore that she had witnessed a magical moment between them when she really believed Bathsheba was actually talking to Emma. How she wished she was able to understand.

"You are my world and you came to my rescue when my life was fading away. That nasty man captured my brother and me from our home in Liverpool. Yes, I have a twin brother and we were named Henry and Henrietta, which we hated. He drove us down to London, putting us in the back of his van without food or water. My brother managed to escape, but I had given up. You are my guardian angel."

There was momentary silence whilst Dawn paused in thought. Meanwhile, Angela and Mike sat motionless, totally spellbound by what she had just said. Dawn continued, saying that after Emma passed away Bathsheba was sadly left with a broken heart and no home. She desperately wanted to have her, but where she lived animals of any kind were not allowed. Out of desperation more than anything else she decided to contact the local branch of the British Shorthair Club and they did in fact have a limited number of places at their boarding kennel, which they rented out on a short term basis. This, if it were possible, would give Dawn a break to think of a more suitable and hopefully permanent alternative.

What she was offered by the Club came as a complete surprise. They pointed out that in all the years of their existence they had never come across an example of a white female British Shorthair as perfect in every detail as Bathsheba. They would love her to represent the club at future shows if Dawn was agreeable. In return they would offer free boarding, provided Dawn was prepared to spend the equivalent minimum number of hours amounting to one day a week at the club, devoting most of that time entirely to Bathsheba. The Club, rightly so, considered it imperative for both their sakes to sustain the relationship between them. In addition to this they stipulated that Dawn carried out all that was necessary in their opinion to maintain Bathsheba in peak 'show' condition. Dawn, a little sceptical at first, knew that in view of the circumstances she had little or no choice but to agree to the request.

Bathsheba naturally had a big problem in adapting to an enforced new way of life. Dawn knew she missed Emma terribly so she did her utmost to spend as much time as possible with her. Commendably, they both made a valiant effort, and eventually with some additional input by the club a proud Dawn and a very beautiful Bathsheba were ready for their first show. For everyone on that day it was an unprecedented experience. No one, but *no one* could touch Bathsheba. She not only stole the show, claiming the most prestigious award of all, The Cat of the Show' award but she also stole everyone's hearts as well. When Dawn finally and proudly presented her to the audience in general there was not a dry eye in the house.

From above, Emma had seen it all, and with love in her eyes she whispered, "That's my girl. Bathsheba you are more than one in a million!"

Dawn had nothing left to say and once more there was silence, filled with anticipation. It was Angela who spoke, with obvious deep concern,

"Well Bathsheba has done it again – her second show. But this time there is a difference, a huge difference. Miraculously she has met Buckingham, her long lost twin brother." She paused, looking at Mike Cass for help.

"What on earth do we do now? Where do we go from here?"

Mike Cass looked at both girls in turn and slowly but deliberately said,

"Bathsheba and Buckingham will never be the same again unless they are together. They will pine forever. Bathsheba needs a proper home with domestic love in it, and Buckingham could possibly become a sullen recluse, which would result in a threat to Cozy Cats Cottage and everything it stands for. The answer lies with some sort of agreement between the two of you. Realistically, Angela is the only one able to give Bathsheba a home and a life with her brother, but then there are the other cats to consider. Rightfully she belongs to Dawn and therefore the final decision must lie with you Dawn."

Dawn, a little taken aback, looked at Mike Cass and then turned to Angela.

"Angela there's no question about it. Mike is absolutely right in that Bathsheba and Buckingham, now that they have found each other, must be together. The bond is too great, especially as they are twins. I have a strong feeling, knowing what you have already achieved, that you will be able to cope, and the other members of the family will eventually, given time, adjust to the new addition."

Before Dawn could say anything more, Angela intervened,

"Well, TC was a recent addition and they have all managed to adjust to him. Truthfully, I would really love to, in fact I would be honoured to have Bathsheba, and for Buckingham there couldn't possibly be anything greater. Lily might be a problem, but they'll have to deal with that between themselves." She turned to Dawn,

"But Dawn, Bathsheba's your cat. She's also an exceptional show cat, which you have painstakingly groomed, cared for and loved."

Mike Cass, who understood the dilemma perfectly, offered a possible compromise.

"Angela, you have Bathsheba. She lives with you and the cottage is her home, but she continues to do the cat shows and continues to represent the Cat Club. Dawn, you must continue to groom Bathsheba, preparing her for all future shows or anything similar that might arise. This will ensure that the bond between you and Bathsheba is maintained, which to my mind is really essential. But, and this is really important, you need to take Bathsheba down to the Cat Club for her grooming sessions. It would not be fair to do this at the cottage with all the other cats around, and besides it would also allow you to have time together on a one to one basis."

Angela then said,

"Well I am perfectly agreeable to such an arrangement. I think it would work well if the rest of the family are amenable. That should be fun! It seems that it could be the ideal compromise."

Dawn then commented,

"Mike you're a genius, but then we always knew that and it's nice to know we're getting good value for our money into the bargain as well!"

Dog tired!

Angela and Dawn knew it would be a moment in a million when Buckingham and Bathsheba not only saw each other again, but also when they realised that they were about to live together. Dawn and Angela agreed it would be fun to orchestrate the occasion and to capture it on camera as a memento for all time. A little soiree with food and drink was arranged, inviting Priscilla, Vicki, Bradley, Mike Cass and of course the irreplaceable photo 'wizkid' Denzil Whitehead. The plan of action was for Dawn to bring Bathsheba over early one evening and to place her box with the door open on the centre of the lounge carpet. The real fun would be waiting to see what followed, especially witnessing how Buckingham and Bathsheba were going to deal with this piece of human ingenuity. Of course, the other cat co-inhabitants would no doubt have a word to say on the matter as well, especially Lily!

Angela was usually one step ahead of the game and so prior to this event she had thought a great deal about Bathsheba's arrival and of course the all important sleeping and eating arrangements. Angela had considered herself lucky that there had never been any arguments or jealousies between any of the cats at any time, at least not over anything major. Cozy Cats Cottage, without a doubt, could easily be classified as the ultimate home of harmony, even though Angela would be the first to admit that a substantial amount of praying had been necessary, but then Bradley was always a good shoulder to lean on as far as that was concerned! Angela, however, did lay down the law. Well she had to, and the cats knew that she meant business, even though they had all tried it on more than once. The acquisition of the doggy beds since the wedding was an ingenious idea and went down a treat! There was not a meow out of any of them, so it was pretty obvious and right that Bathsheba should be afforded the same luxury. Cursing at the thought of having to once again face the bark of that mad dog sales person, she had made up her mind that this time the usual ensuing uncalled for cat and dog fight between them would emphatically be the last. However, he always seemed to get away with the final 'passing shot,' implying, of course, that the dog was far superior an animal in all ways to the cat.

Just as Angela was about to leave, he said, selecting the perfect spaniel-like smile out of his vast repertoire of dog faces.

"You know, with that beautiful bed you have just bought, your cat, bless him or her, will always bask in the luxury of feeling 'dog-tired! That's called poetic justice and that really makes me happy."

Needless to say, the appropriate over emphasised doggy head nodding followed the remark.

Together we are beautiful

Twelve pairs of human eyes and ten pairs of cats eyes were hypnotised by the cat box on the floor. Denzil was transported somewhere else whilst displaying some unusual forms of excitement.

For a few seconds there was silence and then all hell broke loose as Buckingham picked up Bathsheba's scent. He meowed at the top of his voice and frantically circled the cage at least six times, whilst Lily on the other hand really seemed frightened, obviously having never witnessed her husband react in such a bizarre way before. She ran and hid behind the settee, whilst Dexter and Miss Pretty, employing every head and eye movement imaginable, attempted to follow Buckingham's solo Wild West floor show. TC on the other hand, not in the least understanding the method in the madness, was asking almost out loud,

"Just what on earth does Bucks think he's doing? He's definitely 'lost it' and who the hell is in that box to warrant such an insane reaction, for cat's sake?"

Whilst Buckingham couldn't restrain himself from showing just how ecstatic he was in seeing his sister again, the most unusual *cat*erwauling noises were coming from inside the box. Slowly yet deliberately Bathsheba emerged. Once outside the box, the feel of the soft carpet was irresistible. She virtually threw herself on to it and, fully stretched, and rolled over and over displaying to everyone how amazingly beautiful she actually was. Buckingham, oblivious to anything or anyone, jumped on her and frantically started licking and kissing her everywhere. Eventually both of them became so exhausted they just lay there in each others arms. TC walked away shaking his head, not understanding any of it, whilst Lily, with a mixture of emotions furtively peered at them from behind the settee. Dexter and Miss Pretty decided to sit on their haunches almost on top of them. They were obviously wondering what was going to happen next!

It was without question a totally magical moment. There was momentary silence whilst everyone came down to earth and returned to some form of sanity. Denzil smiled victoriously, patting the technical paraphernalia hanging round his neck.

"I've got it all. Worry not!" he whispered proudly.

CHAPTER SIXTEEN

Simply the best!

Mike Cass was the first to break the silence as everyone tried to come to terms with what they had just witnessed. In a very matter of fact tone of voice he said,

"Cats are like humans. They feel and demonstrate joy and pain just as we do.

Buckingham and Bathsheba, especially being twins, will from now on, have a very close relationship. In my opinion, and as you can see, it will be little Lily who will have the biggest problem in suddenly finding she's having to share her husband. They'll have to work that out between them, hopefully without a divorce! As for Dexter and Miss Pretty, they will go with the flow, and will have great fun with the new addition to the family. TC seemingly indifferent, but able to adjust to any situation, will have no problem dealing with any threat of interference to his way of life."

Seeing poor little Lily hiding behind the settee certainly pulled at Vicki's heart strings, but both Priscilla and Vicki believed that Buckingham's innermost feelings for Lily were just as strong as those he had for Bathsheba, but naturally in a different way. Once he had got over the shock and novelty of Bathsheba suddenly coming back into his life he would probably realise that he had unintentionally completely ignored his wife. Hopefully, being the 'man cat' he was, he would more than make it up to her!

Angela picked up on the conversation and with conviction said,

"My Bucks will come round. Meanwhile, nothing will change at Cozy Cats Cottage. All my precious family, thank goodness, will be occupied with something or other at some time or other. Bathsheba won't be a problem either since you, Dawn, will be taking her down to the Cat Club, spending time with her and getting her 'tarted' up for her future show work. That should be great fun!"

Dawn responded,

"I'm looking forward to it and I have heard on the grapevine from the powers that be that Bathsheba might well be in line for some TV ad work as well."

Bradley was particularly moved by all that he had seen:

"It was God's wish for Buckingham and Bathsheba to be together again. If there was such as thing as perfection in this world then it would certainly be Bathsheba, but my prayers at this moment are for little Lily. She needs some support and reassurance."

Denzil had to have his say, and looking at Angela, said,

"Tillsie, I've said it a hundred times before, Troy is grateful. We all are, for what you and those clever little creatures have achieved. Tina Turner said it – "you and they are simply the best!"

As everyone prepared to leave, having been more than satisfied with the evening's spontaneous and unpredictable entertainment, Mike Cass fired the final passing shot, directed at Angela and Dawn

"Of course, you should know that Bathsheba has never been spayed and so she could easily breed. Now that's food for thought!"

Bed talk!

It had been a wonderful evening, but now that everyone had left, Angela was experiencing the distinct feeling of an anti-climax. Whilst she was wondering what she should do next, Buckingham opened his eyes, stretched, got up and slowly walked out of the lounge, making his way towards the bedroom. Amazingly Bathsheba followed with Dexter, Miss Pretty and TC not far behind. Annoyingly for Angela, she was left wondering what on earth she was going to do with Lily. With further verbal persuasion and with Angela virtually pleading on her hands and knees, Lily still adamantly refused to budge from behind the settee. Angela knew very well that Lily was emotionally upset and obviously could not understand the significance of the situation at all. Witnessing Buckingham's amorous behaviour towards Bathsheba, Lily was probably thinking that Buckingham couldn't believe his luck in suddenly having come across some old flame from somewhere or other!

Angela was now exhausted, but had one final word,

"Lily, it's your choice to stay here all night, but I'm telling you, Bathsheba is Buckingham's twin sister and they have not seen each other for a very long time. Sister, Lily, *sister*, do you understand?"

On that note Angela retired to bed.

With the sudden arrival of Bathsheba into his life, Buckingham naturally had no thought for anyone or anything else. It was an endearing moment witnessing Buckingham making his way to the bedroom, amusingly followed by everyone else in procession. For some reason, like a magnet, he was attracted to Bathsheba's new bed and, settling himself down, with Bathsheba immediately following suit, he decided the time was right to offer everyone present some sort of an explanation.

Looking at each of the family in turn, he said,

"Well guys, this is my twin sister Bathsheba, and we haven't seen each other for a very, very long time. In fact I really believed she had gone to that pussy place in the sky with all her nine lives taken from her at the same time."

He then turned to Bathsheba and said,

"Bath, I want to officially introduce you to my two creative masterpieces, Dexter and Miss Pretty. Oh and not forgetting TC over there, who is my best friend. Lily, my wife, has decided not to be with us because she is doing 'a female thing' in the lounge and I am in no mood to sort her out."

Bathsheba responded, and looking at Dexter and Miss Pretty said

"Just like your Dad, you two look like a lot of fun. Knowing your father and his chequered past and seeing your mother, it has obviously produced a winning combination of good looks, beauty and, of course, intelligence! Your father used to be called Henry and I was named Henrietta. Those names were awful and we hated them. Now he's gone and got married, which is totally out of character. He was never 'the marrying kind', but wonders will never cease. Your mum must be very proud of you."

Miss Pretty decided to speak:

"You arriving so suddenly and everything has all been too quick and too much. Mum doesn't understand. Once she gets an idea in her head it is very difficult to get her to change her mind."

Dexter intervened:

"But she'll get over it. It needs explaining slow…ly. She's a great mum and we love her very much."

TC, having taken on board everything that had been said, made a suggestion, which was directed to Bathsheba:

"Bathsheba, please don't think I'm interfering or anything, but it might be a good idea if **you** could go into the lounge, and by offering a suitable explanation, persuade Lily to come back and not to be so silly. You would probably do better than Bucks under the circumstances. I think you have a special way with you, and Lily might just listen."

Bathsheba acknowledged the compliment and then replied,

"TC, you could well be right, and I don't want to fall out with Lily or be the reason for upsetting a happy marriage. I just want to be part of this lovely family, but I'll have a go and we'll see what happens."

She then turned to Buckingham and said,

"Bucks you had better get back to your own bed. If you don't and Lily returns she might well get the wrong idea and your life will **really** not be worth living!"

Bathsheba made her way tentatively down to the lounge since the layout of the cottage was totally new to her. She found Lily in exactly the same spot behind the settee, so she lay down a short distance from her, but so she had her in view. On seeing Bathsheba, Lily responded with two or three silent meows, obviously voicing her disapproval.

Bathsheba opened the conversation:

"Lily, I don't think you understand the relationship between your hubby and myself. We are brother and sister, and not only that we're also twins. I have not seen Buckingham for a long, long time and we have always been very close. We have shared joy and pain all our lives. We never thought we would see each other again after an unforgettable and terrible experience, but now that we have miraculously found each other we never want to be apart again. I do not want to come between you and your husband. I know Buckingham loves you with all his heart and I want you and me to be friends. We could have so much fun doing things together."

Since Lily responded with two or three more silent meows, Bathsheba thought enough was enough and returned to the bedroom. She got into her new bed and gave Buckingham and TC a look of despair, since there was nothing more she could do.

However, five minutes later Lily wandered into the bedroom, climbed into bed with her husband and started to lick him, seemingly leaving nowhere untouched!

TC and Bathsheba, on seeing what was taking place, made eye contact.

Bathsheba smiled and TC winked accordingly. *'What a result'* were the unspoken words!

Dexter, who also knew exactly what was going on, turned to Miss Pretty and said,

"Thank God all that boring stuff is over with Mum and Dad. Now perhaps we can all get some sleep!"

Wakey Wakey

It was later than usual when Angela awoke the following morning, but strangely there was not a sound to be heard anywhere in the house. Angela immediately checked the pussy boudoir to discover that all of her little darlings were still out to the world. However, she smiled to herself when she saw Lily and Buckingham with paws round each other. She was thankfully relieved that they and especially Lily had somehow managed to resolve their differences in dealing with the sudden and unexpected arrival of Bathsheba.

"I'll give them ten minutes," she said to herself.

The clock chimed. Time was up!

"Wakey wakey boys and girls. Breakfast and then work as normal. Bucks and Lily, you're going to Tillsworthy House as usual to spend time with Oliver, Margaret, Sinead and Linda, and Dexter you're off to the day care centre, and Miss Pretty, Princess Alicia Hospice needs you today, unfortunately for me. Meanwhile TC, I want you to look after and keep Bathsheba company. You can show her around her new residence, being the gentleman that you are."

Angela actually felt a little uneasy leaving Bathsheba and TC by themselves, but then Dawn offered to pop in to check on them and deal with anything that might have arisen or been overlooked.

As soon as everyone had left the house, TC, faithfully followed by Bathsheba, immediately made tracks towards the lounge, with sights set firmly on the two arm chairs. TC was adamant that as far as he was concerned the 'getting to know you' process between them should take place somewhere that offered the facility of above average comfort. The two chairs in question were the perfect answer. TC made the appropriate gesture and Bathsheba graciously complied and made herself comfortable on one of the chairs.

TC then said, slightly nervously,

"You know what, if Bucks could see us now my five lives, because that's all I have left, would be reduced to two rather quickly and quite dramatically. He would lose it big time!"

Bathsheba looked at TC, and with a smile filled with admiration said

"You shouldn't be scared of him. He's a big softie really, but I must say you're the perfect gentleman TC. I'm very impressed, and you could be the answer to any maiden's prayer. I want to get to know you better. Will you show me around my new home?"

TC answered without hesitation,

"Your wish is my command my lady."

It was nice that TC and Bathsheba had a lot of quality time for each other. He felt flattered by her remarks and really played the role of the perfect host, showing her around the home as if it was his own, and then taking her into the garden, down the steps and finally showing her the church and its beautiful surrounds.

*"The church is my second home and I often stay with Bradley, the lovely vicar who, by the way, is **rather** friendly with Angela. I also have a very responsible job in that I am the security guard for all this area, and Troy for that matter. Bucks is good for a laugh and often keeps me company and from getting bored."*

Bathsheba, obviously impressed, replied,

"Well TC, my darling, you can guard me any time. I feel very secure being with you and I am very pleased to know that you and Bucks are such good friends. I shall have to find a way of getting into Lily's good books!"

On hearing Dawn's voice anxiously and loudly calling them, they hurried back to the cottage.

"Where have you two been – sightseeing I suppose? I was getting really worried, Bathsheba. We have your next show coming up in four weeks time so we are going to have to spend some time together – excited?"

Angela was relieved to hear from Dawn that Bathsheba and TC had seemingly hit it off and had become close friends rather quickly, with Bathsheba making all the positive moves. Angela remarked that Bathsheba might be rather disappointed if she had any ulterior motives. TC, unfortunately, much to his probable frustration, would not be able to speak the same body language or play the same ball games if that's what she had in mind!

All that aside, Bathsheba felt she should be more concerned with her relationship with Lily, so for the moment that became her prime concern. However, she found herself and TC becoming closer and more affectionate towards each other every day. Bosom buddies was not too far from the truth!

Lily had, in fact, after Bathsheba's lecture the previous night, seen reason and had to accept the fact that it was only natural that her husband needed to spend time with his sister. Just before dinner the following evening Lily found a moment to have a word with Bathsheba.

"I hope Angela will bring you over to Tillsworthy House with us. You'll get to meet Oliver, Margaret, Sinead and Linda and they are all lovely guys. Our lives wouldn't be worth living without them and we know their lives wouldn't be worth living without us. Oliver and Margaret got married at the same time as Bucks and me and it's funny, because Margaret and Sinead are also twin sisters."

Coincidently, the following day Angela said, quite emphatically,

"Bathsheba, I'm going to take you over to Tillsworthy House the day after tomorrow with Bucks and Lily, because I want you to meet the rest of what I call family."

Of course Vicki and Priscilla had proudly spread the news of Bathsheba's forthcoming visit to Tillsworthy House. Margaret was particularly enthralled because apparently she was now well into her promised commitment of creating the cat family caricatures and Bathsheba must certainly be included. Linda was also quite besotted with Bathsheba, since she could not get over how beautiful and regal she actually was, and of course seeing Buckingham and Bathsheba together was like seeing something out of a fairy story. There was a magical moment in the foyer when Lily, not to be left out of anything, quite innocently yet deliberately, positioned herself between Buckingham and Bathsheba, whilst the three of them sat on their haunches directly facing Oliver, Margaret, Sinead and Linda as if to say,

"*So, what's new?*"

Vicki, who had witnessed the whole thing, blurted out quite spontaneously,

"Look at them! That's something not to be missed! Denzil where are you? We need a camera!"

It was a shame that Oliver could not enjoy the moment. Angela was curious to know if Oliver could actually feel the difference between Buckingham and Bathsheba.

As Angela placed Bathsheba on Oliver's lap, the look on Buckingham's face was a sight for sore eyes, and if it hadn't been his sister, such a move would have been met with some positive disapproval. Bathsheba, with no hesitation at all, positioned herself comfortably on Oliver's lap whilst Oliver's hands started to caress Bathsheba's beautiful white fur coat. By the look on Oliver's face he knew immediately it wasn't Buckingham, but he must have felt a connection. Everyone agreed that by the way he moved his hands across Bathsheba's back he was experiencing something different, yet something familiar. What made Angela's experiment so worthwhile was witnessing the pleasure on Oliver's face, even though there was an obvious element of confusion or misunderstanding. Margaret was quick to notice Oliver's expressions

"He thinks more of the bloody cat than he does of me! What do they say? Familiarity breeds contempt." She gave him an affectionate pat on the hand and said, with a touch of sarcasm.

"Never mind, enjoy the moment darling. Things will be back to normal tonight with your old bit of fluff!"

It was sad, but lucky, that he couldn't hear a word!

Clicker training

When Angela first read about clicker training she smiled at the stupidity of it, but then realised that she had to find out if it really worked. Bradley one day casually asked her how Dexter was getting on with the kids at the play school, and suddenly there it was – the ideal situation to find out if things really did 'click' into place as the journal had said.

Angela had phoned Fiona, pre-warning her of something new she wanted to try out with Dexter and the children on her next visit. She roughly outlined the gist of it, which was more than enough to ignite Fiona's enthusiasm, especially as the children themselves would eventually be able to participate. So, armed with several biros, some specially selected morsels of food, a stick and Dexter, of course, Angela arrived at the school. She had deliberately restricted Dexter's breakfast so he would be feeling just a wee bit hungry!

Angela placed Dexter, who was still in his box, in the centre of the room, but did not let him out as she usually did. Dexter was obviously anxious, a little confused and decided to let everyone know it by meowing rather loudly.

"What on earth is Angela playing at? I'm hungry. I've had no breakfast and I want to get out of this cage. Something's just not right."

Fiona then addressed the children.

"I want you to sit down and form a semi-circle, because today we are going to learn about clicker training, which will hopefully teach our little Dexter some fun new tricks, which you will also enjoy. Listen to Angela carefully."

Angela smiled and calmed the obvious anxiety on the children's faces concerning Dexter's apparent distress.

"Don't worry about Dexter meowing. He'll be ok in a minute. Now in my right hand I have a biro and when I press the top of it down like this…. it makes a double click sound. I want Dexter to know that when he hears that sound he will get something nice to eat… like this."

She opened a small tin and showed everybody a collection of yummy cat treats.

"Now, I'm going to let Dexter out and we'll see what happens."

Dexter cautiously stepped out of the box, looked at everybody in turn and finally focused his attention on Angela, especially as he smelt something rather good.

"Angela, you're messing about with me. I can smell food. Why are you making that clicking noise?"

Suddenly he was all over her as she endeavoured to offer him a small piece of fish.

"That was good, but a bit mean. Don't I get any more? There's that clicking noise again. Oh she's giving me some more food. So it would seem that if she clicks I get food. I guess I can live with that."

Angela continued,

"I think Dexter has got the message, but now I am going to show him the target stick, which as you can see is a chopstick. I am going to offer it to him…like this. He will come to investigate…see that, and when his nose touches the end I will click the biro but only once and then I will immediately offer him a treat….just like that. Look how he loves it. Now I'm going to do that all over again, but this time I'm going to move the stick further away."

"She's moved the bloody stick further away, but if I touch the end and she makes the click noise maybe I'll get some more treats."

Dexter got some treats.

"Now she's doing it again, but has moved the stick in a different place altogether. I'm bored with this now, so I am not going to bother with it any more, treats or no treats."

Angela had read the article several times and was warned that if the cat became bored the process should be stopped and left until another time. Dexter had responded well to the stick and had also realised that hearing the click meant a treat. Now the idea was to use the stick to lure Dexter into doing other things, like jumping onto, or even through, objects in pursuit of the yummy target. However, Angela and Fiona's ultimate objective was to involve the children, whereby they could all participate in the fun. Clicker training was a wonderful idea, since it provided motivation, a sense of achievement and it was great fun doing it. Dexter and the children eventually proved it in no uncertain fashion. It was mission accomplished as far as Fiona and Angela were concerned.

CHAPTER SEVENTEEN

Sinead

She had been perfectly all right for some considerable time, so the news that Sinead had suddenly been taken ill and transferred to hospital came as a shock, especially to those close to her. Margaret's concern for her sister's health was clearly visible and even Lily showed obvious signs of distress at Sinead no longer being physically present at Tillsworthy House. But there was worse to come.

Just as Angela was having to think seriously about what to do with Lily and Tillsworthy House, Priscilla phoned to inform her that Sinead had now been transferred to The Princess Alicia Hospice. Her condition was serious, but no prognosis had been given. This was an even greater shock for everyone to cope with. Angela suddenly realised how important it was for Lily to go to the hospice and spend as much time with Sinead as possible. She could organise her visiting time to coincide with Miss Pretty's, as she would be seeing her own patients as normal. Out of courtesy, Angela felt obliged to ask the hospice if this arrangement could be made and Vanessa Middleton, who simply adored Miss Pretty, was at first a little lost for words, since it concerned Miss Pretty's mum. Displaying genuine sympathy, she naturally had no objection.

On seeing Sinead, Lily knew immediately that there was something radically wrong and so she deliberately snuggled up to her as if to reassure her that everything would be all right.

Stroking the back of Lily's head, Sinead said softly,

"Oh Lily you don't know how much I love you and how much you mean to me. I know Margaret loves you as much, but since she also has Oliver, bless him, you have become my life."

Lily looked at Sinead and simply said,

"*Sinead, I love you.*"

Of course, Angela had witnessed and realised the emotion of the moment. Uncontrollable tears, which she endeavoured to hide, came to her eyes. She had to go out of the room to regain her composure, so she said to Sinead,

"Sinead, I'm going to leave Lily with you whilst I pop over to see what Miss Pretty is getting up to. I'll be back shortly."

Whilst on her way, Angela happened to bump into Vanessa, who asked if she could have a quick word.

"You know Angela, it is a touch ironic that we now have both mother and daughter here making somebody's life worth living. Did you know that practically every patient in this hospice has a signed picture of Miss Pretty by their bedside? Not only that, the two other hospices associated with us would like a visit from Miss Pretty. However, if her mother could come too that would be an incredible bonus."

Angela thought for a moment.

"That might well be feasible, in fact it would be lovely. Lily and Miss Pretty would go for that, I'm sure. The one reservation I have is that I would like Lily to devote all her time to Sinead at present, for obvious reasons."

Vanessa smiled at Angela and said confidently,

"I will ensure that happens, so don't worry."

Three weeks later during the night, Sinead quietly but peacefully slipped away.

Angela was greeted with the news on arrival at the hospice the following day. It was a shock and Vanessa did all she could to ease the pain of the moment. By the look on Lily's face, she certainly knew something was wrong and Angela, who was holding her in her arms, endeavoured to explain.

"Lily, last night God called Sinead and told her that it was time she was with him. He would take care of her from now on and she would have no more pain or suffering. Now it's Margaret who will especially need our love even more. We must do everything we can for her."

Lily looked back and forth at Angela and Vanessa several times, hoping for an answer

"I know Sinead has gone to heaven. What are you going to do with me now? I love Margaret and I will try to make the loss of her sister less painful for her. I think my Bucks will be upset when he knows what's happened."

Vanessa looked at Lily and consolingly said,

"I don't expect Miss Pretty to work today. I think Angela should take both of you with her to Tillsworthy House. This is a big shock for everyone, but Miss Pretty's patients and I will be thinking of you with love, sympathy and understanding in our hearts, and Lily…there is always a welcome place for you here too."

Angela looked at Lily, nodded her head in approval and thanked Vanessa for her concern.

On arrival at Tillsworthy House, there was little sign of the usual hustle and bustle of activity. An eerie silence hung over the noticeably deserted foyer, imparting the feeling that the world had suddenly stopped. Words were not necessary as Angela looked sympathetically at Margaret, who was distinctly pale, seated in an armchair in Vicki and Priscilla's apartment. Lily, on seeing her, immediately jumped up on her lap and brought the semblance of a smile to Margaret's face. Priscilla and Vicki tried to be realistic, saying that life must go on and Sinead would want it to once the initial grieving was over.

Angela, a little concerned, asked,

"Where are Oliver and Buckingham?"

Margaret replied,

"They're in our room. Oliver wouldn't understand and it is not worth the effort in trying to explain, but I am sure Buckingham will realise very soon. Oh, by the way, Bradley phoned and I spoke to him. He was very consoling but he would like to speak to you regarding the funeral arrangements. I have told him to go ahead with whatever is necessary. I have a good idea as to what Sinead would have wanted."

Once back at the cottage, and the family having been suitably fed, Angela called Bradley and suggested he came over. He told Angela that he had seen Sinead two days before she died and she had indicated that when the time came she wanted more than anything to be buried in the grounds of All Saints Church in Troy, if that were possible. She also wanted Bradley to conduct the service, which would be small and intimate.

Bradley paused whilst Angela got to grips mentally with the situation.

"I agreed that her wishes would be met if the occasion arose. Sinead, bless her, gave me a list of people she would like to attend. Margaret also knows who they are. She even gave me the wording that she wanted inscribed on the grave stone and I have put this in hand already. Lastly she gave me a sealed envelope which she wanted me to open and read out aloud at the funeral service."

Angela found it very hard taking all this in, and Bradley, knowing that only too well, tried to do it as gently as he could.

Angela, with tears in her eyes, turned to Bradley and said,

"You know, what's so ironic about all this is that some time ago it was Margaret who was diagnosed with the health problems. Not that I wish for one minute that anything happens to her. For Sinead it was so sudden and unexpected. Sometimes God works in mysterious ways." She paused for a moment in reflection.

"I wonder what's in the envelope!"

Bradley continued,

"I think the service and burial should be in a week's time. I have allocated a lovely spot in the grounds of the church. The invitations to the selected few should come from Margaret, so if you could make sure she does that it would help. I will arrange for food and drink in the vicarage after the service."

Angela responded,

"Oh Bradley thank you so much for all you have done and are doing. You are indeed a Godsend!"

Bradley answered protectively,

"Well, I care about our community and I particularly care about you."

Angela smiled inwardly to herself at the sincerity of that remark.

Loved and Missed

A funeral is certainly not a joyous occasion, but for those concerned there is the joy of knowing that the departed one was very much loved and will be missed. Even so, witnessing the lowering of the coffin into the ground is always a particularly harrowing experience. However, Margaret, on behalf of her sister, had requested that it was quietly carried out without being openly witnessed.

The church service for Sinead was beautifully and cleverly orchestrated by Bradley, even though there were no more than a dozen people present. Sinead had requested two special hymns and selected a simple array of flowers which were effectively placed by Bradley within the main body of this beautiful little church. Denzil Whitehead, dressed unusually soberly and immaculately with the help of the ever grateful Jamie, had arranged the funeral cars with almost military precision, transporting Margaret and Oliver, Priscilla, Vicki, Linda and also Seth, believe it or not, from Tillsworthy House for the drive to Troy.

Needless to say, Oliver did appear to be somewhat confused, but he knew very well that he had no option but to accept the fact that everywhere Margaret went he went, but then they loved each other so there was no reason at all to question anything.

For the little time there was to organise everything, nothing had been overlooked, including the welfare of the cats. Dawn, who had become very close to Angela, had once again offered to stay at the cottage and look after them whilst the funeral was taking place. Angela was extremely grateful for this.

The simplicity of the service, the message it carried and the way Bradley delivered it was a highly emotional affair. After Bradley had given a short but uplifting résumé of Sinead's life, he informed his audience that she had requested that he opened and read out the contents of the envelope that he held in his hand.

It read as follows:

"One of the greatest, if not the greatest, love of my life has been Lily, a darling, adorable and beautiful little cat who was lucky to be just one of Angela's extraordinary family of cats. I have to admit that I was initially jealous of Lily's love for my twin sister Margaret. Margaret always had everything, and I wanted to hurt her and so one day I kidnapped Lily, but she has never known that it was me who put her in one of those washing machines in the laundry room at Tillsworthy House. Although I had the good sense not to set the machine in motion, I eventually could not live with the guilt of this dreadful deed on my conscience and I had to own up to what I had done. I have had to live with the torment and guilt of my action for the remainder of my life until now, my almost dying day. Margaret, I want to say how sorry I am yet again and I wonder if you have managed to finish the caricatures of all the cats. You were so good at it! I want you Angela, with Lily in mind, to accept the small enclosed donation from the bottom of my heart in support of the TTPCC. I feel I can now rest in peace."

Bradley paused allowing time for those heartfelt words to register. He then said

"Sinead's torment is over. We shall always remember her with love in our hearts. God bless you all."

During the course of the evening get-together at the vicarage, Margaret managed to have a quiet word with Bradley and Angela.

"I am so upset that Sinead felt the way she did, especially about me, because it was all so unnecessary. It was a lovely service Bradley, and what you said about my sister was beautiful. By the way, I have finished the caricatures, but I have lent them to Denzil because he pleaded with me to let him borrow them. He desperately wanted to photograph them for his collection. It is such a pity that Sinead will not have seen them, since it was she who actually inspired me to do it. Angela, you told me that Sinead had insisted upon a certain inscription on the grave stone?"

Bradley replied,

"Yes it is very simple and very sweet. It will read:

Dear Margaret and Lily
You'll always be with me
In my heart and in my mind.

Angela then remarked,

"Ironically, poor Sinead made a rod for her own back. She had a cross to bear and she bore it well. I am looking forward to seeing those caricatures. Do you know that the cheque of a small donation to the trust was no less than five thousand pounds! That was indeed a huge shock!" She paused. "Bless her."

Angela was no different to any other normal human being when it came to weaknesses of character, or paying attention to things that were just not important enough and yet should be. Her major problem was trust, or rather having too much of it, which created some concern to those around her, especially for her own security and safety, and even more perhaps for Cozy Cats Cottage and her beloved family of cats. Leaving the house unlocked and windows open provided an open invitation. She had, however, invested in a cat flap which allowed access onto the front lawn but she could never decide on when it should be closed or left open, so it was always left open. She was somehow under the impression that the cats should not be treated as prisoners, but have freedom of choice. They would know when it was safe or unsafe to go out or when the weather was good or bad. Bradley had mentioned it a million times that once all the cats were in, the cat flap should be shut! He reminded her that she had already had one rather nasty surprise in finding Dexter and Miss Pretty cavorting in the grounds of the fair one particular night. In case she was wondering, Bradley then pointed out that the circumstances were slightly different for him because he was blessed with only one cat and he was out most of the night doing guard duty and protecting the interests of Troy. Obviously his cat flap had to be left open most of the time.

To the delight of some and the disgust of others it was that time again. The fair had arrived and, as always, Bradley and Angela could not resist the temptation of a night out to thoroughly enjoy the fun of it. Angela, without thinking, had done it again and left the cat flap open. However this time there was a nasty shock in store for her, as she was about to learn the hard way of the do's and don't's of cat flaps!

Satan

He was a 'bad boy.' He knew it and he enjoyed being it. Satan, the apt name selected by his equally 'bad' master, loved making trouble and usually big trouble. He was big, black and ruggedly beautiful, but if aroused he was also aggressive and wild. He had been born and bred on the fairground, but as far as fairground cats were concerned, he was the 'king' and if you valued your nine lives you just wouldn't want to mess with him. He had his own special way of doing things and he had quite a little army of followers, including a string of 'cat fair groupies.' Every place the fair went, he knew what was going on in and around it, but more importantly he knew specifically what the local cat talent was up to. Satan, often nick-named Marlon Brando for obvious reasons, had a soft spot for Troy, but there was a little annoying matter in the local community that had been on his mind for a while. On this visit he decided to make the time and effort to deal with it.

Satan called a meeting with two of his henchmen, Jake and Jasper, another couple of little devils.

"Boys, I've always liked Troy, but there is an ex member of our crew here who a little while ago jumped ship. I don't like that and he should be made to realise that you just don't do that sort of thing without some serious repercussions. His present name, I believe, is TC. You'll know him by that rather swish leopard skin fur coat of his".

Jake hissed,

"What's the plan boss? Do we take him out?"

Satan replied,

"We teach him a lesson, that's for sure, but there is method in the madness. He lives in a posh cottage called Cozy Cats up on the hill with some other posh bodies, so we have to be careful and we have to have a game plan, even though it will unavoidably be a bit of a 'hit and miss' affair. Also living there is a white female pedigree person who ponces about, obviously thinking she's God's gift, so I want you two to show her some of your special disrespect."

Jasper commented with a devilish smile, showing two rather large fangs,

"I've always fancied a bit of posh."

Jake was quick to add,

"A bit of rough might be just what she wants!"

Satan continued,

"The lady owner of the cottage, without fail, always has a night's fun at the fair. That is when we strike, because thankfully she never ever closes the cat flap. You two will lie in wait whilst I will try to entice TC outside. If he is in

there he will know it's me by my exclusive smell and I will give him some 'Satan special,' which he won't get rid of in a hurry!"

Jake and Jasper, almost in unison, said,

"What about the white one, boss? Can't wait to deal with her!"

Satan answered,

"I'm banking on her coming out to see what's going on, so you stay out of sight until I give you a cat call. Then you pounce and give her some of your best fairground verbal and then rough her up a bit, so she doesn't look so good anymore. She likes winning awards at cat shows, if you know what I mean!"

Jasper commented,

"Don't you worry boss. She'll be having a couple of different awards coming her way by the time we've finished with her."

Jake had to have the last say,

"What cat show? She won't even know the meaning of the word!"

The scene was set.

TC never slept *soundly*. Harry had been the *purr*fect tutor in educating TC on the finer points in the art of becoming a 'number one' cat security guard. He had many amazing tales to tell, but Harry was equally fascinated listening to TC describing his years of suffering with the day to day fiascos of fairground life. However, Harry had perceived that this might be in TC's favour, since past bitter experiences would have undoubtedly made him very aware that danger might suddenly be lurking round any corner in the dead of night. Sleeping *soundly* was not recommended in the book of cat security guard rules, which if not adhered to could often invite plenty of uninvited trouble!

For Angela and Bradley the fair was almost an addiction and they were not ashamed to admit it. Now it was 'all the fun of the fair' time again and the night was young, but Angela true to form, had once again left the cat flap open, but this time trouble was brewing! On this particular night it was Angela's turn for TC to stay at Cozy Cats Cottage and Satan had no problem in finding that out, since he had perfected the finest tuned Cat Communication System in the business.

It was eleven o'clock at night when Satan, Jake and Jasper made their way stealthily towards the cottage. On arrival, their entry activated the security light so the entire front of the cottage was flood-lit. They stood still for a moment on the grass almost mesmerised by the open cat flap. They looked at each other with a wink of the eye and a smile on their faces, confirming the success of the first part of the operation. Jake and Jasper then disappeared into the bushes to wait for Satan's call that the 'white one' had emerged. Meanwhile Satan, quite fearless, advanced towards the cat flap then gently pushed it and stepped inside the dimly lit kitchen. He knew TC would acknowledge his presence any second and, of course, TC did!

TC, who always kept his cool in any situation, could not contain his anger with the sheer audacity orchestrated by Satan, who had never instilled anything in him but really bad and painful memories of his past life. He hissed loudly,

"Get out of my home, you evil black creature. You've got some nerve coming in here like this."

Satan, always one step ahead and rarely frightened, turned around went back through the cat flap, followed by an angry TC. Both cats, with looks that could kill, faced each other with backs arched, showing their fangs and hissing loudly.

Satan calmly shouted with due sarcasm,

"Your home was the fair with us or have you forgotten? You're a traitor and I hate traitors. I looked after you all your life at the fair and got you out of trouble many times, or have you forgotten that too? What does TC stand for?

Trash Cat! So it's all cozy, cozy life and cozy, cozy cottage now is it? I hear you've even got a bit of cozy white fluff on the side. You make me sick!"

TC answered angrily,

"Go to hell Satan, where you belong. Jealousy won't get you anywhere and you leave her out of this. Life at the fair is evil and spiteful and I was not prepared to put up with it any longer. You're way too stupid to realise that."

Satan sarcastically replied,

"Talk to the paws 'cos the face ain't listening!"

At that moment, what Satan had hoped for happened, and as luck would have it he was able to play his trump card. Bathsheba, concerned for TC's welfare, knew something was wrong and came out to see what all the fuss was about. Satan let out his infamous cat call and Jake and Jasper suddenly and magically appeared from nowhere and pounced on the poor unsuspecting Bathsheba. During the next few seconds all hell broke loose, with Jake and Jasper shouting and attacking Bathsheba with open claws.

"She thinks she's a real Madame, Jake."

"She thinks she's better than us because she's white, Jasper"

"White trash more like, Jake! Cat shows!"

"She might not be doing any more, Jasper!"

At that point the scene changed dramatically, because Buckingham came out joining the fray, chasing and screaming loudly,

"Get out of here you bloody lot of evil, horrible creatures."

Satan knew it was the right time to quit. Calling Jake and Jasper, all three of them, like streaked lightning, vanished into the night.

Satan knew very well that it had been a major victory – a justified 'devil's delight'.

The aftermath of this evil confrontation was that it had left Bathsheba lying on the grass obviously severely shaken, with Buckingham and TC not knowing how badly she had been hurt and both of them wondering what they should do now. They were extremely concerned and started to lick her to let her know that they were there and everything would be OK. They prayed, and luckily their prayers were answered with the return of Bradley and Angela, who as usual had walked to the fair. However, on their return, as they walked up the steps through the trees, Angela had noticed that the cottage security light was on.

"Bradley look, something must have activated it."

After another five minutes, the light had still not gone off. Angela said,

"That's strange. Something must be wrong. The light doesn't normally stay on for that length of time."

Bradley and Angela almost ran the rest of the way and as they approached the lawn they had the shock of their lives. They saw Bathsheba lying on the grass with Buckingham and TC frantically licking her.

Angela said emotionally,

"Oh God, what's happened? Bathsheba, what have you done?"

Bradley quickly examined her and said,

"I think she's all right. She's been hurt though."

With that he gently picked her up and carried her into the house, placing her on the kitchen table.

Buckingham and TC sat patiently on the floor looking desperately up at Angela and Bradley for some assurance.

Angela anxiously said,

"Do we call Mike Cass?"

Bradley answered,

"Well she is in shock and she has two or three bad scratches, which we can treat ourselves. They don't need stitches. Give her a little while then put her in her bed and see what she's like in the morning. I'll make some coffee."

Angela looked in frustration at Buckingham and TC in turn.

"How did this happen? You know don't you? If only you could damn well talk. Oh no! I've just remembered she's got a cat show coming up very soon. What am I going to do?"

Bradley, showing little sympathy then said,

"Well Angela, I hate to say it, but you did it again. You left the bloody cat flap open and to my mind another cat or cats have done this, by the look of those scratches. We'll never know the true story, but let it be a lesson that in future the cat flap is *shut shut shut* once everybody is in."

Angela, really frustrated and annoyed with herself, then said

"Oh Bradley, I'm such a fool. How could I do it? She might have been killed. Dawn will be furious and extremely upset. I just daren't tell her."

Bradley, attempting to console her, said

"Have no fear, Bathsheba will recover ok but if you feel that there is still something wrong in the morning you must get Mike Cass to check her over."

CHAPTER EIGHTEEN

The Wounds of War

Two days had gone by since that dreadful night. The incident deserved a full scale feature in the local paper with a poignant heading such as 'Assault on Cozy Cats Cottage,' or just plain 'Cat Attack'. The way it was executed with no warning at all, and the speed and precision of it, was actually highly commendable and could certainly be likened to any military campaign. It would have made an interesting read! Angela, of course, could not forgive herself for her stupidity in providing the ideal opportunity for the whole thing to be planned in the first place.

After Bradley's 'common sense' treatment, Angela was quite prepared to stay up all night keeping a vigil on this precious bundle of white fur. As she left the room, feeling more than uncomfortable with so many eyes staring at her in a way she had never seen or felt before, she said quite emphatically and with obvious concern in her voice,

"If Bathsheba is in trouble during the night TC, you come and wake me up immediately. That's an order!"

With a big sigh of frustration, she said to herself, but out loud,

"I wish I knew how this had happened and who the hell had done it."

Buckingham turned to TC on Angela's exit and said, with restrained anger,

"There you go TC, you and your bloody fairground friends. They're a load of yob cats, always taking somebody for a rough ride!"

TC, trying to keep his cool, answered,

"They are not my friends Bucks. Their favourite ride is named the 'tunnel of hate'. Satan, the black one, is the Godfather and with his two favourite 'devil's advocates' in tow, come hell or high water, nothing was going to deter

them from giving me a lesson of a lifetime. I had committed the ultimate sin by turning traitor and breaking the golden rule of turning my back on 'family'. You just do not do something like that without taking the risk of some terrible reprisal. Satan, the clever sod, not only physically attacked me but also enticed Bathsheba to 'play the game' too, since he knew how much that would hurt me. He had done his homework extremely well."

Lily intervened and, quite mesmerised by TC's words, said,

"I admire your courage TC, having to live every day knowing that something like that might happen sometime. Anytime. That's very scary and a high price to pay for freedom. Angela's action, or lack of it, didn't help, but thank goodness I had the sense to stop Dexter and Miss Pretty from jumping in there too, especially after Bucks decided to get involved."

TC looked at Lily and then at Bathsheba and said,

"I feel really bad. Poor Bathsheba, she didn't deserve any of it."

He then turned to Buckingham and said,

"Thank God you appeared when you did. The timing was perfect, but sadly the deed had been done, but it could have been a lot worse."

Buckingham had not missed a word and, obviously deep in thought, had kept strangely quiet for some time, but then said quite philosophically,

"TC, sometimes you even amaze me! I wasn't about to see any of my family and friends getting 'done over', especially like that. That was below the belt."

And then looking at Bathsheba,

"I think Her Majesty will not only live to see another day, but will live to win another show! There are plenty of lives left in that old girl yet!"

Lily had to have the last devilishly sarcastic word:

"Old? She's your twin sister...... old boy!"

Close encounter

Angela was more than worried as Bathsheba still didn't look right. She called Mike Cass, explained the strange 'goings on' of that unforgettable night and cancelled all cat work for the day. She gently placed an unresisting Bathsheba in a cat cage with a blanket and as she went out of the door she said to five anxious little faces,

"Well it's no work today, because this young lady does not seem to be very well at all and I feel Uncle Mike should have a quick look at her. I know. I know. The cat flap is shut… ok? Be good till I get back."

Mike Cass, funnily enough, was not that surprised with what Angela had told him. He had seen it before and he knew Satan was a bad 'dude' but a clever one too.

After careful examination he confirmed that Bathsheba was basically still in shock and it was unpredictable as to how long it would take for her to fully recover. Bradley had done the right thing with the treatment of the scratches, but the most serious concern was her being fully recovered in time for the next cat show, which was one of the biggest, incorporating the Cat of the South award. He confirmed that if there was the tiniest thing wrong she should not be entered. To suffer the humiliation of being disqualified was not worth taking any risks. She had already emerged as being the outright winner of two highly acclaimed awards at two prestigious cat shows. She needed to win this third one, the most important of all, as all sorts of lucrative opportunities could follow. Mike Cass turned to Angela and said,

"Give her one of these tablets each day for seven days. She's in God's hands and it's a waiting game. Unfortunately, I am not the show's resident vet this time round and it's a big, big show. It's in two weeks' time I think".

Angela replied,

"You're right, it is. Dawn will be round to collect Bathsheba in ten days' time and will then get her fully prepared."

Mike Cass thought for a minute and then said consolingly,

"Angela, bring her back the day before Dawn is due to collect her and I will give you my opinion. Fingers and everything else crossed. Hopefully she'll be fine.

If by any chance she won't take those pills, then I'll give you something to put in her food. She'll be fine!"

Behind closed doors

It would be an understatement to say that the day to day scenarios involving Angela and her six cats were unusual and unpredictable.

There always seemed to be something out of the norm going on. However, realistically speaking, behind the closed doors of Cozy Cats Cottage, daily life was presumed to be *purr*fectly normal and *purr*fectly peaceful…..or was it?

Bradley, who frequently spent more than one evening a week with Angela at the cottage, was always amazed at how each of the cats had jealously guarded their own claimed space in the lounge. One of the two armchairs, which Angela had retained from the old 'Odd Acres' days, Buckingham had clearly and rightfully made his own. The words 'If you value your life, keep off!' were clearly etched on his face.

No one as yet had dared to challenge it. This arrangement was fine until Buckingham and Lily had taken their marriage vows. Lily had decided that they should now share one chair between them, as this would be much more conducive in showing the world their love and 'togetherness' and that they were indeed happily married. Buckingham was not quite as amenable, as naturally, he wished to retain some manly independence, but he didn't want to rock the boat so early in this new relationship, so he kept quiet and gracefully accepted the situation. The other now vacant armchair was immediately pounced upon by Dexter and Miss Pretty, but being kittens, damage to the upholstery did not take long to appear. Angela understandably could not contain herself. She suitably screamed and shouted at them, which had little or no effect, so as a last resort she had no alternative but to put a throw over the chair to protect it. This was not the best solution, since Dexter and Miss Pretty decided they really got a kick out of making Angela angry and so they methodically kept pulling the throw off the chair. The arrival of TC put an end to that little fiasco, when he made up his mind that the chair was going to be his. Dexter and Miss Pretty sensibly left well alone and went off to make trouble elsewhere, primarily targeting the kitchen.

Strangely, with the arrival of Bathsheba, TC proved himself to be the perfect gentleman by offering her the undisputed comfort of the armchair and relegating himself to the rug in front of the fireplace which happened to be just as comfortable. TC was in fact a rather strange cat in many ways. As Angela had already experienced, he was wild and aggressive to begin with and then in time, leaving his insufferable fairground days behind him, he became the gentlest and most loving of souls. Often unpredictably, and with no rhyme or reason or set routine, he would, during the night, sneak into Angela's bedroom and then position himself comfortably on her chest. Having nibbled her ears, nudged her chin and purred for a while he would then put his paws round her neck and fall asleep. Although Angela loved what he did, she had to virtually grit her teeth not to object. The problem was his weight on her chest, but she hadn't the heart to move him. After all, love conquers all, so they say.

The day that Angela decided to delegate the second bedroom for the exclusive use by her rapidly expanding cat family proved to be a major 'catalamity'. She had told Buckingham in no uncertain manner that he was in charge of all activities in that room and was responsible for keeping the peace and keeping things clean and tidy. Bad move. Buckingham was not a human being! The room very quickly began to look like a 'doss house' with food and litter box grit all over the place. It was a nightmare. Out of desperation Angela had the inspiration to transfer everything, except the bed of course, to the kitchen, where she managed to tuck things away under kitchen units. However, Dexter and Miss Pretty were not going to let Angela get away with that one! They knew very well that the litter tray provided the ultimate fun in grit spreading, all over the kitchen floor and even on to the lounge carpet. This was indeed the best way to bring out the worst in Angela, who had to quickly find some method of counter attack. Suddenly she remembered a TV programme where children played with water, knowing that cats particularly hated it. So it was down to the shops to invest in a child's water pistol. She waited for the moment when she could catch Dexter and Miss Pretty red handed. She gave them both a quick burst of water power. What a result! The reaction was immediate and they literally went flying! Almost dying of shock and disbelief, they raced into the lounge, made straight for the rug and then rolled over and over on it frantically trying to get dry. After two or three further courageous attempts, Angela's ingenuity finally paid off, and it was not soon enough before that little trick was dead and buried.

However, Angela knew it would only be a matter of time before the devious Dexter and mischievous Miss Pretty had some other outrageous idea up their sleeves to drive her completely insane!

How time flies!

It was Sunday night, and much to Denzil and Jamie's delight it was the usual full house at The Wooden Horse in Troy. This did not deter Bradley and Angela from going down there to enjoy a 'loud' drink! Bradley thought to himself, "Had she or hadn't she?" The penny must have dropped! Miraculously, Angela had not forgotten to shut the cat flap. Bradley smiled to himself and thanked God accordingly!

Being the vicar, and a very caring one at that, Bradley always commanded great respect from the locals as did Angela, for all they had achieved in helping the less fortunate. With open arms and big smiles, many of them offered them a place at their table but Denzil, always one step ahead with his usual impeccable decorum, of course kept a quiet spot 'out of the way' for emergencies. On and off during the next hour between serving drinks and food, Denzil and Jamie alternated casual 'talk' time with Bradley and Angela. For some reason or other the subject always eventually came round to those irresistible but not always '*purr*fect' creatures!

Denzil, in a reminiscing frame of mind, proudly said to Angela,

"Out of curiosity more than anything else, I happened to be going through my ever growing photographic library a short while ago. I really believe I have a memento of every single one of your cats at some occasion or other, right from the very first day I met you. You know how much I love them. I bet you had forgotten that in three weeks time it will be not only Buckingham and Lily's, but also Margaret and Oliver's first wedding anniversary. To my mind, that's an excuse for a huge celebration of some kind, with no expense spared."

Angela excitedly interjected,

"Such words of wisdom! What would we do without you Denzil?

You're absolutely right. This calls for something very special, but needs some thought and careful planning. Margaret and Oliver have had a wonderful year together. For sure Buckingham would rise to the occasion without a second thought and Lily, bless her, would have no problem in enjoying the luxury of them being the stars of the show....again!"

Bradley responded with an upbeat tone of voice,

"Well, whilst love is in the air, how about setting up an afternoon garden party in a marquee? A reasonably sized one could be erected in the church grounds. There's enough room and I wouldn't object to it, and those already under the ground nearby wouldn't have any say in the matter. In fact they would probably enjoy it too!"

There were smiles all round at that remark, after which Angela commented,

"That's a really nice gesture Bradley, but the weather would have to be kind and we would have to get someone to do the catering."

Jamie decided to join in. He turned to Denzil and said,

"How about the room upstairs, Denzil? It would certainly be big enough and pretty convenient with the drinks and food a few yards away, I would have thought."

And then with a wicked smile Jamie added,

"You know what? Buckingham deserves a nice big medal for devotion to duty in having come through his first year of er....... marital... bliss? virtually unscathed!"

Angela commented,

"Jamie, that's a bit harsh. What about Lily, a lady in love having to suffer those...... spasmodic chauvinistic antics...... often with no warning at all."

Denzil interjected and said slowly and deliberately,

"Oliver's wheelchair would be a problem. I actually have a better idea up my sleeve about the whole thing, but I need time to sort it out, if that's all right with all of you? Trust me, you won't be disappointed."

At that point the subject of a wedding anniversary was suitably dropped, whilst Denzil turned everybody's attention to his other favourite pastime, local news and gossip. This time he seemed unusually excited, apparently having had personal confirmation of the arrival of an interesting new resident.

"You must have heard of those five rather exclusively expensive houses, each boasting no less than a minimum of five bedrooms and a swimming pool. They're tucked away amongst the picturesque woodland on the top of Troy Hill. You never get to know or see who owns them and they never come up for sale, that is until now. One of them has been on the market for just one week and has already acquired a new owner. His name is Miles Melford and, believe it or not, for no particular reason other than to meet me of course, he was in here the other day and we shared a very nice drink and chat together."

Bradley interjected,

"Miles Melford! I've seen him on TV and have read about him in connection with all sorts of known and unknown faces. Troy has more than one star in its midst, eh Denzil? A bit of competition is a good thing, keeps you on your toes!"

Denzil smiled accordingly, and looking at Bradley, continued,

"You know me too well Bradley. This guy is, in fact, a highly respected publicist, but strangely he comes across as being so quiet and unassuming. Most unusual when he is dealing with celebrities and such influential and money minded people every minute of the day. But, dare I say, for me the fascination was that he quite casually said he adored cats, especially one his mother had. He was completely taken aback when I told him about the wedding. He just couldn't believe it and how bizarre it must have been. Then he came out with something really interesting. He is apparently working on a brief for an independent film company, which entails finding strong and unusual ideas for a series of short animated films, the key word being animated, that carry some kind of hidden message or meaning about life, for example 'Charity begins at home'. The overall title for the series is 'That's Life', which to my mind is catchy and says it all.

Angela commented accordingly,

"Sounds extremely intriguing, but those sort of people are hard to judge. I don't really trust them, but that maybe a little unfair. Still, he loves cats so he's one of us. It might be worth him having a tête-à-tête with Margaret."

Bradley, also impressed, then said with an ever so slight hint of sarcasm,

"That's a good idea. I hope you're going to invite him to the 'do' Denzil, whenever and whatever that might be!"

Denzil answered,

"Of course I bloody well am, oh sorry Bradley I didn't mean to say that. I am also contemplating showing him some of my collection, especially the wedding, so he can see my expertise for himself! After all – that's life!"

Fingers and Paws crossed

"She looks all right to me, but I still have a slight reservation and I can't put my finger on it."

Mike Cass had just finished examining Bathsheba and that remark was not what Angela wanted to hear. He continued,

"As you know, I am not the vet or one of the judges on this coming show, but personally I would take the chance, and if she doesn't make it, so be it. I know it's the Cat of the South award show but there'll be another one next year."

Angela responded,

"Oh God Mike, I wish this had never happened to her. I'll never go to that bloody fairground again."

Mike philosophically answered,

"It's not the fairground, it's the people, or I should say a minority of people who have no responsibility when it comes to animal welfare. These poor creatures like Satan have to fight for themselves. Everyone deserves to have love in their lives. It is not really a natural way of life. We tend to regard cats as household pets, rather than wild animals."

Angela showed little compassion.

"Well poor Bathsheba was obviously an innocent victim of a spitefully conceived attack. I have learnt a bitter lesson."

Mike kissed Angela goodbye,

"Fingers and paws crossed. I'll be thinking of you. Let me know how you both get on."

Dawn arrived as usual to pick Bathsheba up and take her to the kennel for her grooming sessions. Angela, with due common sense, did not say one word to her regarding the nightmare of the last couple of weeks. Angela lovingly kissed Bathsheba goodbye and as usual all the other cats, by the look on their faces, could not really understand why she was being taken away.

Angela had to say something:

"You know how much of a star our beautiful Bathsheba really is, especially you Bucks. She has already won two awards and now she is going to get her third and most important one, The Cat of the South Award, with Auntie Dawn's help. She'll be back very soon. We might all have to kiss her 'bum' when she returns!"

Initially, Dawn didn't think Bathsheba looked her usual self, but after three days of nurturing her with a mixture of dedicated love and skill, Bathsheba looked totally stunning. 'Glamour puss' was an under statement and even Marilyn Monroe would have had a job to compete! Dawn was pleased with the result and was looking forward to the show. As luck would have it, little Lily picked up something and became quite sick. Angela had no choice but to stay with her, so Dawn and Bathsheba regrettably found themselves on their own. Dawn, of course, having done it all before, was very conversant with all the necessary red tape. She felt proud and confident, since Bathsheba already had two rosettes under her belt.

This particular show was twice as big as any of the others and it was, in fact, the most important and influential show of the year. The Cat Club were joint sponsors of it, but also being Bathsheba's sponsor, they came down heavily on Dawn, impressing upon her that winning this show would achieve one of the highest accolades possible, bearing in mind the nature of the ultimate prize. The winning cat would be one of four, namely North, South, East and West, chosen to be auditioned by one of the best known cat food brand names, with respect to a major TV ad promoting a new product line. It would be worth a considerable amount of money to the lucky owner, but the prestige would be priceless.

The day of the show had arrived. With all the preliminaries over and no foreseeable problems, and with Bathsheba lying quietly in her cage, Dawn made her way to Bathsheba's allocated place and aisle number. The show's vet, Chris Jenner began to make his round, checking on every contestant's health before the show's judges got down to the serious business of thoroughly assessing each cat individually from every aspect imaginable. As usual they left no stone unturned.

Chris Jenner arrived at the cage next to Bathsheba's, which housed a beautiful British shorthair named Georgie Boy. With no pre-warning at all, a mini drama was about to unfold. Having completed Georgie Boy's examination, Mr Jenner turned his attention to Bathsheba. He gently extracted Bathsheba, and whilst carefully and methodically examining her, for no apparent reason she began to tremble quite violently and uncontrollably. Dawn, who was watching the whole procedure, could not believe what Bathsheba was doing.

With considerable concern in her voice she said,

"Why is she trembling like that? She was fine a minute ago."

The vet was quick to reply,

"For some reason she's frightened, almost terrified, of the black cat next door. Other than that her health and condition are excellent."

Dawn began to get rather agitated,

"Well we'll just have to get her moved away from er…Georgie Boy. She's got to be moved somewhere else, for God's sake."

The vet, feeling more than sorry for Dawn's dilemma, calmly replied,

"I understand how you feel, but I don't think the judges will allow it. If they allow something out of the norm for one, they would then have to allow it for all and then there would be chaos. I don't want to be the voice of doom and gloom, but she could possibly be disqualified. I will do my utmost to persuade the judges to re-locate Bathsheba, but I can't promise anything."

Dawn was speechless.

"Disqualified? I don't believe it!"

CHAPTER NINETEEN

The Denzil Whitehead Show!

Denzil always secretly liked to believe he was a genius when it came to conjuring up ideas for something unusual. He also liked the world to know the extent of his skill, and often went out of his way to ensure that they did. The double wedding a year ago was a fantastic achievement, but this occasion, the celebration of two wedding anniversaries was going to top that, otherwise his name was not Denzil Whitehead!

He believed that once again Tillsworthy House should be the catalyst for this event as Tillsworthy House had, in fact, first opened its doors a year ago, and Angela had also inaugurated Cozy Cats Cottage plc about the same time.

Vicki looked at Priscilla, who in turn looked at Denzil, who looked at both of them demanding their full attention.

"This celebration – no this multiple celebration, has got to be done properly. We need to get as much publicity out of it as possible. Invite the press and local radio. I will gladly compere the event, and this dear ladies, is how I see it."

For the next hour, it was the Denzil Whitehead show. He was most definitely centre stage, making Vicki and Priscilla laugh, and not allowing them to get a word in edgeways as he excitedly painted the picture he had envisaged. It was plainly obvious that he had given a great deal of thought to the whole idea. When he had finally finished, Vicki jokingly said she would send him a bill for the hire of the hall! However, what he had said made a lot of sense. This celebration should be a celebration never to be forgotten. It was more than right to locate it at Tillsworthy House and use the downstairs area that had accommodated the two original weddings.

Vicki said excitedly,

"We are blessed with some beautiful grounds here, so why don't we have a huge barbecue, and organise some stalls and games for the kids. We will need banners shouting out what the celebrations are about, and we need the building floodlit."

Priscilla got the message too.

"Why don't we have all Tillsworthy House staff dressed up as cats, just as they did in the musical?"

Denzil was beginning to get excited.

"Now we're on a roll. It's sounding much more like it, although something like the cats would be a cute idea, but maybe a bit 'pantomime'. It depends on how subtle we could be with it."

Denzil continued,

"We should use that beautiful wooden wall in the foyer once again as the main focal point and.....wait for it...we could hang all Margaret's caricatures on it. How great would that be?

Priscilla and Vicki almost said in unison,

"But no one knows if she's done them yet. She's not said a word."

Denzil said with a smirk on his face,

"Well.. nudge, nudge, wink, wink. I do. I have seen them and they are out of this world. Margaret should present them to Angela to commemorate Cozy Cats Cottage, but being a permanent fixture on that wall, they would also signify a life long commemoration to Tillsworthy House. A double whammy if you get what I mean."

Vicki excitedly continued,

"I think we should name that part of the room Cozy Cats Corner and we'll have a beautiful gold name plate made. The framed caricatures should be carefully placed and spaced. We should then cover the whole wall with a drape or something like that so Margaret can do the honour of unveiling them and presenting them to Angela in the evening on the day."

Denzil continued with the seemingly endless list of ideas.

"Eight o'clock should be the time for the inside event which, as such, should be dedicated to the two wedding anniversaries and Cozy Cats Cottage. The outside activities throughout the day would be in commemoration of the anniversary of the opening of Tillsworthy House. There's a lot to organise. We need to have a meeting with both Angela and Margaret, preferably separately."

Priscilla, looking at Vicki, added,

"It all sounds too good to be true. We should start to make a list of invites and think about making contact with the local paper and radio station right away.

Georgie Boy

Angela was getting really worried. Dawn had not yet returned with Bathsheba. It was now two days after the show and she had heard nothing. By the look on their faces, the family also knew something was not quite right. It took a while before Angela finally managed to track Dawn down through the Cat Club. Dawn was profusely apologetic and agreed to come over to explain the situation.

"Angela, I'm really sorry for not having contacted you, but there have been big dramas at the show surrounding Bathsheba and I did not want to worry you as I thought I could resolve the problems myself."

Angela, responded with immediate concern,

"Where is she? Why isn't Bathsheba with you, for goodness sake?"

Dawn answered, seemingly rather frightened with what she was about to say.

"Well, there are two things, the second of which is by far the worst. To start with….. the show. A rather beautiful British shorthair named Georgie Boy came second. He happened to be in the next cage to Bathsheba and as soon as Bathsheba caught sight of Georgie Boy she started to tremble uncontrollably, rather reminiscent of when she caught sight of Buckingham, but different. Chris Jenner, the vet, was very concerned and could not really understand it. I insisted that Bathsheba be moved immediately, since Georgie Boy was obviously upsetting her. Chris did not think the management would agree and that she ran the risk of being disqualified. With obvious disapproval, she was finally moved and she went on to win the Cat of the South award. Amazingly, since the judges were not universally in agreement, this was then withdrawn! They have decided to convene at a later date when they will review and reassess the matter, in which case Georgie Boy could possibly become the winner with Bathsheba being disqualified!"

Angela, listening to every word, then said,

"That's disgraceful! Tell me Dawn, was Georgie Boy a black cat?"

Dawn responded,

"Yes he was. Jet black and beautiful."

Angela, looking shocked and frightened, then said,

"Well, that's why…. that's why Bathsheba was trembling so badly. A few weeks ago she was deliberately attacked in my garden by that nasty big black fairground cat. I think his name is Satan, and it would seem he was ably helped by two of his fiendish friends. TC was also involved, but it was the appearance of Bucks that saved the day. However, poor Bathsheba suffered some nasty scratches and obviously severe shock, which she is still struggling to deal with".

Dawn, very surprised at what she had just heard, answered,

"I thought there was something strange about her when I picked her up. Well, that explains everything, and we can only pray that the judges will understand and show some leniency. Other than that, there was no question that she was the star of the show. But now, unbelievably, we have no Bathsheba. She was kidnapped from right under my nose."

Angela could not believe what she was hearing.

"Kidnapped! Oh God, no! That's the second time in that cat's life! How the hell did that happen?"

Dawn frantically painted the picture for Angela:

"Bathsheba was in her cage, ready to go home. I had placed it on a table next to me whilst I had a parting chat with Chris Jenner. When I turned to pick Bathsheba up she and the cage had gone! I was absolutely frantic, almost crying with despair. Subsequently a big search was carried out by all concerned and even the police were called in, but not a sign of Bathsheba. Her disappearance is top priority as far as the police and The Cat Club are concerned. Apparently they are pretty certain who might have taken her and they hope to find her within two weeks."

Angela shouted in despair,

"Two weeks! We must do something now! She can't just vanish into thin air just like that."

Dawn responded, trying to keep calm,

"As we all know, Bathsheba is an exceptional cat. She is also worth a great deal of money. I have a strong hunch that the police and the Club know where she is, so I think we should wait until they come back to us. And remember one other thing; you sensibly agreed to allow the Club to have her microchipped and that could well be a life saving factor."

Angela, appearing to be a little calmer, then said,

"I'm really glad I agreed to that. I must get the others done. Anyway, for all we know Bathsheba might still win the Cat of the South award, if they decide not to disqualify her."

Dawn answered emphatically,

"Well, that would be ironic..... considering we have no cat."

Hell and back!

Without the presence of Bathsheba, the atmosphere within Cozy Cats Cottage felt distinctly subdued. Angela noticed that even Lily, who had in a way always maintained a subconscious jealousy of Bathsheba's beauty, was showing signs of missing her. But it was Buckingham and TC who felt it the most. Buckingham ensured that he accompanied TC every single night on his guard duty round. They both obviously thought that with rational thinking and CCS, they would eventually locate Bathsheba's whereabouts. Angela, who inwardly felt quite sick, begged Bradley to pray for her safe return. Bradley assured her that he had done so from the day he had known she was missing.

Two weeks went by with no news of Bathsheba at all, then suddenly on Wednesday evening the following week Dawn was excitedly knocking on Angela's front door.

"Great news, Angela. Bathsheba's been found and is at the Cat Club, resting after her ordeal. She's fine."

Angela, more than relieved, then said,

"Oh, thank God she's all right. What happened to her?"

Dawn explained:

"Apparently she was taken from our cat show by a jealous lady competitor who, ironically and luckily, looked after her as if she were her own for two weeks. She then entered Bathsheba into a local cat show about fifty miles away from here, which Bathsheba of course won. However, the vet discovered the microchip and contacted the Club. They came round with the police and retrieved Bathsheba. Apparently all that this lady wanted, and needless to say was obsessed with, was the glory of winning a cat show. She made everybody, including herself, believe it was her cat, but she knew very well what she was doing when she cleverly and deliberately selected Bathsheba."

Angela responded abjectly,

"Somehow I feel sorry for her, because in a way it was a back-handed compliment in her realising what a priceless cat Bathsheba really is."

Dawn continued with excitement in the tone of her voice,

"There's more good news. Bathsheba has won the Cat of the South award.

They decided that there was no case to support her being disqualified."

Angela, with joy written all over her face, said,

"I knew she'd do it. What a priceless pussy she is!"

Dawn continued,

"Well, now she's got the chance of the biggest prize of all. She'll be in the final four, namely Cat of the South, North, East and West, with the opportunity of being selected by a leading cat food brand to advertise their new product line. She's got some really tough competition and I have no idea what type of breed the other cats are. But if she wins that she'll not only earn a fortune but her face will be everywhere! There's nothing bigger. It's the highest accolade of all!"

Angela could not immediately respond, and then with concern said,

"It's all too much to take in. More important is when can she come home? I think she needs some good old fashioned plc before she gets into anything else. She has literally been through *hell* and back over these last few weeks, and so have both of us for that matter."

Dawn added with a smile of reassurance,

"I hope to be able to bring Madame home tomorrow."

Catitude!

Angela always believed cats had a sixth sense, as well as nine lives. As her family grew she had living proof of it on numerous occasions and enjoyed witnessing the hidden communication system that was always going on between them.

On Bathsheba's return, it was painfully obvious how much they had all missed her. Cat chats were taking place all day and every day, but usually at bedtime.

Buckingham looked at Bathsheba in a kind of protective way.

"Well sis, you have certainly turned this place upside down during the last two or three weeks. We're glad you're home, but Angela's been behaving like one of us on a hot tin roof. Even Dexter and Miss Pretty have not been up to their usual tricks."

TC was quick to respond,

"Satan has a lot to answer for and I hope he and those other two little devils go back to hell where they belong. This all started after that happened."

Bathsheba, looking rather forlorn, said,

"I've just suffered being kidnapped for the second time. I seem to cause so much heartache, worry and so many problems for everyone. Why does it always happen to me?"

It was Lily's turn to voice an opinion,

"Bathsheba, I was once very jealous of you and your relationship with my husband. That was so stupid and is now in the past. You are very beautiful and we all love you. I can't complain. I have two beautiful kids who are bringing love and happiness into the lives of others who are less fortunate. What more can I ask for?"

And then looking at Buckingham she said,

"I love my husband dearly and I have little to complain about, but every so often, and it is noticeably becoming more frequent when he seems to...... ..how shall I put it....ration the passion. It must be a sign of advancing years!"

She gave her husband 'that look' waiting for an answer. Buckingham responded indignantly, feeling that his male cat ego was being threatened.

"*Ration the passion! What are you talking about woman? My time is limited in that respect these days. I am keeping the peace, helping TC out with his guard duty, and that, my love, is also time consuming and requires a concentrated* **catitude**".

Dexter, listening to all that had been said, had to voice some kind of defence with respect to his father:

"*My dad is the best dad in the world. He has told me and Miss Pretty lots of things about life. He knows and we know when to say yea or nay, don't we Miss Pretty?*"

Miss Pretty condoned Dexter's remark:

"*We do, that's for sure,*" and turning to Lily said, "*but don't worry Mum. You're the greatest Mum in world and we do love you and that's also for sure!*"

TC had listened and taken it all in, and summing things up, so to speak, said,

"*The good news for us all is that our darling Bathsheba is back safe and sound and in one piece. We will take care of her as we do for each other because we are family.*"

If you get my drift!

He looked at them with those piercing journalistic eyes before producing the indispensable big cigar, lighting it and blowing the smoke in their seemingly innocent faces. With a reluctant sigh and a semblance of a smile he said to the young wannabes sitting before him,

"You managed to pick up the crumbs from the table and produced an edible piece of journalism with your effort on the cats' wedding a year ago. Not a bad result at all, but now I want a proper piece of journalism. Believe it or not, you're going to do it all over again, because it is those blessed cats' anniversary, in addition to the anniversary of Cozy Cats Cottage plc, the company formed by that mad woman Angela Tillsworthy. Extra brownie points for guessing what plc stands for?"

He paused for a second. "Of course you two are not clever enough to suss that one out! 'Pussy loving care', would you believe!" He laughed at the underlying significance of that remark and then waited for a moment or two to make sure that what he had been saying had registered. Hoping that it had, he took a deliberately long drag on his cigar again, slowly blowing it across their faces before continuing.

"Now…apart from what I have just told you, Tillsworthy House is also celebrating its own anniversary. I've heard there's going to be a barbecue located in its beautiful grounds, with stalls and fun games for the kids and so on, and most importantly, food and booze will be free! Annoyingly, I have found out that the local radio station is also going to cover the story. Rather than having a continuous and frustrating feud carrying on between the two of us I decided that it would be far more practical if we could work amicably together, at least on this occasion. What was needed was a brilliant idea so…. conducive to the position of being the Editor of this journal," he smiled accordingly, " I have naturally come up with one that is, of course, nothing but ingenious and they have agreed. We will both run the same competition over the same period of time before the event. The very worthwhile prize will be a weekend family trip for four to Disneyland in Paris. The question will be, 'What is the name of the local Hospice that has a Cozy Cats Cottage kitten as a mascot'?" He paused for a moment, so the impact of the gesture could sink in. "Commendably, Tillsworthy House is also giving the nominal entrance fee, which is only two pounds, to the TTPCC a charity for the prevention of cruelty to cats. It's a good cause….. if you're not allergic to cats of course!"

He looked at both his victims in turn, and with that usual editorial grin said,

"I hope you have taken all this in. Sensibly you haven't said a word and I don't want you to, but I do want you to give me a shit hot report on this event, making sure it's on my desk without fail first thing the following morning. On a more serious journalistic note, and in my professional opinion, your piece should focus on the fact that Angela Tillsworthy, with all due credit, has recognised the cat as being an animal with considerable therapeutic power. By all accounts, from what I have heard from local hospices, schools and the community generally, she has achieved some incredible results with the cats that are in her care. Our readers need to know that. That is the big point of sale that will get them, you and us where it matters the most....right here, if you get my drift." His right hand tapped his heart a few times.

He paused for a few moments more before getting up from his desk, indicating the end of the meeting. He then said, but still a touch begrudgingly,

"I felt good about what you did before, but I want to feel bloody marvellous about what you're going to do now. Remember, delivering newspapers also carries a certain amount of alternative responsibility..... if you get my drift!"

How he loved that expression! He smiled, nodding his head and blowing yet another deluge of smoke in their direction.

"The door is open. You can see yourselves out."

As they were about to leave, as an after thought, he said,

"Oh.... and I want pictures!"

CHAPTER TWENTY

I'm in charge!

The date had been set. The local paper and radio station had been notified and now Tillsworthy House had to be suitably prepared for the time of its life.

The concept of incorporating various types of stalls was agreed by all to be a quaint and picturesque idea, providing it was borne in mind that there would undoubtedly be children present and they would have to be catered for. However, there was a worrying question – was there enough suitable space in the grounds to accommodate such an ambitious event?

Denzil, of course, came up with a brilliant and perfect answer.

The driveway to the entrance of Tillsworthy House was unusually long. One of the features left by the previous owners, and luckily still intact, was a line of historic statues placed at equal distances from each other on each side of the driveway. This provided Denzil with the ingenious idea of placing the stalls between each of the statues. This would then have the effect of making the driveway a large and interesting, fun walkabout area. The driveway would, of course, be closed to any motor traffic, with parking having to be established elsewhere. The local police would have to be contacted and hopefully they would agree to police the event on the day in question. They also agreed that there should be a nominal entrance fee of two pounds per person, which would be paid to the TTPCC.

After much deliberation, the final twelve participating stall holders were agreed upon. They would provide some wonderful, varied forms of fun for young and old, which would, of course, also include the proverbial ice cream, soft drinks and hamburgers.

Practically a year ago, when Vicki and Priscilla first bought Tillsworthy House, the grounds, which covered almost an acre of land, were in a dreadful state, being allowed to run wild and become drastically overgrown. It looked an impossible task, but with careful costing, a lot of fortunately free help, dedication and sheer hard work, Vicki and Priscilla had managed to bring back life and beauty to these wonderful grounds. They had the whole area landscaped, which resulted in the creation of rockeries, ponds, vivacious flower beds and manicured lawns, but sensibly they retained the mystery and density of the wooded area that occupied one corner of the grounds. Always with the residents who were lucky enough to be there in mind, they created a number of quirky pathways that provided some attractive and interesting walks.

As Denzil, Vicki and Priscilla strolled through the grounds to determine a suitable place to locate the barbecue, Denzil was totally overwhelmed by it all.

"You two have almost created paradise. The grounds are breathtakingly beautiful. Such imagination! I strongly feel the barbecue, which needs to be fairly large, has to be located near the house. I suggest putting it on the patio, which would be more than adequate, even allowing space for tables and chairs"

On returning to Vicki and Priscilla's apartment, Denzil continued verbalising as if there had been no break at all.

"Now, when the presentations are made during the evening, the foyer area will be full, so I want to arrange for two big screens, as they do with a celeb music gig these days, to be set up so the people outside will have the chance of seeing and hearing what's going on inside. One of the screens will be placed over the entrance of the house itself, whilst the other will be somewhere near the barbecue. It all sounds a bit technical, but it should work."

Vicki answered, feeling a touch left out,

"I think it's about my turn to have a bit of commendation. I have arranged for a huge banner to be stretched across the front of the building, announcing the reason for the festivities. I have also arranged for the building to be floodlit during the evening."

Amazingly there was silence for the first time. The three of them looked at each other with a 'that should do it!' look written all over their faces.

There was a knock on the door.

"It's only me, Angela. Hope I'm not too late. Lily is with Margaret and Buckingham has gone to say hello to Linda in the foyer, so they'll be all right for a while. Well, how is it all going?"

Denzil responded with obvious excitement:

"Tillsie, if nothing goes wrong on the day it's going to be sensational. Now, this is what's going to happen and also what you'll be doing..................

Having listened intently to Denzil's every word, she then said,

"It all sounds fine to me, as long as you know what you're doing. Margaret told me you wanted to have a word with her, so I will go down and tell her. I will rescue Buckingham, see Oliver and I will also keep and eye on Lily until Margaret returns. It's certainly exciting and, dare I say," smiling smugly at Denzil, " ambitious."

Margaret arrived and the three of them discussed the set up for the evening. Denzil, of course, did most of the talking, emphasising the reason for Angela not being present. Vicki could not resist it, so looking at Margaret and wagging a finger in the direction of Denzil she said,

"He, the crafty so and so, is the only one here to have seen your apparently wonderful caricatures of Angela's cats."

Priscilla smiling, interrupted,

"We were literally *dying* to see them. Anyway, it looks like we're going to have as much of a surprise as the audience."

Denzil retorted with a slight touch of comic sarcasm,

"I'm no fool, am I? Margaret and I made a deal. Now Margaret... this is what will happen and this is what we want you to do."

Margaret smiled and quietly said,

"I can't wait."

The Big Day

Bradley was not the only one praying that the anniversary to end all anniversaries had the perfect summer's day for the celebration to end all celebrations! His prayers were not in vain. By midday the grounds, or to be more exact the driveway down to Tillsworthy House, was virtually vibrating with the sounds of fun and laughter. It was wonderful seeing young and old mingling around the multi-coloured stalls and their various diverse activities. Even the statues seemed to be joining in.

As Denzil surveyed the scene he congratulated himself on its obvious success. However, for him there was, as such, a small price to pay. He had no choice but to swallow his pride and close the doors of The Wooden Horse for the day and evening, much to the annoyance of some of his regulars. But it was an exceptional occasion and, of course, he knew exactly how to put the smile back on their faces! More important was that he wanted Jamie to see and spend time with his mother and enjoy the day, but to be nearer the truth he wanted him to realise just how bloody clever his boss actually was!

The banner was huge, colourful and impressive, almost covering the entire front of the building. Denzil smiled as he saw what it said. Congratulations to Oliver and Margaret, Buckingham and Lily, Cozy Cats Cottage and Tillsworthy House on their First Anniversary. The two giant screens had been installed and the barbecue was beginning to get really busy.

Denzil quite rightly presumed that he had meticulously covered everything, leaving no stone unturned. He got more than he bargained for when he heard the strains of music coming from the direction of the driveway's entrance. "Music!" he said almost out loud to himself, "I don't bloody well believe it! Someone's trying to pull a fast one on me! Well, they're not going to get away with it."

Sure enough, Denzil discovered that it was, in fact, a four piece street band playing Dixieland jazz, even emulating the original New Orleans attire. They were slowly making their way down the driveway, followed by a cortege of young admirers. Much as he hated doing so, he had to admit it was a wonderful sight and it certainly added enormously to the overall atmosphere. They were, in fact, pretty good. However, what really frustrated him was who had bloody well arranged it?

Denzil, with a vaguely insincere smile, fired the question directly at Vicki and Priscilla.

"OK you two, who hired the band?"

They answered almost simultaneously,

"They hired themselves Denzil. They appeared from nowhere and just started to play, walking down the driveway. As you have seen, everybody loves them so we left them to it. Apparently they play other stuff as well, so we're thinking of using them this evening."

Denzil responded as if talking to himself,

"I really think I'm losing it!" Then, directly facing Vicki and Priscilla, he said with that incomparable Denzil touch of sarcasm of joking but not really joking,

"Oh, by the way, if you had the time to tear yourself away from other distractions, you might have noticed that Margaret's caricatures are up on the wall now, and so is the gold plaque, which I suppose I will have to agree looks the business. It's all covered, ready for the big cord pull tonight. I had to wait until you were both hopefully enjoying sweet dreams before I could get away with erecting it."

Priscilla responded,

"Well if tonight goes as well as today, my dreams will be realised and I'm sure Vicki's will too. So far, seeing is believing and we do really appreciate your attention to the smallest detail....except the music of course. You really are an indispensable gem, Denzil."

Denzil answered smiling, deliberately ignoring the music remark,

"An indispensable genius actually! I've even asked Bradley to say a prayer for me....no I mean us, just in case!"

With the usual vocal harmony of disapproval Angela managed to transport all the residents of Cozy Cats Cottage in their 'doggy' boxes over to Tillsworthy House in the afternoon of the big day, arriving via the tradesman's entrance. They were given the freedom of Vicki and Priscilla's apartment, where there was ample food, water and toilet facilities readily available, but unfortunately no 'automatic paw dryer'!

Whilst Priscilla, Vicki and Denzil were busy organising the evening show, Angela decided to find Linda, and with Oliver and Margaret take advantage of some afternoon sun and fun at the stalls.

Evening was approaching. The foyer of Tillsworthy House was

virtually unrecognizable and had the appearance of being about to host the Oscars. It was tastefully and impressively decorated with flowers placed thoughtfully throughout. Banners carrying various messages of congratulations were also evident, individually proclaiming a particular anniversary. The familiar oak panelled wall was now covered with a heavy maroon drape. However, it was the base of the wall that was commanding an unusual amount of attention. There appeared to be a raised platform about two feet wide running the width of the wall, which was strangely labelled – Denzil's Catwalk. Two of the staff, wearing cat face masks, stood at each end of the platform.

Showtime!

House lights dimmed, giving way to spotlights which dramatically picked up the catwalk and the maroon drape above it. The introduction to the show was announced through the loudspeaker system. "Ladies and Gentlemen, Tillsworthy House is proud to present your host for the evening, the incomparable Mr Denzil Whitehead."

Denzil, dressed more flamboyantly than ever with what most people would cringe at as being a terrible clash of yellow and orange, was totally in his element. He was unquestionably an incredibly good speaker and was blessed with an amazing sense of humour. He introduced Vicki and Priscilla, humorously describing how they had initially got together and subsequently how they had suffered the traumatic journey in bringing their dream of Tillsworthy House and HALE to a positive and fruitful conclusion.

After the applause had died down Vicki imparted that on the very spot where she was standing one year ago, a very unusual event had taken place.

Priscilla continued, and with excitement in her voice, proudly introduced the Reverend Bradley Smith, who had found himself in the fortunate, or unfortunate, position of agreeing to marry two very different couples at the same time.

"God was with me on that day. The occasion will stay in my

memory for all time. We had to orchestrate a special service because I had never married two cats before." He paused momentarily. "It was the most extraordinary request, but the look of love was in their eyes, blessed with purring, clearly being heard loud and clear. How could I refuse? So with dear Margaret and Oliver, whom by the grace of God Buckingham and Lily have religiously and lovingly been caring for over the past year, it is indeed an honour to have all four of them here again celebrating their first wedding anniversary."

Margaret then appeared from the left, proudly pushing Oliver in his wheelchair, with Buckingham and Lily for once both sitting quietly on his lap without either of them, thank goodness, voicing their usual marital back chat. The four of them appeared as though they had just done a 'shoot' for 'Hello'!

Enthusiastic applause followed.

Denzil had always thought the world of Angela, from the first day he met her. He would never admit it, but in his own strange way he probably actually loved her. He was certainly her greatest fan as far as her achievements were concerned and he more than just adored the cats. He regarded it an honour to introduce her and in doing so having to announce yet another anniversary celebration, this time in respect of Cozy Cats Cottage plc, a venture Angela had envisaged a year ago.

Angela, slightly embarrassed, thanked Denzil for his glowing remarks.

"For the past year cats have been my life. I have witnessed their incredible therapeutic power time and time again. Cozy Cats Cottage plc was specifically formed to help those afflicted or less fortunate, young or old. Buckingham and Lily were the company's first two employees and then, unbelievably, they produced Miss Pretty and Dexter. Please welcome Vanessa Middleton from the Princess Alicia Hospice and Miss Pretty and also Fiona from the Little Kids Day Care Centre and Dexter."

Once again enthusiastic applause followed.

Angela, realising the audience were hanging on to her every word, proudly introduced Dawn and Bathsheba, explaining that Bathsheba was Buckingham's long lost twin sister. Luckily, she had been found. To cap it all, she had recently won the Cat of the South award, the most prestigious award of all.

As the applause subsided, Bradley reappeared with TC in his arms, paws around his neck.

"Ladies and Gentlemen, this is TC – Top Cat and he is definitely all that. A short while ago I lost the love of my life, Harry. He was a big, lovable black cat with a heart of gold. He used to guard my church as well as the streets of Troy. TC, being his best friend, has, as such, replaced him and taken on all of his duties. Like Harry, TC is one in a million."

The audience seemed as if they were going to clap forever. Denzil reappeared and proudly said,

"Well there they are.......all together for the first time ever. This is a magical moment, probably never to be repeated! However, if any of you want to see them or talk to them individually you can do so in a little while when they are back in their boxes over there." He pointed to the left of the stage.

"Meanwhile stay where you are, because…. the show ain't over yet!"

CHAPTER TWENTY ONE

The Presentation

Denzil, knowing he had the audience in the palm of his hand, made that pleasure last for as long as he could.

"You lucky people.......you very lucky people are going to have the pleasure of enjoying the outstanding talent of a certain beautiful and charming lady. Once again I am honoured.... truly honoured to present Mrs Margaret Tillsworthy."

Margaret appeared, obviously in 'command' mode, and sounded as confident as she looked:

"I am really proud to have the name Tillsworthy, which I acquired on this very spot a year ago. I am also fortunate to be living in this beautiful house, also named Tillsworthy, thanks to Vicki and Priscilla. However, my life has not been without considerable trauma, especially when I lost my twin sister Sinead to cancer a short while ago. But I have had a long and successful professional career working for a national newspaper as a caricature journalist. I am lucky to have won several prestigious awards. The day Oliver and I made direct contact with Buckingham and Lily, two of Angela's amazing cats, our lives changed dramatically and the four of us have almost never been separated since. Angela has given her life totally, with unselfish love and dedication, to helping others by realising the therapeutic power of the cat. You have now met all six of her remarkable employees. Surprisingly, it was Sinead who persuaded me to do it, and when I finally committed myself, I knew Harry had to also be included, as he had become an important part of the family. All this must sound double dutch, but in a minute all will be revealed."

Margaret then moved across to the right hand side of the stage and placed her hand on a beautifully braided sash-like cord. Directly addressing Angela, Vicki and Priscilla she said,

"It gives me great pleasure to present these seven caricatures to each one of you in thanks from the bottom of my heart for all you have done for Oliver and myself and are doing so for so many others. I have really relished the opportunity to re-create and re-live something that has always been very close to my heart" With that she pulled the cord, and the thick velvet maroon drape fell to the floor, displaying caricatures of all seven cats arranged as if depicting a family tree. Placed above them was a striking gold lettered plaque which read – Cozy Cats Corner. There was a gasp from the audience, who then enthusiastically gave Margaret a truly justified standing ovation. Bradley was totally overwhelmed with the inclusion of Harry, and remained momentarily speechless with a tear in his eye, which was most unusual. Angela had a serious problem with emotion as well. The reality of what Margaret had achieved with each individual cat was quite remarkable. After studying each one in turn, Angela literally ran over to Margaret and gave her a big thank you hug and kiss. Vicki and Priscilla followed suit, supported by a strong reaction from the audience. Even Denzil had to admit that it was all very moving and a very suitable ending, which more than justified all the effort and hard work by everyone that had contributed to making the entire event such an outstanding success.

Front Page News

There was no doubt about it. He was the local newspaper and the local newspaper was him. However, he had the most annoying habit of making anyone, no matter who they were, feel like a naughty school boy or girl called before the headmaster to receive a major bol……..king. This time, however, was a little different. Looking at both his 'minions' in turn, he condescended to offer them a chair and, having inhaled on the ever present nauseous cigar and then blowing the smoke deliberately in their direction, he said,

"First of all I have to tell you that the competition run between us and the local radio station on that Tillsworthy gig was a huge success. There were in fact over a hundred correct answers, so Angela Tillsworthy and those creatures must be doing something right.....if you get my drift! I have to reluctantly concede that in my opinion your article is right on the button and deserves front page. In view of what you have achieved on this assignment, I am going to promote both of you as the number one feature writers with anything to do with animals. I mean animals world wide, which would include wild life, farms, zoos, domestic creatures and so on......if you get my drift!" He paused as if he was trying to remember something. He then suddenly said,

"Oh yes! Photographs of the Tillsworthy do? I told you they were important and necessary."

The answer came back like a pistol shot.

"We did a deal with a certain Denzil Whitehead, who was the main organiser and brilliant with the camera. We have some superb images coming shortly. We thought it astute to negotiate for them......if you get our drift!"

It's called 'tit for tat', but there were smiles all round!

Recovery

The celebration of the anniversaries would be remembered for a long time to come. It took a good week for everything and everyone to get back to normal. However, the press and radio were determined to keep the whole thing alive for some considerable time, which of course provided Angela and Tillsworthy House with a flow of really welcome continuous publicity. Angela had even been asked to do an interview on one of the station's prime time programmes, and she was really looking forward to doing it.

Vicki and Priscilla were thrilled with everything that had taken place at Tillsworthy House. There had been no big dramas and all credit was solely down to a brilliantly concerted effort, orchestrated by Denzil and his meticulous eye for detail.

Cozy Cats Corner in the foyer of Tillsworthy House looked sensational, with a daily audience nearly as good as a major art gallery. Even the national newspaper that Margaret had worked for wanted to come and see what all the fuss was about. Seth Jones, who had previously learnt his lesson in good manners and become a gentleman once again, could not resist voicing his opinion quite openly for all to hear:

"Charge 'em, I say. Nothing's for free these days, not even for looking at bloody cats!"

Linda looked at him somewhat surprised and quietly said,

"Seth, Seth! Come on now, we don't want any of that. You promised no more old Seth, besides those caricatures are quite something else. You've got to admit that."

"Well... I suppose I have to give Margaret her due. They are pretty good, even charismatic and funny, that is of course.......if you like cats!"

Linda commented quite firmly,

"You said you did now that you and Buckingham had come to shall we say – an understanding between you."

Seth replied,

"Linda you're right. I was only joking. I have changed my mind about cats. I really hate them."

He smiled at a very shocked Linda,

"No, no, don't worry. It's just my sick sense of humour and I just couldn't resist getting you going. I didn't mean to upset you. With hand on my heart, I really didn't. Margaret is extremely clever and very talented and I genuinely mean that."

So proud of you

It had been such a long day and it was practically three o'clock in the morning by the time Angela had got all her family safely home and indoors, said good night to Bradley, who had very kindly offered to help carry them in, and finally shut the front door. She knew the poor little devils must be tired and hungry, having not eaten anything for some time.

"You all deserve a big, *big* treat because your performance today was nothing short of outstanding. You stole the show, and thanks to you, Cozy Cats Cottage and what it stands for will be imprinted on everyone's minds for a long time to come. I am so proud of you."

Whilst Angela was preparing their food their joint purring

sounded just like the tick over of a farm tractor engine! At the same they were all anxiously looking up at her and impatiently walking around in circles rubbing her legs. Finally she placed all six dishes on the floor and, just for fun, put each cat in the order that she had acquired them – Buckingham, Lily, Miss Pretty, Dexter, TC and last but not least Bathsheba. With them all sitting contently in front of their dishes with their tails stretched out, it was a sight for sore eyes. Angela luckily found her camera to capture that magical moment, one which might have even made the mighty Denzil feel a little jealous.

Almost immediately after eating, Buckingham led the way to their bedroom and they all followed without a sound. Angela made herself a cup of coffee, and reminisced for a while on the settee before retiring herself. She was exhausted but very thankful and very satisfied.

Silence reigned

They were obviously all grateful to be in their beds but Dexter, renowned for never really being able to totally relax and always hyper, was the first to make comment.

"Did you see those awful pictures Margaret had done of us? Even the kids at my day care would have had a good laugh. I don't understand why everyone thought they were so wonderful."

Buckingham answered in a fatherly like fashion:

"Well my boy, professionally speaking they are called caricatures, which are not meant to look exactly real, but to portray a bit of fun. They are in fact classified as serious art and not intended to take the piss!"

Dexter wouldn't leave it at that and then said,

"That big maroon curtain was asking for it. To jump on that and hang on for dear life would have been Dexter's delight, and not only that, I would have saved Margaret the trouble of pulling the cord to expose those things. It was only the thought of Fiona having a heart attack or something as dramatic that stopped me from doing it."

Lily intervened,

"You would have put us all to shame and the last laugh would have been on us. Angela would have been devastated, but thank God all of you were

244

little stars and behaved so well," and looking at her husband, *"Don't worry darling as always you were a big star!"*

TC added,

"And Bradley remembered Harry, which was really nice and so right. Cozy Cats Cottage has nothing to be ashamed of. We set the purrfect example and no one will argue with that. Well Miss Pretty's asleep, Bathsheba's asleep and now it's my turn. Night Night."

Silence reigned. There was not a sound from anyone for a very long time!

Quiet evening drink

Even though the anniversary celebrations were still on everyone's mind, the weekly work schedules were calling for attention. Angela had envisaged problems, but amazingly there were none, and all the cats were back into work mode almost as if nothing had happened. They, in fact, seemed to be pleased that they were back. Excitingly, Dawn had received a call from an agency desperate to have Bathsheba on their books for future animal feature work. Angela felt quite elated with that request.

For Angela and Bradley, a quiet evening drink down at the local was almost certainly out of the question. The combination of The Wooden Horse and Denzil Whitehead was quite lethal, but Denzil, as usual, never failed to play the perfect host and greeted them with open arms. He was still re-living his much applauded celebration achievements and apparently many Troyites had found their way down to Tillsworthy House, spent the day there and had a whale of a time. At this moment, however, he seemed even more excited than usual, saying that he had 'prayed' Bradley and Angela would appear because there was someone who was desperate to meet them. Denzil had, in fact, mentioned Miles Melford before, in that he had just purchased a rather lovely property in the neighbourhood and that he was the publicity agent for a number of well known faces and…. he loved cats!

With the hand shakes and hellos over, Miles Melford opened the conversation.

"Courtesy of Denzil, I went to the show and naturally had a

fantastic day. I loved the stalls and barbecue, but the highlight of the whole thing was definitely what you, Angela, have achieved with those incredible cats. I spent some time looking at them individually afterwards and they are so charismatic. Every one of them is different. Needless to say, Buckingham gave me the, 'What the bloody hell are you looking at?' sort of face. Great stuff!"

Angela, looking more than pleased, answered accordingly,

"Well Miles, if I may call you that, it has been a lot of hard work with a lot of patience and understanding, but now there are signs of it becoming all worthwhile with many already benefiting from the work we do."

Bradley intervened,

"And you know what? She makes nothing out of it and basically does it totally for love and charity, which is very commendable."

For once in a blue moon, Denzil decided to remain quiet during this conversation, probably to ensure that the outcome whatever it may be, would happen on its own accord without any persuasion from him.

Miles, having taken all of this on board, responded accordingly,

"In view of what Denzil had previously told me and what I have seen and learnt from the celebration day, I do have something concrete in the way of a proposition. One of the most successful companies I broker for is interested in doing an animated feature as part of their 'That's Life' forthcoming documentary series. It would be based on your story Angela, Cozy Cats Cottage and the cats, of course. Both the company and I feel it would have very strong universal appeal. Anything to do with charity, helping those less fortunate, and the amazing cats of course, are all the right ingredients for potential success. The film would ultimately go out with some major release right across the country."

Denzil could not resist having his say:

"Tillsie, this must be the biggest break you could possibly ask for. Imagine the amount of people, maybe around the world even, who might get to see the final masterpiece. It would open up unending opportunities. It's very exciting."

Bradley interjected, and commenting specifically to Miles said,

"I know the therapeutic power of the cat has not gone unnoticed and is universally pretty well known. What is so incredible about all this is the fascinating way in which Angela has used it to promote and expand it to impart love, light and happiness into the lives of those with seemingly little to live for."

Miles continued,

"I fully appreciate that, but the real stars of the show are the cats themselves. Their almost human-like characters will be exploited strongly in the film. My head is full of so many ideas that could emanate from this project. I would like to set up a meeting with you and myself with the film company, who are, by the way, brilliant at this sort of thing, as soon as you have the time."

Denzil was genuinely overcome by all that had been said and having fixed celebratory drinks for everyone, imparted his own special news.

"I have now developed all the pictures from the anniversary celebrations and they will be on display in this pub and of course also at Tillsworthy House. Needless to say, they are out of this world and are obviously the work of a genius!"

Miles was quick to answer,

"Having such a set of great images of each individual cat would be invaluable help at this forthcoming meeting. No one's questioning the fact that you're the genius Denzil!"

At that moment, as if from nowhere, an out of breath Dawn suddenly appeared. She was more than just excited.

"Oh Angela, thank goodness I've found you. For some reason I had a hunch you'd be here. Don't worry, it's not bad news, in fact it's quite the reverse. I have been tracked down by the British Shorthair Club, who have told me that Bathsheba has won the overall award between North, South, East and West. She will be representing a major cat food brand name with a new product they are bringing out called Paws for the Purrfect Cat. Her face will soon be all over the country, as this food product will be available through every major food chain. It's totally unbelievable!"

Denzil could hardly contain himself.

"Oh my God Dawn, sit down. I'll get you a drink. This is Miles, by the way. That's really fantastic news, but wait, just wait till you hear what we've got to tell you!"

Angela and Bradley, totally exhausted, finally arrived at Cozy Cats Cottage at almost midnight. The earlier envisaged quiet drink at last became a reality with a welcome self made cup of coffee on Angela's comfortable settee. For some while they sat in silence, unable to believe all that they had heard and witnessed. Bathsheba was the icing on the cake. It all seemed like a glorified fairy story.

Bradley broke the silence.

"You know what Angela, I really do believe all this will happen. In my special prayers for you, God has given me signs, and remember the cats are God's creatures. They should not be underestimated. Of course, you will soon have to *paws* for thought when feeding them, after all it will be the food for the *purr*fect cat!"

Angela answered, looking affectionately at Bradley,

"You make me feel that everything is worthwhile and even done for a purpose. There have been many problems and no doubt there are more to come, but since my arrival in Troy and meeting you I have got through everything with a great deal of strength and determination. With the proposition from the film company and the support from Miles, let alone Bathsheba, my family and I have a lot to look forward to, with so much thanks to you."

Bradley quietly responded,

"Angela, one proposition deserves another. You and I have come through a lot together. I often think and talk to Harry, and I know he would be really happy and honoured, as I would, if you would give serious thought to yet another proposal. One that is very close to my heart."

It was a long and lingering farewell before Angela was able to say goodnight to Bradley that night. There was something very different about it to anything she had experienced before. She had a lot on her mind, but of one thing she was certain!